Meda

Cyrus visibly relaxed, fl... wardrobe and regarding Kyle seriously. *"You will do, young man. Despite your unfortunate Randall lineage, you appear to be a decent, upstanding man. You have my blessing to court Miss Carey. Mind you, do not hurt her. I have the feeling she has been through more heartache than most."*

Kyle shook his head. This was damn unreal. He waited quietly, willing the ghosts of Bliss House to say more—but they did not. Before his eyes, their images faded. As he left the room—as fast as his feet would carry him—he thought he felt an almost motherly pat on the top of his head.

"*Heavenly Bliss* is a tender, moving love story... compelling and hypnotic. Sara Jarrod is one of the best writers of ghost romance today." —*Affaire de Coeur*

Praise for Sara Jarrod's
Heaven Above

"A spellbinding tale of love, loss, and redemption."
—Susan Wiggs

"A superb romance." —*Affaire de Coeur*

"You'll laugh. You'll cry. You'll fall in love... Definitely a winner!" —Barbara Bretton

"A fascinating debut novel! Sara Jarrod skillfully draws you into the complex plot and brings a fresh, unique voice to women's romantic fiction." —Virginia Henley

Turn to the back of this book for a special preview of
Shadows in the Flame
the next Haunting Hearts romance!

HEAVENLY BLISS

SARA JARROD

JOVE BOOKS, NEW YORK

HAUNTING HEARTS is a registered trademark of
Berkley Publishing Corporation.

HEAVENLY BLISS

A Jove Book / published by arrangement with
the authors

PRINTING HISTORY
Jove edition / July 1997

All rights reserved.
Copyright © 1997 by Sara Brockunier and Ann Josephson.
Shadows in the Flame excerpt copyright © 1997 by Terri Sprenger.
This book may not be reproduced in whole
or in part, by mimeograph or any other means,
without permission. For information address:
The Berkley Publishing Group, 200 Madison Avenue,
New York, New York 10016.

The Putnam Berkley World Wide Web site address is
http://www.berkley.com

ISBN: 0-515-12100-2

A JOVE BOOK®
Jove Books are published by The Berkley Publishing Group,
200 Madison Avenue, New York, New York 10016.
JOVE and the "J" design are trademarks
belonging to Jove Publications, Inc.

PRINTED IN THE UNITED STATES OF AMERICA

10 9 8 7 6 5 4 3 2 1

To our editor, Judith Stern Palais—

For seeing the possibilities in Sara Jarrod,
and trusting us to make our "spirits" come alive;
for holding the hands of not one but two neophytes,
yet giving us the freedom to tell our tales . . .

No writers could ask for more. Thank you, Judy!

—Sara and Ann

Chapter One

"Stop!"

Jill Carey knew the moment she saw the derelict of an ancient house, perched on a gentle rise above the road, that this was it—the refuge she had seen in her dreams, the home that had called out to her! She pictured fragrant jasmines climbing the stout, square columns that marched across the front, clumps of mountain laurel brightening the sloping yard that was now a maze of unkempt brambles.

"You don't want Bliss House." As he pulled his car into the overgrown driveway, Jill sensed terror in the portly realtor's rumbling voice.

"Yes, I do. This is just what I've been looking for. It will be perfect after I renovate it. Is this place on the historical registry? How old is it?" Jill could hardly contain her excitement about the old house, outside the little town of Gray Hollow high in the Smokies, yet not too far from either

Greensboro or Charlotte. Wanting to see more, she opened the door and started to get out.

None too gently George Wilson, the realtor, grabbed her arm. "You don't want this place," he repeated, his voice shaky. "It's been haunted for nigh onto a hundred years. Been on the market, off and on, since long before I started selling real estate around here."

Jill laughed. She had always heard mountain folk were superstitious. And now she was seeing it firsthand. Haunted houses and ghosts. What a joke! If she could live with the mess she had made of her own life, she could certainly make room for these figments of George Wilson's active imagination!

"I'm not afraid of a few spirits, George. Come on, I want to see the inside." She extricated her arm from the realtor's grasp, slid out of the car, and headed briskly up a weed-filled path to the porch.

When George caught up with her, he was huffing and red-faced. "I can't let you go in there by yourself," he grumbled, catching Jill's arm and placing himself in front of her. "Watch out for those rotten porch boards." He reminded her of a very reluctant knight of old she had once seen in a movie, the way he stood there, as if scared to death but determined to shield her from her own perilous folly.

They made their way across the sagging porch, and George fit an ancient, rusty key into the lock of the front door. When he opened it, the creak of long-immobile hinges made Jill jump. Still, the house called out to her, like a living thing too long deprived of the warmth of human care.

"Might be able to salvage some old heart pine," George muttered as he made his way across wide board planks that hadn't seen a broom, much less wax and nourishing oils, for years. "Guess you could build a mighty nice place here after you tear this one down."

Jill could practically feel the old house shudder. "Tear it down? That would be a crime! I'll have it restored! See this detail? It looks as if it was all carved by hand." She knelt and traced a dust-filled crevice in a baseboard, revealing a design of delicate, interwoven leaves and vines. When George made his way down a wide, empty hallway, she stood and followed, taking in the charming ambience the deserted rooms still exuded as the realtor opened doors and stood back for her to look.

"Miss Jill, you don't want to live here," he said again, opening another creaking door and practically leaping back, as if he thought he was in mortal danger. "Here's the very room where they got what was comin' to them. Nobody ever fixed it, just boarded it up and left it to the ghosts." In a shaky voice, hands trembling, George related the tale of ill-fated lovers who had died in the still-charred ruins of what must have once been a cozy bedroom. "You know, they say th' bed burned first," he concluded, closing off the room with a trembling hand and making his way as fast as he could to the gaping front door.

The story—and the sight of the gutted room, where repairs had been limited to the outer walls—shook Jill for a minute. But she had made up her mind. This was where she would mend her life and her battered heart. She wasn't going to rest until Bliss House belonged to her.

Chapter
Two

THE GHOSTS

Later, after the sun faded behind a mountaintop west of Bliss House, its ghostly occupants settled in the ruined parlor—as was their habit of a late summer evening.

"Dry your tears, my dear," said the ghost of Cyrus Bliss. He wished he could do more than whisper in the wind to the spirit of Laura Randall, his love in life and now his companion in death. Silently he cursed that harebrained excuse for a snake-oil peddler who had been halfheartedly trying to sell this place for close to thirty years—and the others who had preceded him, trying with little enthusiasm to unload the place he guessed must have become an albatross around the necks of his heirs.

He had felt Laura's spirit grow sad every time the realtors brought some prospective buyer to the decaying pile of wood and mortar that had been her pride and joy in life. And they all did a damn fine job of scaring anybody away who might have bought Bliss House, what with their tales of bad luck and ghosts.

Cyrus reached out, as if he could comfort Laura with a touch, and he felt her spirit settle beside him in the dark of the moonless night. *"Will she buy it?"* Laura asked, her voice high and reedy, like the sound of tinkling bells.

Cyrus felt her fear. They had been given one hundred years—it had nearly passed. Still, his and Laura's scandal lived, fueled by the legends of the hill people and fired by hatred and shame passed down through generations of Blisses and Randalls.

He would have thought, after his family had moved away from Gray Hollow, that the talk would die down. But it never had. And now he and Laura had just three months left to right mistakes that had brought them to this, a limbo where they floated, not living yet not dead. To end the curse on Bliss House or meet the fiery pits of hell.

"Cyrus?"

"Yes, my dear?"

"She reminded me of your Prudence."

Cyrus shrugged his ghostly shoulders. Years had dimmed his memories, he supposed, for he had seen little in the woman that could compare with his daughter, the only one of his or Laura's children who had stood by them when they had defied convention and flaunted their ill-fated love for all to see. *"Really?"* he asked as he tried to picture Prudence in his mind.

"Imagine the lady with lighter hair, long like Prudence's instead of cut so short, my love. And with skin untouched by the sun. Heaven knows what the world outside has come to, when ladies ruin their soft white skin by baking in the sun like darkies—and try to look like men with their pants and cropped-off hair."

"Hmmm." Actually Cyrus liked the way the woman's scandalous denim pants hugged her trim, taut thighs and

buttocks. Her hair wasn't bad, either, with wispy curls that drew his attention to high cheekbones and big, dark eyes that reflected none of the modesty required of young unmarried women in his day. Still, he couldn't imagine running his fingers through a tousled mop of curls no longer than his own.

"Didn't you see the resemblance?" Laura asked, her tone anxious now.

"Perhaps."

"She looked wanton, though. Prudence was always the perfect lady." Laura drifted over to the weathered mantel where a faded daguerreotype still rested in its tarnished silver frame. *"But there was something about her . . ."*

"The woman is not of my family. Remember the legend, Laura. We will know when a Bliss or a Randall returns to Bliss House."

"Always the legend," Laura murmured, her tone conveying a bitterness rare in the woman who had risked everything to share his love, and who had died for it, only to remain trapped here with him for a hundred years. *"She has known love and pain, Cyrus. I believe she is the one we have waited for. Do you think she will buy the house?"*

"Time will tell." Cyrus would not raise Laura's hopes too high, but he could not bring himself to dash them by mentioning what he knew Laura had already seen. The woman who came today had been alone—and she was neither a Randall nor a Bliss. But he had seen one encouraging sign— the woman's finger, where he might have seen a wedding band, was bare.

To break the spell that bound them to Bliss House, he and Laura must entice another pair of lovers, one of whom had to have descended from either Laura or himself, to settle here in Bliss House. And these lovers had to be free to say the vows fate had denied Cyrus and Laura so many years ago.

But Cyrus had felt the young woman's excitement as she knelt and raved over hand-carved baseboards long obscured

by dust and grime, and when she followed the reluctant realtor through dingy rooms that made his Laura fret and cry
for the way they used to be. He had a hunch this woman
would be the one to buy Bliss House. Perhaps fate would
bring a modern-day Bliss or Randall here as well. If it did,
he and Laura would do their best to see that romance
bloomed between that as-yet-unknown man and the new
owner of his ill-fated home.

Gathering Laura's fragile spirit gently to himself, Cyrus
allowed them a bit of hope.

Chapter
Three

Six weeks later, as summer gave way to the soft, cool breezes of fall, Jill arrived in Gray Hollow, all her possessions stuffed into the shiny new Bronco and dilapidated trailer she pulled behind it. Bliss House was finally hers! Settling on a price had been ridiculously easy, compared with the chore she'd had persuading George Wilson she really wanted to buy the haunted house.

"It's all yours," George said as he handed Jill her copies of the deed to Bliss House and the ten acres that surrounded it. "Though heaven only knows what you're going to do with it."

Jill smiled. It didn't matter that the realtor thought she had lost her mind, and she certainly didn't care that her friends in Atlanta were certain she would lose her shirt, running a home-decorating business from an isolated old house high up in the Smoky Mountains. Bliss House was hers, and she couldn't wait to see it emerge, like a butterfly from its ugly cocoon, into the refuge she knew it would become for her wounded soul.

"Can you recommend a contractor around here?" she asked, anxious to begin renovating her new home.

George scratched his head. "I can make a few calls. But like I told you before, folks around here don't want to go anywhere near that haunted house. They're not going to jump at the chance of working on it."

Jill looked around the old-fashioned café and general store next to the courthouse in Gray Hollow where she had met with George to close the sale. It was ten in the morning, a time when most folks would be working, yet she saw at least twenty able-bodied men lingering over coffee as if they had nothing better to do. "I'd thought about simply making enough repairs so I can move in now, and holding off on the major restoration work until spring," she told him, shifting her gaze from the idle townspeople back to George.

"You could pin up a note on Maida's bulletin board over there, and maybe at the grocery store," George said doubt-fully, "but that old house is going to need more than what some handymen can do to make it fit to live in."

Jill figured George was right about that. Still, she didn't relish spending the winter camping out in her tiny travel trailer. She spared a glance at it through the rippled plate-glass window. Even though the trailer had appeared roomy enough when she'd bought it last week, it appeared to grow smaller every time she looked—certainly smaller than it had felt while she was towing it here from Atlanta behind her Bronco. "I'll find someone to do the work," she said hope-fully. "I'd best be going home now so I can get the trailer set up before the electric company gets there to hook up the power."

"I'll look around for someone to work on the house for you," George said in parting, but his tone didn't convey much hope that he would be successful.

As she pulled into the driveway Jill decided George must

be feeling guilty for having sold Bliss House to her as she recalled how hard the man had tried to steer her away from the place he must truly believe was haunted.

Briefly she wondered if she should have revealed the modern-day ghosts she lived with every day, just to reassure him that she had no reason at all to fear spirits departed a century ago. Then she shrugged. Her past was hers and hers alone; she had no need to fuel old local legend by embellishing it with the tale of her own personal hell.

As she came home Jill felt a sense of rightness. She was starting over, building her life on a firm foundation rather than on the shifting sands where she had spent the last ten years. She would prove everybody wrong: not only the folks around here who thought she was tempting fate by taking on this place and its century-old legend, but friends she'd left in Atlanta who had said she was throwing away all she had there to escape the memories of her marriage and its tragic end.

She hadn't told them the whole story. She hadn't told anyone. As she brought Bliss House back to life she would exorcise the shame and hurt. By doing so, she would come to life again.

Full of energy, Jill dug right in to the chore of cleaning up her new home. But the job was daunting. And in the next two weeks no one came or called to respond to the ads she had posted. She had planned to make the house livable, spend the winter planning how she would renovate, and hire a construction crew in the spring. To make Bliss House fit to live in, though, she had to have at least a few people willing to help scour off decades of grime.

"Come off it, Jill," she muttered as she plunged a stiff scrub brush into a pail of water she'd heated on the tiny stove in her trailer and hauled to the house. "George was right. This place needs a damn sight more than a thorough cleaning. You've got to find some contractor willing to start restoring it *now!*"

She stood and lifted the bucket, her other hand reaching

around to rub her aching back. Tossing out the water the minute she stepped outside, Jill headed for the trailer to clean up and go to town. With all the city people buying land and building houses around Gray Hollow, she figured there had to be several building contractors around, and that she could hire one now, since their business must be slacking off in anticipation of winter. George *had* told her he would ask around.

"Someone actually bought that pile of rubble and wants to restore it?" Kyle Randall asked longtime acquaintance George Wilson as they sat in Maida's, having lunch.

"Yes. Lady from Atlanta by the name of Jill Carey. She's young. Kind of brittle like, but pretty. Not more than thirty, I'd guess. Crazy, though. She actually intends to live there this winter. Don't know how she's going to manage that, because she hasn't had any luck hiring folks to help clean and patch up the place." George motioned toward the bulletin board on the wall by the antique cash register. "That sign's been up for two weeks now, and not one single soul's been brave enough to go earn good money, working in the haunted house."

That hardly surprised Kyle. Folks in Gray Hollow had been scaring their kids for generations with tales of the wicked ghosts of Cyrus Bliss and his own great-great-grandmother, Laura Randall. "She wants to restore the house?" he asked idly.

"Yeah. She'd be better off to tear it down and start fresh, I told her. But like I said, she's downright nuts. Insists she's going to get somebody to fix it up. You think it can be done?"

"I've never been inside the place. Don't intend to be, either." It wasn't that he was afraid of ghosts. He just didn't need a reminder of the taunts he'd endured as a kid growing up in Gray Hollow, about how he was descended from Gray Hollow's legendary adulteress and the cuckolded husband who had blown her and her lover away one wintry night in the distant past. Besides, if the county commissioners accepted the bid he'd just put in to restore the crumbling courthouse in Gray Hollow, he would have all the work his crew could handle this winter.

"Didn't think you would," George commented. "You know anyone who might be desperate enough to work on Bliss House?"

Kyle shrugged. Since city dwellers had been buying up mountain land for vacation homes, decent building contractors in western North Carolina had as much work as they wanted. "Not offhand."

"Could you ask around? I feel bad, bein' I was the one who showed Ms. Carey Bliss House in the first place. Hell, I had no idea she'd be crazy enough to want to buy it."

"I had no idea anyone would ever be crazy enough to buy it. The place has to be ready to collapse. No one's lived there for nearly a hundred years." Pausing, Kyle tried to think of contractors he knew who specialized in restoring old houses and might be hungry for business. He came up blank. "George, I don't know who this woman might hire to fix up her haunted house."

"She's got cash money," George said, as if that might spark Kyle's interest. "Paid for the place outright—didn't blink an eye at the asking price. Not that Margaret Bliss up in New Jersey was askin' much for it, since the family's been trying to sell it for longer than I can remember."

Kyle's gaze shifted toward the front door of the café, and Helen Smith, the county commissioners' rotund secretary, who had passed through it and was headed toward their table. "I'll let you know if I think of someone," he said, rising to greet Helen as she waddled up to him.

"They've got an answer for you, Kyle," she said, turning and heading out the door, obviously intending for him to follow her back to the makeshift courthouse the commissioners had been using for five years now, since the fire marshal had condemned the two-hundred-year-old structure he hoped to restore. He rose and, after telling George good-bye, caught up with Helen in three short strides.

Jill's trek into Gray Hollow had netted her absolutely nothing. She might as well have kept on scrubbing. At least if she had, she would have been another square foot or so closer to having her home clean enough to sleep in!

"I'll probably have to import a firm from a thousand miles away," she muttered. George hadn't given her a bit of hope that she could hire someone to restore Bliss House now. And after she'd spoken with some of the locals in Maida's, she had started believing there wasn't a soul within miles who would risk riling up the so-called ghosts by intruding into the house where they had died.

Jill snorted. She had been living in her travel trailer just outside Bliss House for two weeks, and she hadn't seen the first thing that made her believe in those elusive ghosts!

Still muttering when she heard her phone beep, she clicked on the speaker and said, "Hello?"

"Ms. Carey?"

"Yes?"

"I'm Kyle Randall, with Randall Contractors out of Greensboro. I understand from George Wilson you may need some renovation work done on an old house near Gray Hollow."

Jill smiled. "Bliss House." Better to get *that* out in the open from the start, she thought, wondering if this man with a deep, pleasant drawl shared most everybody's terror of "her" haunted house.

"I know. George mentioned it. My firm specializes in re-creating old buildings."

"Re-creating?"

"That's how I like to think of it. I work from pictures and old plans and build from scratch so folks can't tell the new from the old," he explained.

"I'm planning to renovate the existing house," Jill said

firmly. "Of course, there will have to be some rebuilding. I'd be interested in getting your opinion and bid."

She thought she heard him let out a big breath of air. "Would tomorrow be convenient for you?" he asked after a minute's silence.

"That would be fine. Ten o'clock?"

"I'll meet you at the house," he confirmed before hanging up. Jill sat there for a while, wondering if during the fifteen or so hours between now and ten tomorrow Mr. Kyle Randall would decide he had best not brave the ghosts of Bliss House. If he did, she thought ruefully, he would certainly not be the first of his kind to shy away from her beautifully decrepit folly.

Kyle settled back with a beer and wondered why the idea of going back to Gray Hollow—to Bliss House—made his guts churn. Hell, it was only a house!

What had gone on there nearly a hundred years ago was ancient history, doubtless without a bit of meaning to anybody except the Randalls scattered about the North Carolina mountains. No one now would give a damn that his great-great-grandma had been the infamous Laura Randall, or that she had died with her lover, Cyrus, at the house that still bore his family's name.

Hell, who was he kidding? He figured parents in Gray Hollow must still scare their kids with stories about the ghosts of Bliss House, the same way *their* parents had been doing for generations.

He should just call this crazy Jill Carey and tell her he didn't have time for her damn pet project! But if he did, he knew he'd regret it. He'd won the bid to restore the Gray Hollow courthouse, but the commission had voted to postpone having the work done until next spring. That meant he had to find a project now.

Earlier today he'd told George Wilson he didn't know any contractor desperate enough to take on the ghosts of Bliss House. Boy, had he been wrong! In ten short minutes Kyle had gone from being overbooked with work to a state of minor desperation. Big jobs were few and far between this time of year, especially ones in this part of the country, where he could work and still be close enough to visit Alyssa every weekend.

Kyle's gaze settled on the child in a picture on his coffee table. His little girl looked so pretty, laid out on a blanket underneath an old oak tree, her dark eyes wide open as if she was looking at something far off in the distance. Knowing Alyssa would never see anything, never walk or talk or be able to learn her name, ate him alive.

He would never have to put on a monkey suit to walk his baby down the aisle to some guy who could never be good enough for her. Or hold her baby in his arms. But one thing was for sure. Alyssa would need the total care of people like the ones at Angels' Paradise School as long as she lived—and that care didn't come cheap!

"Damn her to hell!" Kyle tried hard not to think of Tina, Alyssa's mother. Or the way she had passed the results of her lousy drug habit on to his daughter seven years ago, before she checked out on him—and life—with one final trip on God only knew what. But when he thought of Alyssa and the bleak future she had in store, he couldn't help wishing Tina was still alive so he could have the pleasure of killing her with his bare hands.

Like they say Harry Randall did to his faithless wife and her lover.

Kyle shook his head. Where the hell had that thought come from? Was the idea of going to Gray Hollow, bidding on fixing up the house where his great-great-grandmother had died, starting to drive him nuts?

Like it or not, he had to bid on that job. Winter was coming—and no matter what the season, Alyssa's special school expected to be paid. Draining the last of his beer, Kyle tried to push those odd, scary feelings out of his head.

Chapter
Four

Jill yawned. Glancing at her watch, she saw it had been nearly four hours since she had begun poring over the blueprints of Bliss House she had found tucked away in a moldy wardrobe. She wanted modern comforts along with authenticity, yet the house itself seemed to call out and beg her to restore it to the way it was when Mortimer Bliss built it in 1858 for the bride he had expected to arrive that year from England.

Perhaps Kyle Randall would be able to suggest how she might bring to Bliss House the best of both old and new worlds. For a moment she tried to picture a face to go with the deep, sexy voice that still rang in her ears. Then she laughed. She was visualizing young and ruggedly handsome, while Randall was probably ugly as sin and old enough to be her dad. Besides, Jill reminded herself, she had sworn off men—not just Rob, but everybody else of the male persuasion!

Still, the memory of Kyle's voice made her tingle, and she felt her nipples stab insistently against her soft silk robe. Idly Jill ran a finger back and forth against one aching nub, gasping when the flesh swelled and pushed against the slight, warm pressure. With determination, she got up and willed the aching need to go away.

After washing up and brushing her teeth in the closetlike bathroom of the trailer, she crawled into her narrow bed. Damn Rob for having taught her never to ignore her own sensual needs, she thought as she caressed herself until the tension broke. When she finally slept, she dreamed.

Bliss House shone bright, and sounds of joy came from within. Jill stood in the doorway, waiting for a sad-faced butler to take her velvet wrap. Her gaze wandered from a beautiful chandelier twinkling above her head to the modest ballroom someone had created by opening the front and back parlors of this gorgeous old home to create one highly polished dance floor.

Suddenly she felt naked. All the other guests looked positively Victorian. This black silk minidress didn't cover nearly enough of her, she decided, wondering if she had missed the words *costumed ball* on her invitation. She watched dancers twirling gracefully to a distinct three-beat tune that sounded as if it came not from a stereo system, but from a small live orchestra.

She looked around. Where had Rob gone? Annoyed, Jill stepped alone into the ballroom and searched for his angel face. She couldn't find him. Instead, her gaze settled on a couple whose quaint costumes reminded her of a Victorian picture postcard.

The woman's rose crushed-velvet gown featured a bustle and train that dripped with ecru lace. More of the lace peeked out from a low, heart-shaped neckline and the cuffs of fat leg-o'-mutton sleeves. Her partner wore tails, stark black, with pristine white linen at his wrists and throat—too much, Jill decided, for even the most formal of Atlanta balls. Feeling out of place, she hid behind the French doors that normally would have separated the two rooms, and searched again for Rob.

But her gaze kept returning, as if without her direction, to that mesmerizing couple who seemed to have stepped out of yesterday. The way they looked at each other, the graceful way they moved together, kept Jill enthralled. Then a stranger found her, and the spell broke. He pulled her onto the dance floor, seemingly unaffected by the sense of the past that surrounded her.

He was tall and rugged, and he made her tingle from head to toe, but mostly deep inside her where she needed to be filled. But then he changed, became Rob again. Suddenly she relived the horror that had sent her running from Atlanta—and her memories of how her marriage had begun—and ended.

"No!"

Her own scream startled her from her dream. She couldn't stay in her sweat-drenched bed another second. Pulling on a robe as she ran, Jill sought peace in Bliss House. For some reason, she felt that there she would be safe from the nightmare that tormented her.

In his lonely bed, Kyle was dreaming, too.

He had come to Bliss House, in the gray hour before the dawn. It was early, too early for his appointment with the husky-voiced woman who'd been fool enough to buy this place of sorrow and death. Still, he was here, on land he hadn't set foot on since he was a brash kid, proving he wasn't afraid of the ghosts or bothered by what people kept telling him was his family's shame. Why had he come so early?

Maybe I figured that if I spent a little time here, I'd realize the stories about this place are all a bunch of bull, he thought as he pushed aside a bit more of what his mind insisted had to be unwarranted fear. Kyle ventured into the bramble of untrimmed hedges and shrubs that ringed the house. And then he heard a scream.

"Oh, no!" That cry came right after what sounded like wood splintering—and a few words he would almost swear had sounded like ones he wouldn't dare to use in mixed company.

The sounds came from the porch. The hair on the back of his neck stood up, and for a moment he thought of the so-called ghosts and felt tempted to get the hell away and not come back. But the angry voice sounded female—and very much alive. Kyle had been raised better than to run away from a woman in distress, so he gathered up his courage and sprinted toward the house.

"Can I help?"

It was a female—from what he could see in the faint light of the rising sun, a damn attractive one. And it was obvious she could use some assistance, getting out of that hole she'd made in the rotten porch boards and up onto firm ground.

"Yes. It seems I suddenly got too heavy for this section of porch," she said huskily with what sounded like a brave try for a grin. "Be careful. You don't want to fall through, too."

Kyle turned on the flashlight he had been carrying and aimed the beam at the hole. "Looks like I will, if I try to get to you that way. I'll just pull off the latticework out here and come in from the ground."

The woman hesitated, as if the idea of tearing up this old porch upset her. "All right," she finally said, turning around to face him while he ripped off ancient strips of lattice. "Don't tear up any more than you have to."

"I won't." In short order Kyle had torn off enough latticework to make a hole big enough to squeeze through. "I'm coming with the flashlight. See if you can wiggle through that hole." In his experience, women didn't much like the dark—or places where there might be creepy, crawly creatures, either. Of course, Tina had seen those things even where they weren't likely to be, Kyle reminded himself as he ducked to keep from hitting his head on the porch floor above him. Carefully he made his way toward the trapped woman.

Their fingers touched, and he felt electricity clear down to his toes. "Are you willing to do it?" she asked when they reached solid ground.

Willing to do what? He raked her trim, inviting body with his gaze and decided he'd been celibate too long. This woman was a dream come true.

"Do you think that bottom step is safe enough for us to sit down on?" she asked, moving awkwardly, as if she had a bug inside the gaping lapels of that damn silky black robe.

Kyle knelt and ran a hand over the ancient wood before tentatively putting his weight down on the step. "Seems okay," he finally said, and he watched as she settled down beside him. He caught a glimpse of one plump, white breast before she pulled the lapels of her robe closed and met his gaze with dark eyes he thought looked unnaturally excited this cool, misty morning.

"You want me?"

He noticed her gaze had settled on the crotch of his pants, and that her tongue was darting out to moisten pink, inviting lips. "You're serious, aren't you?" he asked as he felt his cock begin to throb and grow under her close scrutiny.

"Dead serious." She sounded as if she was about to come already.

He knew he had to be dreaming, but he reached out and traced a finger down the exposed hollow between her breasts. She certainly felt real. She felt like silk. And she smelled like some musky tropical flower. He watched her eyes darken before long, dark lashes fluttered shut, and her mouth opened slightly as if in invitation to his tongue.

He stood and scooped her into his arms. Making his way carefully, he got to the front door of the house he had never entered before. "Open the door," he said. When she did, her robe fell open, baring full, lush breasts that seemed to beg for the touch of his fingers and lips.

He stepped inside with her before dipping his head and flicking a distended nipple with his tongue. The pebbled nub seemed to strain for more. *God, how she responds,* he thought as he looked in the dim light for a place to set down. He deliberately rubbed his cheek against her nipple. He was ready to explode.

He set her down slowly so he could feel her softness slither down his body; and he gasped when she pressed her hips tight to his, as if she was checking how much he wanted her.

"In here," she whispered, and she led him into a room that seemed to have escaped the ravages of time. He watched, throbbing harder with each breath, as she pulled back a faded quilt and knelt on the sleigh bed with knees spread apart, shrugging out of her robe and holding out her arms to him like some naked, gleaming goddess.

There was something pagan about her, something that beckoned him to taste her honey. As he stripped down, his gaze fell from those impudently tip-tilted breasts to . . .

Jesus, she took his breath away! He feasted his gaze on the soft downy mound and lower, where he could see the throbbing of the tight little bud of her throbbing cleft. Before collapsing on his knees before her, he managed to jerk a condom packet out of his pocket with shaky hands and toss it on the bed.

She reached out and touched him, her fingers as hesitant as her invitation had been bold. "Ooh," she murmured as her hands moved between his legs and traced the length of his cock before drifting lower to weigh his balls between her palms.

"Don't stop," he told her, pausing to savor the silky feel of her mound while his other hand toyed with a straining nipple. "Does that turn you on?"

"More like I hope it turns you on."

"Baby, I was already hotter than a firecracker. But your hands are stokin' the fire hotter."

"I know." She traced him from base to tip, then circled him with both her hands and stroked back and forth. He felt damn near ready to come even before she bent and took him into her mouth.

His fingers worked at her nipples, tugging and pinching lightly, bringing them to straining points. He felt her lap up beads of moisture from the tip of his cock, and he barely registered her question. "What's his name?"

"Huh?"

"This beautiful guy. What's his name?" He felt her tongue flick the tip and her finger trace around the base of his sex.

"Big Al," he said gruffly as he lay back and made her straddle his face so he could drink her honey. He laved her with his tongue until she screamed. When she would have moved, he stopped her, letting her turn just enough that she could play with him while he feasted on her. He heard her rip open the condom wrapper and felt her smooth the rubber over his pulsing cock.

When he paused to catch his breath, she swiveled around, coming down on him and taking him inside her tight, hot little body. God, it felt too good, the way she milked him as she moved, slowly sinking down to take him all the way to his balls before rising up again until she nearly let him go before doing it all over again, faster and faster until all he could do was clench her soft little butt and hold her there while he came a dozen ways from Sunday.

"Again?" she asked when he finally quit breathing hard and lazily started suckling at a handy nipple. He grinned when he felt himself twitching and swelling again inside her.

"Yeah. How do you want it this time, honey?" He sucked harder, flaying the tip of her nipple with his tongue as he found the other breast and weighed it in his hand. He felt himself getting harder, felt her inner muscles teasing and caressing him. God, but she could fuck!

"On my knees." She was panting now, as if she couldn't

wait. So she could move, he pulled out and waited, getting harder and hotter as he watched her settle, butt in the air, belly and tits pressed against the quilt along with the flushed face that rested on her folded hands. "Now," she begged as he teased by rubbing Big Al up and down the crevice of her gorgeous backside.

He pushed into her slowly while his fingers toyed with the tiny nub of her sex. When they were completely joined, he drew her upward, freeing her breasts for one hand while the other possessively cupped her smooth, soft mound. This time she came first, screaming out her completion the fourth time he thrust hard and deep into her honeyed sheath. He followed close behind, pulled along by the strength of her wild climax.

Then he fell back into a deep, dreamless sleep.

When he woke up to the incessant beeping of his alarm clock, Kyle wondered why he was tangled in sweat-drenched covers when he had spent the night as alone as he had been every night for the past seven and a half miserable years. And why couldn't he stop remembering pieces of what had to be the most erotic dream he'd ever had?

A cold shower and a pot of hot coffee had him feeling almost human by the time he climbed in his pickup and headed over to meet the crazy lady who'd bought Bliss House. If it weren't for the way his own family's history tied in with the old legends about the place, he could get excited about the prospect of restoring the former post house that had been around since before the Civil War.

He stopped the truck on the scenic overlook directly in front of the house and got out to size up Bliss House from a distance of about two hundred yards. The house had a kind of timeless grace about it, he had to admit as he took in its square-columned porches that ringed both sides as well as the front. Even from this distance, though, Kyle could tell the place was in sorry shape. He would do his damnedest to persuade this Jill Carey to let him tear it down and rebuild from scratch, using as many of the original materials as he could salvage.

Glancing at his watch, he decided he might as well go on over to the house. He shrugged off the feeling that he'd been on that porch before, and that there was something he should recall about this place other than its connection to the scandalous story of his long-dead ancestor and her illicit relationship with Mr. Bliss.

Jill glanced out the open front door and saw a shiny pickup truck bouncing up the cleared-out track through brambles that masqueraded as a driveway. Then she looked at her watch. Nine-thirty. Kyle Randall must be coming early.

Sighing, she set aside the dry mop she'd been using to brush years-old spiderwebs and dust from water-stained walls. Wiping at the dirt she knew was smudged across one cheek, she watched as a tall, powerfully built man with longish, dark blond hair got out of the truck and headed toward the house with long, decisive strides.

God, he's gorgeous. The breeze tossed his clean, light hair across his brow, drawing her attention to eyes the color of pine boughs in the forest. Only a tiny scar that ran through his right eyebrow, and his nose, which she guessed must have been broken sometime in the past, kept him from being pretty-boy handsome. She couldn't fault his big, tough-looking body, either, or the way he set it off with a deep green button-down shirt and khaki slacks that fit him as if they'd been tailor-made.

"Ms. Carey?" he said politely in that deep sexy drawl that had kept her up half the night.

"Yes." She could barely find the will to speak.

"I'm Kyle Randall." He fished in his pocket and came up with a business card.

So he wasn't going to apologize for being early, she thought, mentally excusing him because, after all, he was a male and not expected to kowtow to any woman, prospective customer or not. "And you're early," she retorted as sharply as she could manage while he stared at her as if she were some treat he was sizing up for a possible meal.

"The better to get started deciding what has to be done to this old girl," he said casually, holding out both arms as if he were trying to encompass the entire house.

She noticed, though, that Kyle's gaze stayed fixed on her—and she wished she had worn something besides this old aerobics outfit that left little to anyone's imagination. "I should go change," she murmured before she could call back the words.

"Don't do it on my account." Kyle grinned as he met Jill's gaze, and she noticed that when he smiled he looked good enough to eat.

"All right. What do you want to see first?"

"We might as well start inside. You wouldn't happen to have blueprints, would you?"

"Yes. They're in the trailer."

Kyle nodded. "Good. We'll look at them last."

For the next two hours they toured the house, and for the first time since she had bought Bliss House, Jill felt as if unseen eyes were watching their every step. She didn't say anything, though, for fear she might scare Kyle off.

When she'd called George Wilson last night, he'd told her Kyle was a Gray Hollow native, related to the Laura Randall who had died here with her lover. She couldn't imagine a big, rugged guy like Kyle putting a whole lot of credence in tales of ghosts and haunted houses, but she wouldn't take the chance of mentioning this eerie feeling to him, since he was her best, maybe her only, hope of making her home livable before next summer!

Jill had saved the bedroom that had been destroyed the night the so-called ghosts had died for last. She winced when Kyle shook his head after making a thorough examination of weakened floorboards and walls.

"Have you considered tearing this place down and re-creating it with new materials?" he asked as they strolled back into the front hall.

"No." Jill had had enough of things and values that were new and brittle. She had bought Bliss House to get back in touch with herself and a past much older than her own. But she didn't know how to put her feelings into words Kyle would understand.

"It would be cheaper, and easier," he interjected.

She turned to face him. "I don't care."

"You're going for a historical-restoration tax credit?"

His assumption would work as well as the truth she didn't quite know how to express. "Yes."

"It's not going to be cheap."

Jill nodded. "I don't care."

"I need some fresh air. I need to take a look at the exterior, too." Kyle sounded as if he couldn't get out of Bliss House fast enough, and Jill wondered if he, too, had felt the nagging, silent presences that had nudged at her while they explored.

"You'll need to check the porch," she replied, leading the way. "Watch out over there—there's a hole where I fell through rotten boards this morning."

Why did Kyle suddenly look as though someone had walked over his grave? "Is something wrong?" Jill asked, concerned.

He shook his head, then forced a smile. "No." He knelt and looked closely at the weather-beaten boards. "All this is rotten. You shouldn't even try walking on it. Let's get down on the ground." He stood and carefully made his way down the steps, politely turning and offering her his hand.

When their fingers touched, Jill felt the muscles contract in her lower belly as a sudden burst of heat spread throughout her body. She hoped Kyle's gaze was focused elsewhere, because she knew he would see her hardened nipples stabbing against the snug Lycra of her leotard if he looked. No one had ever affected her quite so strongly—not even Rob.

"Jill?"

She breathed a sigh of relief. He hadn't been looking at her, since he had crouched down to inspect the base of a massive square column that framed the porch and held up the cedar-shake roof. "Yes?"

"I think we can salvage the columns. This one looks pretty solid. Of course, there could be rot inside, but I don't think so." He stood up, and she quickly shifted her gaze, but not until she had focused momentarily on the impressive bulge at the juncture of his thighs.

What has gotten into you, Jill? This man is just that—a man. And you swore off them, remember? For damn good reason.

She kept her emotions under strict control, and her greedy gaze everywhere but on Kyle Randall, as they spent the rest of the day inside the trailer reviewing the ancient set of blueprints she had found. When he left, promising to get back to her with a written estimate within the week, she let out a sigh of relief and headed to Maida's café for an early supper.

"Tell me about the legend." The café was quiet, and Maida had sat down with her after bringing her a slice of coconut cream pie. Since Jill had sensed that eerie presence today, "her" ghosts had been playing on her mind.

"Well, folks say it started when no-'count Harry Randall took to samplin' too much of his uncle Burle's moonshine," Maida said, settling more comfortably onto the straight-back chair and giving Jill a piercing glance. "That would've been back in ninety-three, folks say. Apparently Harry didn't hold his liquor very well, and he started in usin' his fists and hurtin' folks. Word has it he bruised up Miss Laura pretty good, and Mr. Bliss didn't take too kindly to Harry using her for a punching bag."

"Were they neighbors?"

"No. Th' Randalls lived higher up in th' hills, a couple of miles farther up that road that goes in front of Bliss House. But Laura cleaned house for Mr. Bliss, had for about three years before the trouble started, ever since his wife took the fever and died."

"Oh," Jill said.

"Well, Mr. Bliss took it on himself to take ol' Harry to task one day when Miss Laura couldn't hide the bruises from folks no more. And Harry took a mule-skinnin' knife to him. Didn't do more than draw some blood, but Mr. Bliss got the sheriff and a circuit judge, and Harry got sentenced to five years' hard labor at the penitentiary over by Boonesburg. Folks say they dragged Harry off in chains, with him cussin' and yellin' that he was gonna kill 'em both—Miss Laura and Mr. Bliss, that is."

"Did he?"

Maida cleared her throat and shifted her ample bulk in the chair. "Not then. You want to hear this or not?"

"Yes. I'm sorry for interrupting." Jill leaned back and looked out the window at the mist that was beginning to settle on the mountainside.

"After Harry was gone, there Miss Laura was, all alone, 'cept for those three wild boys of hers. Oldest was about fourteen, the next one twelve. The baby must have been around three or so, I guess. She didn't have any kinfolk, and Harry's blamed her for gettin' him sent off to the pen. She and those boys would've starved if it weren't for Mr. Bliss.

"At first she stayed in that shack up on Hunter's Mountain, walked down to Mr. Bliss's place every day to cook and clean. She'd take her youngest boy with her, tote him in her arms when his little legs would get tired. After the new year in ninety-four, though, Mr. Bliss built her a little cabin at the back of his land. Foundation of the place is still out there somewhere in your woods."

Jill nodded. So that was what she'd seen the other day, when she had ventured through the brambles to explore her property.

"Laura's two big boys wouldn't budge from Hunter's Mountain. But she brought the little one with her. Folks say she loved that little boy something fierce, him being the only one she had left. But one cold night, in the winter of ninety-four, he got real sick, and Laura called Mr. Bliss down to help her take care of him. The little fellow died, though, in spite of all they and the doc Mr. Bliss brought back from Greensboro could do to save him."

Jill's heart constricted at the thought of Laura Randall's loss of a beloved child. "And after that?" she prompted.

Maida reached over to pour herself another cup of coffee from the ironstone pot on the table and took a long, thoughtful sip. "After that, Laura went into a decline. Wouldn't talk to anybody, do anything except go up to Bliss House to cook and clean. Until one night about six months later . . . ."

Why had Maida paused? Anxious to hear more, Jill leaned forward and rested her elbows against the scarred surface of the wooden trestle table. As if it were her own life being revealed to her, she waited, entranced.

"Mr. Bliss's boy had left for the university over in Chapel Hill, and it was just him and his girl, Prudence, in the big house. Then she went to spend some time with her mama's sister over in Greensboro, and Mr. Bliss was left there with nobody—except Laura. Folks guess it started because of her bein' so distraught over her little boy and him trying to cheer her up.

"Anyway, on the Fourth of July in ninety-five he talked her into joining him in Gray Hollow for the big Independence Day celebration, and while the cannons were boomin' and shootin' off their sparks, he kissed her. Right there in front of the whole town, where everybody could see. Scandalized everybody, that's what they did, what with him bein' the town's leading citizen and her bein' his housekeeper—not to mention she was still married to crazy Harry Randall."

"That hardly seems scandalous enough to—"

"Maybe not to you and me, honey, but remember this was more than a hundred years ago. Folks didn't go kissin' in public, and they sure didn't look the other way when they saw marriage vows bein' violated like that. But that wasn't all Cyrus Bliss and Laura Randall did."

As if she couldn't bring herself to say it out loud, Maida lowered her voice nearly to a whisper. "He took her home and moved her right into his house that very night. Into the room where his sainted wife had died. Same room they died in, it was. And they carried on in front of God and everybody, not even tryin' to hide the fact they were living in sin. His son disowned him—and her two big boys came down from Hunter's Mountain to spit on her and call her a whore.

"When they came to town, decent people crossed the street to stay away from the stain of their sinning. Only his daughter, Prudence, seemed to think they were all right. She didn't remember her own mama, don't guess, and she latched on to Laura right from the start when she started working for Cyrus. She was the only one to grieve when they died."

Jill felt a tear roll down her cheek, and she reached to brush it away. "How?" She couldn't help asking, even though George Wilson had mentioned the circumstances of Laura and Cyrus's ignoble demise while he was trying to dissuade her from buying the house.

"No one could ever be sure, because not a soul saw him do it, but some folks figured Harry Randall sneaked back here and did 'em in. Would've been his right, they said."

"To kill them?"

"Laura played him false."

"But you said Harry was in prison." The idea of him being justified in killing his wife and her lover struck Jill as absurd, but she guessed some people had felt—might still feel—that way.

"About a week before it happened, Harry overpowered a guard and escaped from the pen. Wasn't ever seen again. They say it was like he just disappeared off the face of the earth. That's why a few people believe he could've come back and taken his own justice. But most folks say God himself made Laura Randall and Cyrus Bliss pay the price for their sins."

"God?"

"God." Maida's face took on a faraway look, as if she were in a trance. " 'Twas a cold, dreary December night, about a year and a half after Laura moved into Cyrus Bliss's bed. Although she was old to be carrying a child, Laura's belly had started swelling with her lover's seed, for everyone to see. The mist swirled down from Hunter's Mountain, and the wolves howled. The only light came from a full, white moon and a coal-oil lamp next to the bed where they were sleeping with their shame.

"Then, out of the darkness of the night there came a single bolt of lightning. God directed that lightning bolt, and it seared right through the roof and into the very bed where Laura and Cyrus lay sleeping. They were consumed in fire, like the sinners they had been.

"But God was merciful. He sent freezing rain to quench the fire before it could burn through the walls and kill Cyrus Bliss's innocent daughter. And He left the house standing so that for the years to come, folks in Gray Hollow would be reminded of what happens to those who sin."

Maida bent her head, as if in prayer. For a long time Jill just sat there, thinking about the ghosts of those two ill-fated lovers as she stared out the window at the swirling mountain mist.

Chapter
Five

THE GHOSTS

"I'm glad she's fixing this place up," Laura's spirit commented as they floated downstairs to enjoy the evening in the front parlor where the new owner had cleaned away most of the dirt and dust.

Cyrus settled lightly onto a wooden chair next to the empty hearth. *"Did you hear the man, my dear? He wants to tear the house down. And I could feel he has no love for Bliss House."*

Laura sighed. She knew Cyrus, too, must realize that the big, strapping man the woman had brought here today had to be descended from one of her lost, older sons—the ones who had reminded him so much of Harry, so little of her. *"He's a Randall."*

"I know. And I'm afraid."

33

Drifting over from her place on a drafty window seat, Laura knelt and reached for his elusive spirit. *"This young man—he appeared to be more uncomfortable than evil,"* she said in a soothing tone.

"You were always too willing to make allowances for Harry and his kin," Cyrus ground out, and Laura knew he was right. She *hadn't* really believed Harry Randall was evil, until that night he had broken in the window and stood there like a demonic avenger, taunting her and Cyrus with that blazing torch as well as his filthy allegations, before tossing it into their bed with a maniacal cackle she would never forget and calmly stepping through the broken window from which he had emerged. Now it looked as though Harry Randall might have the last laugh once again.

"I know. I know you expected it would be one of Prudence's children to break the spell. And we could deal so much more comfortably with one like that precious, loving girl. But fate has sent us Kyle Randall. We must trust he is as much my descendant as he is Harry's."

She could feel Cyrus's spirit gathering her gently into his arms, and for a moment Laura imagined she felt the stirring of the child they had conceived so long ago, deep within her soul. When they had been alive, Cyrus had been the brave one; now the duty fell to her to lead, to see justice done and their captive spirits freed at last.

"I felt a sensual pull between him and the woman," she said, hoping that feeling was real and not the result of wishful thinking.

Cyrus grunted. *"Yes. Neither of them took pains to mask their carnal thoughts. It would seem there have been changes in behavior between men and women since we were alive."*

"And attire, as well." The woman had been wearing nothing but some brightly colored drawers, so tight the man could hardly have failed to note how her nipples tightened when she stared at him. Laura blushed as she recalled that while his clothing had not been downright scandalous, she'd

noticed he got hard *down there* after he had stared a bit too long at the immodest display of the woman's body.

"Yes. I take it women are going about in nothing but their undergarments now," Cyrus said, sighing.

In spite of herself, Laura laughed. *"You enjoyed the view, I imagine!"*

"She reminded me of you."

"They both made me miss the sinning that brought us to this," she murmured, and she imagined Cyrus lifting her and carrying her away to love her, the way he so often had when they were alive.

"And me. Would that I could touch your beautiful breasts, lay my head between them, and feel your heart beat fast for me. And that I could love you yet with my body as I will always love you in my heart."

"Would that I could have lived long enough to bring forth your child." That had been Laura's burden for a hundred years, to carry the love child who would never be born, never learn to run and play and become a proud man like his father.

"Soon we will be able to leave Bliss House, and he will be born in heaven, sweetheart."

It was Laura's turn to doubt. *"If the woman and this young Randall descendant cooperate and fall in love,"* she reminded him.

"They will. We must see to it."

And so, through the night they plotted, hampered in their work by the curse that kept them prisoners inside Bliss House. Laura believed that Cyrus, too, felt the love that had brought this curse upon them would also work to set them free.

Chapter
Six

Kyle worked late into the night as well, hunkered down by a fire in his renovated cabin high on Hunter's Mountain. From the notes he had made at Bliss House, he worked on drafting a proposal for its renovation. As he did he tried to dispel the nagging feeling that he had been at that house, and with its owner, sometime before today.

Jill Carey had to be the most sensual creature he'd ever met, and he was damn well sure he would remember if he had ever seen her before. Those long, shapely legs, that lithe dancer's body with surprisingly lush, full breasts would have engraved themselves on his memory even if he had managed to forget her arresting, pixie face.

He felt himself stir inside his jeans as he imagined tunneling his work-roughened fingers through soft curly hair shorter than his own to cradle her scalp. He could almost feel blunt ends of the tiny tendrils tickling his knuckles, sense the slight abrasion of the close-cropped curls against the pads of his fingertips. And he could imagine her dark eyes growing liquid with desire, her full pink lips slackening as if inviting him to sample her with his tongue.

No, he'd remember Jill. And he sure as hell would recall having been inside that house that made him feel as if someone was watching his every move.

"Damn! I should have headed on back to Greensboro. It must be this place that's making me crazy!" Disgusted with himself, Kyle got up and went out on the porch to clear his head. But the eerie feelings didn't go away. And neither did his hard-on.

Jill shivered as she stepped out of the shower. Hearing the story of this place and its ill-fated lovers from Maida had almost made her believe the spirits of Laura Randall and Cyrus Bliss might really still be lingering close by. Especially after she had felt some surreal presence all the time she was in the house with Kyle today.

Kyle. She wished her hunch had been right, that his sexy voice had masked a guy as ugly as sin and old enough to be her dad. If she didn't need him to put Bliss House to rights before winter, she would run away as fast as she could, because she sensed Kyle Randall had the power to hurt her twice as much as Rob ever had.

She took the towel and dried her hair, sparing a glance in the mirror at the little-boy curls she had just about gotten used to seeing. Her hair would grow out, and she wouldn't have to live much longer with the souvenir of her last encounter with Rob—the visible one, at least. Then she shrugged into red silk pajamas and crawled lazily into bed.

She liked Gray Hollow and its friendly people like Maida. Yet Jill wondered if she'd ever fit in as she recalled the café owner's provincial sense of what was right and wrong.

Jill knew her past wouldn't stand up to close scrutiny here in the hills—indeed, it didn't stand up to her own close examination, either. What she'd done, she'd done for love. But she doubted she would ever forgive herself for letting Rob lead her so far down the road to moral decay.

And she felt, deep inside, that if it hadn't been for her catching him committing an act too depraved even for her jaded mind, she would still be with him, following his lead in the futile hope of holding his love. That made her feel dirty. So dirty she doubted anything but time could cleanse her soul.

Because for nearly ten years, I lived a fantasy, in a world where nothing was real. Where what was good was artificial; what was pleasure, illusion.

Gray Hollow had condemned Laura Randall for loving one man not her husband. Jill felt sure they would stone her if they knew even half of what she had done with the demented pervert who had married her the day she'd turned sixteen. As if by doing so she could atone for her sins, she made herself remember that awful night that had ended her illusions—and her love for Rob.

She had practically run into the huge mansion of glass and concrete, anxious to show off her new, grown-up image. An afternoon at an exclusive salon had netted her a sleek, sophisticated shoulder-length hairstyle as well as lessons in applying makeup to enhance her too-young features. She had been sure her new look would revive her forty-five-year-old husband's faltering interest in her, and make him want her as a woman, not reject her as an aging ingenue.

He hadn't, though. He'd taken one look, and those thin, discerning lips had curled into a mask of disgust. She had broken down and sobbed like a baby when he'd walked out. She doubted she would ever forget the sound of slamming doors in the distance or that distinctive purr of his Excalibur as it rolled down the long paved drive.

For two days straight she had cried. Then, the morning of the third day, she had gone out, trying to sort out her feelings. When she had returned, his car had been in the drive. Exhilarated that Rob had come home to her, she had rushed into their bedroom. What she had seen had nearly destroyed her.

He hadn't been alone. And the little girl whose long dark hair he'd been grasping as he held her down on his thrusting hips couldn't have been more than twelve years old. Long-shelved memories had assailed her, and suddenly she had seen herself there with him, alone and frightened yet wanting more than anything for him—for anyone—to love her. She had run blindly from the house and gone hysterically to the police.

Jill had never again set foot in the house that had been her legacy from her grandmother—the place where she had lived with Rob since the old woman had died when she was fourteen. Unable to face the hideous memories, she had put the house and everything in it on the market three weeks later, after the funeral.

Though she hadn't been there to see the carnage, the picture the police had shown her of that poor little girl lying lifeless on the bedroom floor with Rob, both of them drenched in blood—would haunt her the rest of her days.

The child's blood was as surely on Jill's hands as it was on his—for it had been she who had called the police who had stormed the house. If she had simply gone away, Rob might have let the little runaway girl escape instead of killing first her, then himself, rather than being caught in his foul perversion.

All I wanted to do was escape.

And escape she had—yet nothing could still the memories that lingered in her dreams.

Before running to these mountains in search of a place to heal, Jill had replaced the wardrobe of childish dresses Rob had bought her, and the sophisticated designer gowns she'd foolishly thought would entice him back to her. She had chosen bright, sexy things she had hoped would make her feel fresh and new. She'd even had her ears pierced to show off some of the glittering precious stones from her grandmother's extensive collection—ones Rob had never let her wear.

She had made a return trip to that styling salon and demanded that Monsieur shear off her hair to no more than an inch in length. No one would use her hair again to force her to do their will, she had sworn when images of Rob with that little girl—and with her—accosted her in her nightmares each night.

Jill thrust away the awful memories. Bliss House would be her peace, her salvation. She wouldn't run away again. She had begun a real life now. Someday she would overcome her shame. Perhaps she would find her path in life.

Exhausted, she slept away the next morning, awakening to the sound of Kyle Randall's mesmerizing voice calling out to her. Quickly she pulled on jeans and a snug red cotton sweater and met him barefoot at the trailer door.

"I—I'm sorry. I wasn't expecting you so soon," she said sleepily, rubbing her eyes with the back of her hand.

Standing on the ground as he was, two feet below the trailer floor, Kyle's gaze hit right about the level of Jill's thrusting breasts. He forced himself to think of something, anything, other than stepping inside that door and talking her into crawling back in bed—with him.

"I've got an estimate for you," he said as he tilted his head back to look into her eyes.

"Good. Come on in. I'll make some coffee."

Kyle didn't think his self-control was up to another session in that tiny enclosure with this woman who made him think of nothing except how many ways they could have sex together. "Let's drive down to Maida's and go over them there. I could use some breakfast, and I imagine you could, too."

He liked the way the corner of her mouth turned up when she gave him that hesitant-looking half smile and asked him to wait while she put on her shoes. He hoped to hell she'd take time to slip into a bra as well. If she didn't, keeping from staring at those gorgeous tits was going to be damn near impossible.

"I'm ready."

He noticed she'd run a brush through those short bouncy curls, and that she hadn't bothered with a bra, as they walked down the overgrown path to his truck. "I still think you'd be better off to rebuild from scratch," he told her as he closed the door, determined to keep his mind firmly planted in reality.

"No."

"Then I can tell you now, you're talking big, big money to put that pile of wood and bricks into any kind of decent shape. I'm damn near ashamed to let you see my bid."

"You don't want to do it?" she asked, and he suddenly felt he'd heard her ask him that same question before, when she'd been talking about something far more personal than restoring some old house.

"Not particularly. I'm sure someone around here has told you it was some ancestor of mine who burned with her lover there, in your old house. It's become sort of a legend around here, what happened that night. As you can probably imagine, taunting kin of the couple who died has developed into a fine art with kids in Gray Hollow. I don't believe the stories about the damn ghosts, but I still don't feel comfortable in that house."

If his mixed feelings about remodeling her house put her off, so be it. He could always change his mind and accept that restoration job down in St. Augustine, Florida.

"Then why are you giving me this bid?" she finally asked.

He liked the way her short hair bounced when she tossed her head back against the seat. And how her expression conveyed understanding for the cruelties people can inflict on others—even without malice. But that wasn't why he had decided to help her restore her haunted house.

"Because I've gotten into the habit of eating regularly, and I have a crew that likes working year-round. They're good workers. I'd like to keep them working for me and not some other builder," he said shortly as he pulled into the gravel-strewn parking lot in front of Maida's. He got out and strode around the truck to open Jill's door. "And I like you," he added as he rested a hand at her waist to walk her into the café.

He felt her move almost imperceptibly closer. Today Jill seemed reserved, her reactions muted, when yesterday she had shown him an earthy, honest sexuality that he'd read almost like an invitation.

He figured maybe doing without a woman for as long as he had must have messed up his radar. Years ago, before Tina, he'd had good luck, guessing what a woman wanted almost before she figured it out for herself. "Let's sit by the window," he said, shelving thoughts that had no place horning in on a business discussion.

She made it damn hard to concentrate on anything but sex! He decided she had turned the act of eating one of Maida's hot cinnamon buns into a fine art as he watched her tongue dart out of her mouth and spear a little bit of frosting that had stuck on her lower lip.

Kyle forced himself to look away, taking sips of coffee as he set out the bid, detailed cost projections, and a contract he still wasn't certain that he wanted her to sign. If she did, he knew as sure as he was standing here that they'd be in bed together long before the job was finished.

Jill looked up and smiled. "May I?" she asked, picking up the contract and glancing at the numbers he had inserted in the standardized form. "Four hundred fifty thousand?"

"Yeah." Why the hell should he feel sheepish? He'd pared that estimate down as far as he could, but would still make a decent profit. "My workers are experts. So am I. We don't come cheap."

"I wasn't complaining. Just asking. How do you want it paid?"

"The usual way. A third up front, another third when the exterior work is finished, and the rest on completion." Kyle had trouble believing what he was seeing when Jill opened her bag and set a checkbook on the table.

She scribbled out a check and ripped it out of the folder. "Here. One hundred fifty thousand dollars. Where do I sign?"

Kyle motioned toward the contract. "On the last page. But don't do it now. We'll walk over to George's office after we finish eating so he can notarize our signatures."

You should be jumping up and down, doing cartwheels, Randall.

Kyle could tell himself that all day, but deep down he'd been hoping Jill would tell him to take his bids and his contract, tear them into a million pieces, and toss them off the top of Hunter's Mountain to drift like the garbage they were, down into the valley.

Now he was going to have to get used to the damn eerie feelings he got inside that sad old house, not to mention those almost forgotten yearnings Jill had brought back to life in him with a vengeance.

"We'll be starting work on Monday," he told her as he dropped her off after they'd signed the contract. As long as they were on neutral ground, he'd been able to control his compulsive need to touch her, but here outside the porch of Bliss House, he felt caution flying away on the gentle breeze. "Jill," he murmured as he took her head between his hands and bent to align his mouth with hers.

She looked into his eyes, and he was lost. What he had intended as a gentle brush of lips to lips became a feast full of carnal promise. When he finally broke the kiss, he saw her breathing was as erratic as his own. "Take care," he said, and walked away while he still could.

At the cabin, while he transmitted a list of the materials he would need to begin work on Bliss House to his Greensboro office, and later as he wound down Hunter's Mountain toward the interstate, Kyle tried to make sense of all the jumbled feelings inside his brain. He felt out of control, and that was something he hadn't allowed himself to be for years. Since long before Alyssa was born. Even before Tina. Kyle tried to remember the time he'd been free of worries, free to reach out for all the pleasures life had to offer.

He'd been just nineteen, at Carolina on a football scholarship, guzzling beer after watching the Tarheels' baseball team smash archrival Duke twenty to seven, when he had gotten the call. Dolph had been hurt, smashed under a pine tree in a logging accident up on Hunter's Mountain. Kyle would never forget how he'd felt that day, knowing his brother wouldn't have been up there, felling trees, if he hadn't been doing his damnedest to see that Kyle broke the cycle of Randall men's consistent failure and made something out of his lousy life.

That had been the end of Kyle's boyhood, though he'd stayed on and earned the degree that meant more to Dolph than it ever had to him. Later he had stepped in and married Tina Valenti, his brother's girl, after she had torn her life to shreds and turned to drugs because Dolph had thrown her love away.

For months Tina had come to the hospital every day, encouraging Dolph, willing him to live with all her fragile strength. Kyle believed she'd have stayed forever, even knowing the extent of his brother's injury, if only Dolph hadn't cruelly sent her away after he found out he would never walk, or make love, or even be able to control the simplest of bodily functions again. But he had, and Kyle had understood.

He wouldn't have wanted to tie a woman he cared for to a life like that. And he wouldn't have been able to stand seeing her every day, wanting what he could no longer have. But Dolph hadn't reckoned on the strength of Tina's love, or the depths to which she would sink when he sent her away.

Kyle had been twenty-three, just starting his business, when Tina had come looking for Dolph. She had found him, contentedly managing the small construction-company office from his wheelchair, and for a while Kyle had thought the two of them would reconcile. It would have been better for everyone if they had, Kyle thought bitterly as he pictured Alyssa in his mind.

But Dolph had pushed Tina toward him, and he had begged Kyle to give her what he no longer could. They had married in the spring, and before fall Tina had graduated from coke to heroin, and on to the mixture of mind-killing drugs that doomed her to her grave and her baby girl to a living death.

Since then, for going on eight years now, Kyle's life had been a constant grind of working, taking every job he could to get his little girl—and Dolph—the exorbitantly expensive medical care they both would require as long as they lived.

The buzzing of his cellular phone snapped Kyle from his melancholy memories. As he'd guessed, it was Dolph checking on the order he'd sent over his laptop to the office's main computer. "Yeah, that's right. Four thousand square feet of cedar-shake roofing shingles. And two thousand board feet of two-by-eight heart pine."

Kyle paused. "Yeah, I know it's going to cost a fortune. But we're getting plenty for doing the job. What are you doing working, anyhow? Weren't you supposed to spend another week getting over that surgery?"

Kyle laughed, even though Dolph's crude joke about the plumbing job he'd had struck him as sick, not funny. But his brother had damn little to joke about. "So now you can pee without bothering with your dick," he replied as he was sure his brother expected. "Sounds convenient."

They spoke for a few minutes before Dolph hung up. It was damn unfair that Dolph, who loved living, even with his paralysis, and who had so much to give, faced probable death within a few years—while poor little Alyssa, who most likely didn't even know what it meant to be alive, had every chance of surviving to a ripe old age.

Feeling guilty, Kyle pulled off the interstate and made the short trip down a wooded, curving secondary road to stop by Angels' Paradise to see his little girl.

Chapter
Seven

THE GHOSTS

"Did you see them, Cyrus?"

Cyrus looked up from his task of lighting a candle to project an indulgent smile toward Laura. *"I saw them, my dear. The whole shameless display! Would that her father had seen them as well! Our curse would be broken in short order, with the assistance of his trusty shotgun, if necessary."* His mouth curved upward in the sardonic grin Laura knew so well.

"Morals must be more lax now than they were in our day. Besides, I've seen no indication that our lady has either father or mother to guide her. Surely if she did, they would not allow her to live out here, all alone." Laura tried to imagine what mayhem Cyrus would have caused had his Prudence

allowed one of her beaux to give her a lover's kiss like the one her Kyle had bestowed on Jill.

"Perhaps the guidance must come from us. After all, they are in our home. They must abide by our wishes." With his piercing gray eyes, Cyrus reached out and caressed Laura's hair.

If only he could truly touch her! She yearned, more than she had for years, to feel the gentle touch of his hands, the weight of his strong, hard body pushing her deeply into a goose-down feather bed. *"I love you, Cyrus,"* she said, and caressed him with her gaze. *"I think tomorrow will be the time for us to make ourselves known to the very fast, very wanton Jill Carey. I've no desire to wait until December to be with you again in heaven."*

"From your mouth to God's ear, my love," Cyrus told Laura as he blew out the candle in the window before they settled down for a long night's rest.

Chapter
Eight

As Jill took one last look out the trailer window before climbing into bed, she distinctly saw that candlelight flicker, then fade.

Suddenly she believed every tale Maida had told her about the ghosts of Cyrus Bliss and Laura Randall. Except the one that said their punishment had come from God. God wreaked vengeance on the evil, like Rob . . . and herself . . . Jill couldn't believe He would destroy two people for honestly expressing their mutual love.

It has to be their presence I've been feeling ever since I brought Kyle into Bliss House.

I want to meet them. Find out why their spirits are still here after all these years.

Eager now to confront her otherworldly boarders, Jill vowed that tomorrow she would find them and coax them to tell her the real story.

* * *

Every creak of ancient floorboards made Jill jump with apprehension. Each rustling sound of the autumn breeze whistling through trees outside sent tingling sensations down her spine. As she tiptoed through the rooms where Laura and Cyrus had lived and loved so long ago, she felt their ghostly presence.

"Come out here and talk to me, damn it!" It frustrated her that she couldn't will the elusive spirits to join her.

"You, young lady, need your mouth washed out with some of my good lye soap."

Jill glanced quickly in the direction of that stern, yet soft and gentle feminine voice. All she saw, though, was the wall that separated the front hall from that burned-out bedroom where Laura Randall and Cyrus Bliss had died. Suddenly she needed air, more air than she could force into her heaving chest as she hurried to the front door—and safety.

"Come back tonight."

Jill spun around, sure she would see the man who had spoken. But again, nothing was there but the empty hall.

"We will join you then," the masculine voice promised in a soothing baritone. It was almost as if he had realized how eerie she found the disembodied voices.

She *wanted* to meet "her" ghosts. Jill kept reminding herself that she had searched out the spirits that haunted Bliss House as the voices echoed in her mind. Still, a kernel of fear grew larger as she shoveled away the years' accumulation of overgrowth that obscured a stone-paved walkway from the house to what must have once been a carriage road.

As the brightness of the early-October day turned into twilight, she put away her tools and returned to the trailer, as eager for the promised meeting with the ghosts of the ill-starred lovers as she was afraid of their response to her intrusion into the house they had haunted for almost a century.

Later, while she waited in the room that must once have been a cozy parlor, she stared at the flickering light from two fat candles she had lit and imagined how life must have been back then. Cyrus and Laura must have shared a love as strong as the timbers of this venerable home to have defied the rigid codes of Victorian morality to celebrate and declare their love.

Laura materialized first, floating into the room and settling near the empty fireplace. She was lovely, like a porcelain doll, draped from neck to toe in an exquisite nightgown of tucked white lawn, with Belgian lace insertions in a square yoke and at the wide, fitted cuffs of flowing, long sleeves.

"Welcome to Bliss House."

Before Jill could find her voice, an imposing gentleman appeared at Laura's side; tall and well into middle age. Jill shuddered at Cyrus Bliss's resemblance to Rob. Then she looked into dark eyes that appeared to see clear to her soul. She realized then that this man was nothing like the monster she had married. In his old-fashioned robe of maroon velvet brocade, Cyrus Bliss epitomized Jill's idea of the fine Southern gentleman—strong, good, and all those other qualities so lacking in men of the 1990s.

"Yes, welcome."

The soft, deep baritone of Cyrus's voice reminded Jill of honey and moonlight—and Kyle. "You're really here. The legend is true," she murmured inanely. "Y-you're happy that I've come, bought your home?"

"We've prayed you would come for nearly a hundred years. You're the key to our salvation," Cyrus said as he placed an arm lightly around Laura's waist.

"What?"

"Dear, you must tell her." Laura's tone was firm, yet coaxing as she looked up at her long-ago lover.

"Tell me what?" Jill couldn't help the apprehension that washed over her.

Cyrus and Laura sat down together on the cold stone hearth. *"You've heard our story, I imagine,"* he said, his gaze meeting Jill's as he grasped Laura's trembling hand.

"Yes."

"Then you know of the curse?"

Jill sensed Laura's shame. "I think it's ridiculous. After all, from what I heard, you hurt no one, did nothing to regret," she said.

"Nonetheless, we were cursed, doomed to remain here together, not alive yet not free to join the spirits of our loved ones in heaven. You will be the one to set us free." Cyrus cleared his throat as if waiting for Jill's reaction.

She was here to set these ghostly lovers free? Was this to be her mission, the reason for her having felt so instantly drawn to this house? Could she free Cyrus and Laura, and if she did, would this act of goodness help her atone for her own sins?

"How am I to do this?" Jill asked when she found her voice.

Cyrus started to say something, but Laura gently interrupted. *"Let me, my love."*

"Of course."

Laura spoke hesitantly as if carefully choosing each word. *"Almost a hundred years ago we died here, in this house—"*

"We didn't die, Laura. Harry Randall killed us in a drunken rage, destroyed us and our unborn child, and condemned us to remain here in limbo."

"Cyrus, please. One must not air one's dirty linen in public. Miss Carey, it will suffice to say that we were cursed for our sin. Cursed to stay here for a hundred years."

"It's been a hundred years . . ."

"Please, let me finish. A young lady never interrupts her elders," Laura admonished gently. *"It will not have been a hundred years for three more months."*

"What happens then?" Jill couldn't hold her tongue; she had to know!

Cyrus cleared his throat. *"Unless a member of one of our families, one who is in love with one he has the right to claim, returns to live in Bliss House by the hundredth anniversary of our murder, Laura and I will be condemned to eternal damnation."*

"Then I guess you two are out of luck, because I'm not part of either of your families," Jill said flatly. Thanks to her grandmother's obsession with tracing the Carey family's roots, she could state unequivocally that no Blisses or Randalls graced her family tree. Suddenly fear washed over her. Would these seemingly caring spirits chase her away from here? Destroy her?

She searched for answers in Cyrus and Laura's expressions. But she saw nothing but kindness, benevolence—emotions she had rarely read on the faces of her own relatives. Suddenly she wished she could claim these likable ghosts as her own.

"You will fall in love with a member of our family," Laura told her firmly. *"Lord knows, young lady, you need a man to protect you. What were your people thinking, allowing you to move out here all by yourself?"*

Jill shrugged. "I don't have any family. Besides, I'm twenty-six years old. Plenty old enough to take care of myself."

"No young unmarried woman has any business living by herself, without even a servant to guard her reputation," Laura said, letting go of Cyrus's hand to gesture toward the empty rooms of Bliss House.

"Now, my dear, I've told you before. Times have changed. We may have spent nearly a century confined in this house, but we've seen enough people come and go from here to realize many of the rules we lived by have gone. Ladies have more freedom now. They can vote. Work. Even divorce abusive husbands and remarry without being censured."

"Cyrus, that may be. Still, a young woman must behave as a lady to attract the right gentleman. Miss Carey, certainly you agree."

Jill shrugged. She doubted Laura would consider her a lady if she knew half of what she'd done with Rob. "I'm not looking for love. I've had one husband, and that was enough."

"You've divorced?" Laura sounded scandalized.

"My husband died." None of her business *how*, Jill thought.

"You poor dear!" Cyrus stood as if he was planning to step over and comfort Jill.

"If he hadn't died, I'd have divorced him," Jill informed them tartly.

Cyrus sat back down. Jill thought he appeared to be relieved, but she noticed Laura's lips curl into a little frown as she toyed with a handful of her old-fashioned gown.

"What do you think of Kyle Randall?" Cyrus finally asked just as Jill was beginning to become unnerved at the ghosts' silence.

"He's going to restore the house." Jill had a feeling Laura wouldn't approve of the way Kyle made her body tingle with the slightest touch, with a heated glance from eyes the color of the darkest evergreens.

Laura smiled. *"That's good. The years have taken their toll on this place. I wonder which one of the Randalls he's descended from,"* she said wistfully.

"Kyle told me he's your great-great-grandson."

"Oh."

Somehow knowing Laura ached for knowledge about this newly found descendant, Jill told her all she knew about Kyle's business. "I don't know anything about his personal life," she concluded, heading off questions before Laura could ask.

"He's a fine figure of a man," Cyrus interjected.

"Yes. You could do far worse than to fall in love with him."

Jill held up a hand, as if that would stop the ghosts' gentle meddling. "Wait a minute. Nothing against your however-many-times-over-grandson, ma'am, but I'm not ready for another man." *I don't know if I ever will be, at least not on a permanent basis. Although I wouldn't mind finding out if Kyle makes love as well as he kisses.* Jill felt her cheeks begin to burn.

"You will be. But my dear Miss Carey, you must learn to

*dress properly if you're to attract my Kyle or any other gen-
tleman of quality. And to curb your tongue! This morning
you sounded like a veritable mule-skinner!"* Laura cast a
censuring look at the loose slacks and bulky sweater Jill had
put on after her shower a few hours earlier.

"What's wrong with the way I look?"

*"My dear, ladies do not wear trousers. And they certainly
do not step out of their boudoirs in their underwear!"*

Jill laughed. "This is 1997. What I wear is perfectly ac-
ceptable, even for attracting a man, should I be so inclined!
Shall I bring some fashion magazines over here for you to
see?"

Laura didn't appear convinced. *"That would be nice,"*
she murmured as she seemed to consider Jill's offer. *"You
will watch your language, though?"* she asked hopefully.

"Yes, ma'am."

For the next hour or so Jill talked with the spirits of Laura
and Cyrus, revealing more about her family than she'd ever
told anyone before—maybe, she thought later, more than
she had ever even admitted to herself. As she reflected after
her encounter with the ghosts, she realized that while their
meddling had exasperated her, she wished her own family
had cared for her as much as Laura and Cyrus appeared to.
Perhaps if she had grown up with a strong foundation of
love and values, she could have avoided the trap Rob had set
so neatly for her.

Chapter Nine

THE GHOSTS

"A strange but lovely young lady," Cyrus mused as he helped Laura sort through belongings they had found in the attic. *"But you were right. She is attracted to this Kyle Randall."*

"I thought I felt some spark between them. You seem so certain, though, Cyrus. How can you be sure?"

"The look in her eyes when she mentioned his name. The way her body became tense. Miss Carey looked the way you used to when you wanted to make love."

Cyrus thought he saw his Laura blush before she turned to rummage through a small humpback trunk. He floated over to her, abandoning his own search through discarded furnishings and Victorian accessories when she gave a little sigh and clutched some small object to her breast.

"What have you found?"

She met his gaze, and her beautiful blue eyes were brimming with tears. *"This. Dolph and Aaron. And Miles. He was just a baby."*

Cyrus took the faded photograph and studied captured faces that even now, more than a hundred years later, stared solemnly at him with forever-captured youth. Laura's children. The beloved toddler she had lost the year before they died—and the two robust young men she had effectively given up when she had become his lover. Guilt washed over him.

"Which one, do you think, belongs to Kyle Randall?" she asked, her voice shaky as she looked again at the portrait Cyrus had returned to her.

Cyrus looked again at the faded sepia images. *"I can't begin to guess. I think, though, that this picture belongs on the mantel downstairs. Surely it will pique Miss Carey's interest. Her Mr. Randall bears an uncanny resemblance to all your sons, my dear."*

Laura nodded, then turned away. Cyrus felt her pain, as he sensed she was remembering why that portrait had rested here, out of sight, instead of in its rightful place downstairs, beside the framed daguerreotype of his own daughter, Prudence.

They had been wrong, he admitted silently, to seize their own happiness in spite of its effect on their families. Still, as he floated down the narrow attic stairway behind Laura, he wouldn't change what they had done. Not a century in limbo, not even the prospect of eternal damnation, could make him regret having taken Laura Randall as the bride of his heart. But he could and did regret having been the cause of her children's turning away from her in disgust.

Chapter
Ten

Kyle deposited his daughter onto a blanket and sank down beside her, willing himself not to shudder as he lifted her head to position a pillow. Not that Alyssa would know, he thought bleakly. But Dolph would. And he had come along today, as he did almost every Sunday. Kyle figured this was his brother's penance, seeing Tina's beauty in this helpless, pathetic child, conceived not in love, but in desperation.

Desperation? Tina's, for sure, because she had sought out every substance known to man and found no cure for the heartbreak of Dolph's rejection. His, too, Kyle silently admitted as Dolph wheeled up to the edge of the blanket. For he had been young and horny, resentful of feeling obligated to marry his brother's girl and determined to enjoy the only advantage, as he then saw it, of his and Tina's loveless union.

"Hi, Alyssa," Dolph said, and Kyle wondered as he often did whether his brother had some misguided notion that this child could hear him. "Took me a while to get out here," he added. "Worth it, though. The trees are starting to put on their fall coats."

"Yeah." Kyle picked up a brilliant red sycamore leaf that had blown onto Alyssa's chest and looked briefly at it before crushing it in his fist. "I'm going up to the cabin from here. I'll stay there while we're doing the work on Bliss House."

"Are the trucks going to be able to get up close? From what I remember, that property's nothing but a mass of brambles."

Kyle grinned. When they were kids, Dolph had been the brave one, actually sneaking into the so-called haunted house once, on a dare. The farthest he himself had ever gone, before touring Bliss House with its new owner, had been to the edge of the tumbledown porch.

"The access road's passable. George Wilson saw to that when he took over trying to sell the place. I thought I'd take the bush hog from the cabin, get there early in the morning, and clear off enough space so the guys can load and unload the trucks."

"So you've gotten over your aversion to that place, little brother?"

Kyle shrugged. "It gives me the willies, being inside the house. But money's money, and Jill Carey has nearly half a million dollars that tells me Bliss House is worth restoring. Besides, only kids and fools believe in ghosts or that old legend. Generations of parents have kept it going, just to keep kids around Gray Hollow in line." He glanced at Alyssa and regretted, for about the thousandth time, that he would never have to worry about curbing her youthful exuberance.

"Let me hold her."

Kyle scooped Alyssa up, blanket and all, and deposited her in his brother's arms. It damn near killed him to look at them together like that, both terribly flawed in different ways because of him. "She doesn't even know we're here," he muttered as he watched Dolph cradle the child that should have been whole, and his, tenderly against his chest.

Dolph met his gaze. "You don't know that, Kyle. Go on.
You look like you've had about all you can take today. Besides, it's almost an hour's drive to the cabin. I'll stay a
while longer. Alyssa and I will enjoy watching the leaves
turn color. Tell the attendant to come and get us in another
hour."

Kyle left, feeling as guilty as he always did before the reality of his daughter's affliction, even though that reality
never really escaped his consciousness. As he drove to his
cabin on Hunter's Mountain, high above Gray Hollow, the
picture of Alyssa in his crippled brother's arms tore at his
heart.

Chapter
Eleven

THE GHOSTS

"He's back. I can feel it."

Cyrus looked down at Laura, who had settled into a moonlit corner of their burned-out bedroom. *"Who?"*

"Kyle."

"Here?"

"No. But he is close by."

"What is he thinking?" Cyrus hoped Kyle Randall's thoughts would be as focused on Jill Carey as that young woman's wanton musings had apparently been on him.

"He is sad. Riddled with guilt. And he is fighting a fear of this place—and us—even as he denies our existence."

Cyrus floated over and drew Laura's spirit closer to his heart. *"Guilt? For what?"* Was this Randall a chip off old

Harry's block? Had he hurt someone he loved while indulging an obsession for Randall moonshine?

"I—I don't know." Laura turned away and stared at the golden moon. "*I sense the guilt but not the act that caused it. Cyrus, I am afraid. Afraid these young people fate has sent us have lives too complex for them ever to fall in love.*"

"*Perhaps when he is here, in the house, you will be able to tell, my dear. Do not fret. This man, and Miss Carey, will be the ones to set us free.*" Cyrus wished he felt half as confident as he made himself sound as he tried to soothe his Laura's distress.

Chapter
Twelve

Jill's hand shook as she set the mug of hot chocolate back on the little table. Her gaze settled on the cheery red numbers of the digital clock on the microwave oven.

One o'clock. Might as well be morning! Will I never experience a full night's sleep again?

She stood and stared at the twisted linens on her narrow bed, then let her velour robe slip to the floor. She would go up to the house, scrub off another layer of filth from the parlor floor, she decided. Wasting no more time, she pulled on a pair of disreputable sweats and reached for the propane camp light she had bought last week at Maida's.

At her tiny sink, she ran the water until it turned hot before filling a plastic bucket. Then, less concerned about avoiding the friendly ghosts of her new home than about the terrifying ones in her mind, she walked quickly across the yard to Bliss House.

On hands and knees with a stiff, wet brush, Jill scrubbed until her shoulders practically screamed in protest. The ache in her lower back nearly obscured the cramping pains in her knees and thighs. She had to sit down somewhere and rest!

Her muscles creaked and groaned as if they were as old as the house, but she managed to stumble to her feet and make it to the huge sofa that was the only piece of furniture in the room. Stripping off a filthy dustcover, Jill stared at the ugly Victorian piece before sinking onto it. "None of Cyrus Bliss's kin wanted you, I guess," she said to the sofa as if it were a living thing.

She felt her eyelids droop, and reflexively she blinked. Then they shut again, and Jill felt a sense of peace. Maybe I can sleep, just for a few minutes, she thought as she brought her feet up onto the sofa and leaned back against the stiff, curved arm piece.

Jill's mind drifted, and she didn't have the energy to wake up and head off the terror. She saw herself at thirteen, bounding into her grandmother's living room after getting off the school bus and grabbing a handful of honey drops from a crystal dish.

"What are you doing, child?" the old woman asked in a voice that exuded soft Southern culture and masked the hostility Jill had sensed since she had arrived five years earlier—after her parents had died in separate accidents six months apart.

"Getting some candies."

"Put them back."

Jill obeyed and left Martha Carey to her solitary brooding, holing up in her room with a favorite book. A knock at her door brought her back from a world of childish fantasy.

"Rob!"

Her grandmother's nephew gave her a conspiratorial grin. Jill liked Rob—and she thought he liked her, too, even though at thirty-two he was very much a grown-up. Nearly as old as her father would have been if he were still alive. "Come talk with me," she begged, half in love with the only person in her life ever to have paid her any mind.

"Aunt Martha said you tried to make off with some of her honey drops," he said as he joined her on the padded bench beneath her window. "Want some?" He fingered the material of her wool plaid uniform skirt.

"Oh, yes!"

He patted the front pocket of his slacks. "It's in here."

Eagerly she reached into his pocket, but as she tried to retrieve the candy, Rob placed his hand over hers. "Feel what you do to me, baby," he said, his voice suddenly husky and compelling.

When she met his gaze she saw love—love she had searched for all her life and never found before. That was when she gave Rob her heart. Later she gave him more . . . much more . . . all a child's love, however he asked it of her.

Part of Jill knew what they did when he sneaked into her room at night was wrong, if for no other reason than Rob's insistence that she never tell a living soul about their affair. She believed he loved her, though, and loving to her meant giving . . . pleasing . . . sharing everything with the only person in the world who had ever shown her tenderness and caring.

No act, no gesture of love or submission was too much for her to give in return. From that first touch she was his to mold and do with as he would. He made her laugh with his sensual games, games she was too naive to under-stand—games she learned too late that good, decent peo-ple called by ugly names. In her innocence she knelt before him, a child bride prepared again to do her husband's bidding.

"No!" Jill was no longer loving Rob, she was watching him force that other girl—a child as she herself had been not so long ago—to perform what she had done so willingly. The acts of love that once had seemed beautiful now made her retch with disgust. "Rob, no!" she screamed as she ran blindly out of the room and the house she shared first with her grandmother, then with Rob.

"I'm sorry," she sobbed, her hands clutching the fabric of a black summer dress as she watched the county workers shovel red Georgia clay over the plain pine coffin that held the earthly remains of a child they called Jane Doe. "We both would have been better off alone."

Jill bent and took a handful of the soft moist dirt and tossed it into the little girl's grave. As she walked away she stared at her stained fingers. "I can wash away this dirt, but the guilt will stay with me forever."

"You screamed. What is wrong, child?"
At first Jill believed she was still dreaming. Then she realized she had fallen asleep on the dusty Victorian sofa no one had ever bothered to haul away from Bliss House—and that Laura was hovering over her, a worried expression marring her usually serene features. "Nothing. It was only a dream."

"A dream so frightening it makes you call out in the night? Perhaps if you told me . . ."
"No."

"Cyrus and I would never hurt you, my dear. There is no cause for you to fear us."
Jill laughed. She wished it were only ghosts who haunted her nightmares—yet they were nothing she could speak of with the gentle ghosts of ages past. "You don't frighten me. The nightmares come and go—they have

since months before I even saw this house, or you and Mr. Bliss."

"If you need to talk, child, we are here," Laura said softly as she floated back toward the attic stairs.

Gathering up her cleaning supplies, Jill decided she would stay up now. Awake, she could live with her guilt. It was when she slept that it overwhelmed and tortured her.

Kyle tossed in bed all night, tortured by the remorse that wouldn't settle into a dark corner of his mind and leave him the hell alone. There was something else, too, something he couldn't put a finger on—other than that it felt as if someone, somewhere, was trying to see into his very soul. At four A.M., he gave up on the idea of sleeping and decided to get an early start on the overgrown vegetation he had to clear before his crew arrived with their heavy trucks and equipment.

When he got to Bliss House, it couldn't have been much after five o'clock, but Jill was standing there in the open doorway, smiling. She was looking at him with that naked hunger she had shown him when they kissed. From somewhere deep in his brain he recalled how silky soft her high, firm breasts had felt against his palm—his lips.

He tried to quash the sudden hardness in his groin. Where in hell, he wondered, had that memory come from? He damn sure had never fondled Jill Carey's tits. How in God's name could he have so vivid a memory of something that had never happened that he got a damn painful hard-on? Kyle forced down an uneasy feeling that all this had something to do with the house and his long-dead ancestor.

"You're here early," Jill said with that heated smile when he managed to calm down enough to leave his truck and stroll up toward the porch.

"Yeah. I need to run the bush hog, clear out enough space so my crew can get the big trucks in."

"Oh. Would you like some coffee?"

What I'd like, lady, would scorch your pretty brain. "No, thanks. I'd better get this hog unloaded and start to work."

"All right." She sounded disappointed. And his muscles clenched with need.

He'd told himself before he took this job that if he didn't keep a tight rein, he'd break every rule he had ever set for himself by hopping in bed with this client *before* the work got finished. But this frankly sensuous woman with her needy, dark gazes—and appraising glances, hotter than the flame from a blowtorch—turned him on so, he doubted he would last through the first week.

He stared at soft, full lips that had eagerly mated with his own. But it wasn't the kiss he was recalling. It was the feel of those lips sliding hotly down his—

"Shit." Was he losing his fucking mind?

"What's wrong?"

Kyle forced himself to meet Jill's gaze. "Sorry. I was just thinking about—about what a miserable job it's going to be to get that jungle cleared out before my trucks get here. I'd better get started." He turned on his heel and practically ran back to his pickup.

As he rode the bush hog through the overgrowth, mowing it down, Kyle hoped Jill hadn't noticed his arousal—it had to have been blatantly obvious if she'd been looking. He sure as hell would hate having to explain how, every time he looked at her, he started remembering all kinds of erotic fun that had never happened. Particularly since he couldn't even explain it to himself.

The low roar of a lumber hauler distracted him. His workers were beginning to arrive. Kyle steered the bush hog out of the way and watched as the drivers maneuvered their trucks into the space he had cleared. He set the men to tearing away rotten porch boards, and when they had made a good dent in the mess by late afternoon, he began checking the ancient foundation structure.

For the second time he remembered pulling Jill out after she had fallen through this porch. And he felt himself harden as erotic bits and pieces of what came after that rescue flashed through his mind. When Jill came up behind him, he gave up trying to rationalize his weird feeling of *déjà vu* and greeted her with a smile.

"You feel it, too, this heat between us," he told her as he met her gaze. "Come with me tonight, and let's find out what it's all about before it drives us both insane."

Jill forced herself to meet Kyle's gaze. So he felt it, too, this carnal attraction that had begun the moment he'd stepped foot on this rickety old porch of hers. Her nipples tingled, and she felt a sudden hot, damp urgency deep inside her body. She moved her lips to accept his challenge; then she remembered.

Ten years ago she had succumbed to the potent lure of sexual gratification. She had even married the man who had taught her always to answer her body's needs—to explore and exploit them to the limit, heedless of all but the heady pleasure of physical release. She had indulged Rob's perverted fantasies, helped him develop them to the point that he'd finally snapped. In the process, he had destroyed at least one innocent young life.

It was as much my fault as his.

"I can't," she said, hardly recognizing the reedy voice as her own as her body tensed in protest.

"See you all tomorrow at eight."

Vaguely Jill realized Kyle must have been responding to the chorus of "Good night, boss" that had barely registered in her mind.

As soon as the sound of the trucks faded to a dull roar, she felt Kyle's muscular arm snake around to draw her closer. "I—I can't," she repeated feebly.

When he drew her tightly into his embrace, she felt the strength and size and heat of him nudging against her belly, and she had to restrain herself from reaching down and touching . . . caressing . . . kissing that rigid shaft she knew would ease her body's yearnings the way no touch of a hand, no erotic toy, no other man's hot, hard penis ever could.

No other man? Jill jerked away and stared at Kyle. How had he managed to get to her like this? They had only met twice before. They had done nothing sexual—nothing more than share one heated, potent kiss. Never before had a man aroused her simply by his presence. This didn't make sense!

Sure, Kyle Randall was a good-looking guy, big and muscular and blessed with a face that would do justice to a movie star if it weren't for that little scar that bisected one perfectly arched eyebrow. Those deep green eyes and that dazzling grin could make him a fortune, Jill figured, if he were of a mind to storm the New York ad agencies. Still, that didn't explain why her body ached for him to fill her—or why, since they'd met, his compelling presence had found its way into her nightly dreams.

"Jill?" His soft, deep drawl flowed over her like honey.

"Yes?"

"It's going to happen, sooner or later. Neither one of us will be able to stop it. Let's just give in gracefully and put ourselves out of our misery." Kyle sounded puzzled, even a bit put out, Jill thought.

"I told you, I can't. Not now. This is crazy. Do you think it's this place? This house?" If she'd thought he would believe her, Jill would have told Kyle about her visit last night with her resident ghosts—and their hope that she and Kyle would get together and end some century-old curse that bound Cyrus and Laura here, not living yet not really dead and gone.

Maybe Cyrus and Laura are doing this to us, making us

*so hot for each other that we can barely keep from tossing
common sense to the winds and giving in to this animal
urge.*

Not realizing she had done so until she felt the slight
rasp of his beard against her knuckles, Jill touched Kyle's
cheek. She traced his lower lip with her finger. "Don't
think I don't feel this—this attraction, too," she murmured
as she met his heated gaze. "But it's too fast, too hot. I'm
afraid of getting burned."

"You're burning now. So am I. We're going to burn together, honey. Soon. It's inevitable. All you're doing is
prolonging the pain." He took her finger into his mouth
and sucked, never shifting his gaze from her face.

He was right. But she couldn't give in without fighting
harder, longer. *Hard. Long. Thick. Like the heated length
of him that imprinted itself on my belly and stirred up this
crazy need from somewhere in the farthest corners of my
mind.*

"I know," she murmured even as she rubbed her torso
sinuously against the muscled hardness of his frame.

His callused fingers seduced her further as they tunneled through her hair, catching and tugging gently at the
short tendrils. His hot, sweet breath mingled with hers,
and she wanted nothing more than to feel his lips join in-
timately with her own.

"Kyle." His name came out in a husky whisper.

"Come home with me." He punctuated the husky de-
mand with a quick, hard kiss.

She wanted to. God, how her body ached for him! He
had taken her will to resist. Vaguely Jill realized she was
nodding her head.

"Yes. Come on. Oh, baby, we're going to be good together," he murmured against her cheek before grabbing
her hand and heading for his truck.

Baby? Jill jerked her hand free. "I'm not your baby,"
she snapped, but it wasn't Kyle she was seeing. It was

Rob—and that poor little girl, the one he had used then destroyed as if her only value had been as an instrument of his pleasure.

"Jill?" Kyle sounded confused.

"No. Just go. Leave me alone!" she cried as she sprinted for the lonely safety of her trailer.

Chapter Thirteen

THE GHOSTS

"They seemed to be getting together so well. Scandalously so. What do you imagine went wrong?"

Cyrus smiled. Laura had a way with understatement! Had it not been for whatever insensitive remark her hapless descendant had made, he imagined that by now Kyle Randall would have had Miss Carey panting and wild beneath him. He envied the young couple their mortality as he recalled the joys of making love with Laura so long ago. *"I have no idea, my love."*

"Kyle was being impossibly bold—not a gentleman at all. Yet she was encouraging him until . . ."

"Until he said something to frighten her off. It is well that he did, though. They know far too little of each other yet to embark upon a sensual journey."

75

Laura nodded. *"Of course. His boldness must have frightened her. Scandalous! But then Harry's kin were never
known for their sense of propriety. I'd say young Kyle grew
up without a mother to teach him right from wrong, punctuated by a few brisk strokes from a willow switch. Cyrus, do
you think he has frightened Miss Carey away?"*

Not likely, Cyrus thought, recalling how eagerly the new
owner of Bliss House had melted into Kyle Randall's embrace. She appeared sensual, almost wanton by his and
Laura's standards—not the sort to shrink away from a
promise of sexual pleasure.

"I don't think Miss Carey frightens that easily, love," he
murmured, floating away from the open window and down
the hall. *"Come, Laura, we've half the attic to explore before morning."*

Chapter Fourteen

If I don't get some sleep, I'm going to die, Kyle thought as he tossed between sheets he had hoped to share with Jill. Her parting words and abrupt departure bugged him. What the hell had he said that sent her running as if he'd thrown ice water on the fire that had been building between them from the minute they first met?

He pounded the goose-down pillow, then settled his head. Determined to sleep, he made himself lie still. But questions kept popping into his exhausted brain.

She'd been as ready as he. He knew it. He had felt her need in the touch of her fingers on his cheek, seen it in the depths of her eyes. Hell, he'd felt Jill trembling with need— just before she had jerked free of his arms and bolted.

Memories of the sexual encounter he knew had never happened made him sweat, caused his gut to clench and his cock to swell. He couldn't get Jill out of his mind, not with visions of the sexy, appraising looks she was always giving him. Looks that raked his body from head to toe before settling at his crotch.

The woman was going to drive him nuts. Maybe she already had. Why couldn't the new owner of Bliss House have been eighty years old and uglier than sin? Kyle rolled onto his stomach, trying to fight down desire that threatened his sanity.

He tried to remember what the hell he'd said just before she ran. Something about their being good together, he thought, still perplexed. *I'm not your baby.* She had choked out those words, sounding straight-out terrified, right after abruptly pulling back from his embrace.

All he'd done was murmur a casual endearment, one he had used before with satisfactory results. That, or something else, had apparently made Jill go berserk. He'd never figure women out, he decided as he buried his head against the pillow and fell into a restless sleep.

He didn't see much of Jill the next few days, but distance did little to cool Kyle's raging need. At first all he'd felt was lust—but now he was beginning to wonder if there could be more. He missed talking with her, seeing the excitement in her expression when he pointed out the progress they were making with the restoration.

Early the next week, after his crew had finished stripping away the rotted wood outside, he sought her out. "I'm sorry I upset you," he said as they strolled around the house, inspecting the new foundation for the porch.

He watched her eyelids flutter against her pale cheeks, projecting an odd vulnerability at odds with her frank sensuality. "It's all right. I overreacted," she murmured.

"To what?" Suddenly Kyle wanted more than just to take her to bed. He wanted to know what made Jill tick.

"Nothing. Something you said just made me remember . . ."

"What?"

Her tongue darted out of her mouth and wet her upper lip. "Baby. I don't like being called a baby. I shouldn't have gotten so upset, though. Kyle, it's no big deal."

Kyle shrugged. "Then you won't mind going down to Maida's with me for a bite to eat?" He gathered from Jill's dismissive explanation that this was neither the time nor the place to pursue whatever it was she didn't like about that particular kind of sweet talk.

"I'd like that."

That evening and those that followed brought little relief for the yearning that lay just below the surface of Kyle's thoughts as he and Jill shared superficial bits of their lives—and casual good-night kisses before they went to their lonely, separate beds. As he tried to sleep each night, though, his need was for Jill's warmth and companionship as well as for the passion that seemed to bubble in her, just beneath a veneer of casual conversation.

Her lips still tingled from Kyle's chaste kiss, the evening after Kyle's crew had finished the exterior work on Bliss House. The empty ache between her legs told her they were quickly reaching a point where the sexual tension between them would have to break.

Deciding sleep was out of the question, Jill slipped on a robe and sneakers and made her way across a path piled high with crackling autumn leaves to the house. She sighed as she opened the back door.

Making her way gingerly across the creaking floor, she found a rickety wooden chair and dragged it close to the empty kitchen hearth. Her thoughts centered on Kyle, how much she ached for him to fill the emptiness in her body and heart, and how little he had revealed of himself as they had danced some sort of elusive courtship dance these past few weeks.

Who was Kyle? From all he'd told her, Jill could surmise he was a man of simple tastes—a self-made man. He had revealed little of himself when he'd spoken of his roots here in Gray Hollow, his years at Chapel Hill, or the life he lived today in Greensboro. Somehow, though, she knew Kyle left much of his life unsaid, much of his emotion under wraps. All Jill could say for certain was that Kyle Randall was nothing like Rob.

I wonder where Cyrus and Laura are tonight.

No sooner had her mind wandered to her resident ghosts than Laura appeared in front of the window, her image back-lit by a harvest moon. *"Did you and my grandson have a pleasant evening tonight?"*

Jill smiled. "Yes. We did."

"Tell me about him," Laura said, and Jill's heart went out to this kindly ghost who so obviously longed to know about her newly found relative's life before he came here to fix up his great-great-grandmother's tumbledown house.

"I'm afraid I don't know a lot. Kyle isn't very talkative, at least about his family. He did say he grew up here, farther up Hunter's Mountain. He's staying in a cabin he built on the land where he was born."

"About two miles from here?" Laura asked, her expression softening as though the site brought back happy memories.

Jill shrugged. "I haven't been there."

"Of course you haven't. That wouldn't be at all proper."

Times have changed, Jill thought, wondering for a moment whether she might have been happier growing up in Laura's time—protected by strict rules of behavior from her own foolish whims. Earlier tonight, after Kyle had left her at her trailer door with only a gentle kiss, she'd wished as she lay alone and unfulfilled in her narrow bunk that she had asked him to take her with him to his mountain vacation home.

"He isn't married, is he?" Laura's anxious tone drew Jill's attention.

"No. But he doesn't say much about his family." Every time they were together, Jill sensed Kyle had secrets, just as she did—secrets he wasn't anxious to share.

"I sense guilt in my grandson. Sadness. Yet I cannot see its cause."

Jill shook her head. "So far as I know, Kyle has nothing to feel guilty about." *Certainly nothing like the regrets I'll fight with for the rest of my life.*

"The guilt is there. I worry that its roots may drag you two apart."

"We've never been together. Miss Laura, I know you and Mr. Bliss are hoping Kyle and I will be the ones to break the curse. Don't get me wrong. I like Kyle Randall. Maybe I could even love him. And he, at the very least, wants me in his bed. But desire isn't enough to base commitment on." Jill averted her gaze, not wanting Laura to read the regret she felt every time she remembered her life with Rob.

"Of course it isn't," Laura murmured, and Jill looked at the ghost to find her pale cheeks stained a rosy pink. *"Courtship is for building trust, learning about the interests you share. To indulge the passion, you must hold out for marriage. For a hundred years now Cyrus and I have paid dearly for flaunting all the rules. I take it many of your generation reach for the joy without the wedding vows."*

Laura gestured toward a *Cosmopolitan* magazine Jill had left on the hearth, hoping the ghost would bring herself up to date on current female fashion. Apparently Laura had read as well as looked, Jill thought as she recalled an article in that particular issue about long-term relationships that didn't and never would include marriage. "Some do," she confirmed. "Some marry, as well, indulging their passions first and regretting it later."

"Is that what you did, my dear?"

Jill nodded.

"It is no worse than what I did with Harry. I wed him, knowing from the start he had a fondness for strong drink. Knowing while there was some little spark between us, that spark was not true love. I bore Harry Randall three sons without once feeling the joy I learned later could exist between a man and a woman."

Perhaps this quaint spirit from an age gone by might understand. Suddenly Jill wanted to unburden herself, tell Laura all that went on between her and Rob. But she couldn't. She wouldn't risk losing the ghost's respect—that feeling that came closer to love than anything she had experienced with her own parents or the grandmother who had reluctantly taken responsibility for raising her.

"I learned the joy of loving with Cyrus. And I sense that you will learn it with Kyle. I have seen you together, felt the sparks that fly each time you touch."

"You're right about that," Jill muttered, damning whatever force inside her turned her into a quivering mass of need every time Kyle touched her. "But I'm afraid to try to quench those flames, Miss Laura."

"You bank those flames until you two climb into your marriage bed."

"The rules have changed since you were a girl. Today lovers don't think twice about sampling each other fully—even if marriage is not in the cards for them." Jill couldn't imagine marrying again—and she doubted if Kyle had more in mind than a mutually pleasurable interlude while he worked to restore Bliss House.

Laura shook her head, as if she couldn't believe the rules of human behavior could have changed so much in a mere century. *"Really, my dear,"* she said primly.

Then Cyrus joined them, floating into the room as if he'd been waiting just outside the open door. Jill wondered how much of the conversation he had heard—and she felt her cheeks turn warm. It felt strange to fret over how ghosts—not people but disembodied spirits—perceived her.

"You must remember, my love, Jill is of a different world than ours." Cyrus put a ghostly arm around the woman he had literally given his life for as he turned and riveted Jill with a look so intense it made her shake clear down to her toes. *"I understand. Laura does, as well, although she's a bit reluctant to accept that times have changed. Tell me. Has young Kyle Randall stolen your heart?"*

Had he? Jill shook her head. "No. Yes. I don't know." She felt tears begin to burn her eyes. "This place—you—Kyle—all the people in Gray Hollow who have kept your legend alive for generations—you're confusing me. I want Kyle Randall in a way I've never wanted a man—yet the attraction seems so . . ."

"So magical?"

Jill nodded. Cyrus had hit on the words that had escaped her, words that described the otherworldly quality of her dreams—of the feelings that washed over her each time she looked at Kyle, every time she listened to the deep, mesmerizing sound of his voice. She lifted a hand to wipe away her tears.

"There's magic here in Bliss House. Good magic. That magic is coming alive again, for you. And for young Randall as well, I'd wager. Laura, haven't I been telling you for a hundred years, your scoundrel of a husband didn't manage to destroy the mystical power of this place when he damned us to a fiery grave?"

Through her tears, Jill watched and envied the ghostly lovers as their faces reflected an almost heavenly joy. Could Cyrus be right? Could Bliss House possibly exude an aura that intensified—magnified—the natural attraction between a woman and a man?

Deep inside, she envied the ghosts' devotion. She could see that love as Laura looked deeply into her lover's eyes, and as Cyrus took her hand and brought it to his lips.

"I'll be going now," she murmured, feeling suddenly like an intruder in her own house. As she left she sensed them wafting through the closed doorway that led to the bedroom where they had died.

Chapter
Fifteen

THE GHOSTS

"She is coming to love him, Cyrus."

He nodded. While Jill Carey appeared reluctant to express herself in words, she wore her feelings plainly on her expressive, pixie face. From the way her dark eyes glowed when she spoke of Randall, Cyrus could sense the man had touched deeply—more deeply than the young woman's obviously healthy passion.

"Cyrus."

"My apologies, my dear. Yes, I agree Miss Carey has tender feelings for your grandson."

Laura settled near the spot where a washstand had once stood in the gutted bedroom. *"He and his workers have made quick work of the repairs outside,"* she commented as she looked around at the evidence of the fire Harry had set off so long ago.

"I do hope they will restore this room. Remember, Cyrus, how we would sit by the fireplace on cool evenings? I'd work on one of my quilts, and you would whittle a piece of wood with that silver-handled knife? The one I bought for you from the traveling peddler?"

"The simplest of times, my love. Yet the best." Cyrus floated over toward the gaping hole that used to be a fireplace with an ornately carved mantel. *"I heard your young man tell one of his workers yesterday that he would begin the interior work here in this room."*

Laura smiled, that smile that had stolen Cyrus's heart so long ago. He longed for Harry Randall's curse to end so he could touch and hold his love again in heaven. Futile though the effort had been proven in the hundred years since they had died here, Cyrus crossed the room and tried again in vain to feel and touch the soft, warm flesh he recalled so well.

"Miss Carey asked me to describe the way our room was, Cyrus. I tried to remember every detail. . . ."

As if they had loved here only yesterday, Cyrus recalled the walnut sleigh bed with coverlets lovingly created by Laura's talented hands—the washstand with its simple creamware pitcher and bowl—a multicolored braided rug his mother had made one winter when he was still a child.

His gaze shifted to a massive wardrobe, the only piece of furniture that had escaped the blaze that had killed them. *"I remember, Laura. As if it were yesterday."*

The seed of a plan began to take root in his mind. He would think on it for a while—no need to trouble Laura now, not until he was certain he could accomplish ghostly magic—and that the magic would work on mortals now.

Chapter Sixteen

Giving up on sleep *again,* Kyle rolled over and squinted at the fluorescent red numbers on his alarm clock. *Four o'clock.* Damn, if he couldn't manage even one night's sleep without images of Jill intruding, he was going to be an old man long before his time.

The job at Bliss House was going more smoothly than he had expected. But there was something about that place—not so much eerie as enchanted. Or was it Jill Carey who had enchanted *him?*

This courting dance had to go! He was no wet-behind-the-ears high-school kid, and neither, by God, was she. He'd had it with dinners for two and walks through the woods—gorgeous fall colors or not. And he swore he'd given her his last brotherly good-night kiss at the door to that little trailer parked next to her haunted house.

He still hadn't figured out why she'd suddenly bolted

when she had been just as fired up as he'd been. Something had to give! And soon!

Before he did something stupid and asked her to marry him, just so he could get some relief. *Where did that idea come from?* Being horny was frying his brain.

Why not? he asked himself.

Because, idiot, you've got a kid no woman's going to put up with, lying there in that hellishly expensive hospital they call a school. And a brother you're going to be responsible for forever, too. You'll never be able to afford another wife, even if you manage to forget the nightmare your first one put you through.

Thinking about Tina damn sure should have cooled his cock. But it didn't. Painfully hard as he'd been most of the time since he'd met Jill, Kyle stumbled out of bed and pulled on some clothes. Today, they would begin on the inside of Bliss House, in the gutted bedroom where the so-called ghosts had died.

All day Kyle worked right beside his crew, tearing out charred inside walls in that bedroom. Although he had half expected the ghosts to creak and moan as they invaded the room, Kyle heard nothing but the familiar hum of power tools, saw only his men. He shrugged off the feeling that they were being watched to paranoia as they set new French doors in place where a sheet of plywood had been.

"What do you want us to do with that old thing?" Joe Evans, Kyle's crew chief, pointed at a huge, bulky wardrobe. Apparently it was the only piece of furniture in the room left intact by that fire a hundred years earlier.

Kyle strode across the room. What a monstrosity, he thought as he inspected the old-fashioned piece. "Ms. Carey said she wanted to refinish it. Except for a couple of singed spots, it looks fairly sound."

"Do we move it out?" Joe sounded skeptical.

"We'd better not. Old furniture can be more fragile than it looks. Let's shove it over against the outside wall for now." Kyle and three of his crew wrestled the heavy piece carefully across newly placed subflooring and set it against a completed section of the wall by the new French doors.

Kyle thought he heard a plaintive moan, but he told himself he had only heard the autumn wind whistling through as-yet-unsealed doors next to the ancient wardrobe.

"You're coming right along with the work," Jill said later as she and Kyle stood in the doorway of Cyrus and Laura's bedroom. "I thought I'd reward you with a picnic, if you'd like."

"Outside?"

He must think she had taken leave of her senses, since soft cold rain had been falling all afternoon, and mists now had settled, cloaking Bliss House in shadow. "No, inside. Out in the living room, by the fireplace."

"Here?"

"The ghosts won't hurt us," she teased.

"I'm not worried about ghosts. They don't exist, now, do they?"

Jill wished Cyrus and Laura would show up. She had the feeling that once Kyle met them, his obvious unease whenever he was inside the house would disappear. She wanted him to share her love for this beautiful old house, to come to care for its spirits, too.

"Come on, let's eat," she said in a coaxing voice. "When I was down at Maida's this afternoon, I had her pack a basketful of her fried chicken. Potato salad, too, and two big pieces of that wonderful coconut cake she makes. You must be starving, as hard as you've been working today."

The feeling that someone was watching them intensified as Kyle sat cross-legged on a blanket next to Jill. He hardly tasted the food, and the uneasy atmosphere almost but not quite distracted him from the insane physical need he felt whenever they were together.

When they had finished eating, they sat and talked, but Kyle's unease didn't pass. He might not believe the stories about the ghosts of Bliss House, but that didn't make it any easier to maintain a casual pose.

The last thing he wanted was to explore a haunted house at night with Jill or anyone else. Especially when he heard otherworldly, scratching sounds from behind the door in the room where he had been working earlier. Every muscle in his body tensed.

As he strode quickly toward the room he told himself he must have left those new French doors ajar—that a raccoon or other forest creature must have found its way inside, seeking food or warmth this chilly night. But his heart beat faster, and he was wishing Jill had stayed behind when he suddenly sensed her presence right behind him.

He opened the door just a crack, and soft light flowed into the hall. What the hell! He knew damn well he'd turned off all the portable work lights before he'd left an hour earlier. And lights didn't make that noise he'd heard.

"Kyle!" Jill's soft exclamation pushed him into action.

Making sure she stayed behind him, Kyle strode into the room. Not the room he and Jill had left an hour earlier, but a room he remembered vaguely from that first wild dream. His gaze settled on the bed. He had taken her on a bed just like that, in that goddamn erotic fantasy.

He had to be going stark, raving mad! The only goddamn stick of furniture in here this afternoon had been that monstrosity of a wardrobe, and he had moved *it* from its present spot to that empty place beside the French doors.

"It's beautiful!"

Jill bounded into the room, apparently oblivious to the madness that had overtaken them. Kyle glanced around, searching for tools . . . lumber . . . anything that could attest to the fact that he had worked in this room today!

He saw Jill kneeling on the floor, looking at a braided rug that certainly hadn't been there this afternoon. He watched a cool breeze from slightly open French doors ruffle her short, dark curls. And he heard the sound of tinkling laughter and what must have been the creaking of ancient boards from somewhere in the distance—just before all the doors slammed shut.

He didn't care if Jill thought he was nuts. He had to get out! With two long strides he reached the entry to the hall and fumbled with the rusty doorknob.

Nothing! It was locked—or stuck. He put his boot to the ancient wood and shoved, expecting the door to splinter into a thousand pieces. It didn't. This time he kicked harder, slamming into it with the force of two-hundred-plus pounds coming from a running start.

"Kyle?" She sounded too damn calm.

"That door won't budge." If he ever got the hell out of here, he'd have to check the door's construction. "We'll go out onto the porch." He crossed the room quickly and tried to pry each of the French doors open. He had ordered those doors himself, and he knew damn well he had the strength to break them down—but they held up against his furious assault. It was as though someone had reinforced them with concrete and steel rods, he decided after half a dozen attempts to batter through them.

"We could just stay here," Jill said, her voice as fiery and smooth as the shot of Jack Daniel's he had just been wishing for.

The old house creaked again, and Kyle could feel air from somewhere stirring around them. He glanced at the flickering light from a kerosene lantern that bathed the room—and Jill—in golden shadows.

His initial sense of terror left him, replaced by a need—more like a compulsion—to play out this fantasy, to see where it took them. Kyle moved toward Jill, his gaze locking with hers as he reached out and touched the tips of her long, slender fingers. "If we stay here, and it looks as though we don't have a hell of a lot of choice, you know what's going to happen," he muttered hoarsely.

She nodded, but the heated expression in her big, dark eyes as she settled her gaze on the rapidly expanding bulge below his belt said much more than a simple yes.

Letting her hands go but maintaining eye contact, Kyle shrugged out of his denim jacket and began loosening the buttons of his flannel shirt. When he peeled it off and tackled his belt buckle, he watched her tongue dart out and moisten lips the color of azaleas in the spring.

The soft thud of his boots falling onto the braided rug followed by the rasp of his zipper punctuated the silence and gave Kyle hope that this moment was real, not another frustrating dream.

He shoved his jeans and underwear roughly down his legs and stepped out of them, feeling the heat of Jill's gaze on his aching flesh.

"Meet Big Al," he told her gruffly, indicating his needy cock.

He watched her eyes widen, saw that enticing little tongue dart out again to wet her lips. "It's got a name?" she finally asked with a grin.

"Back when I was a horny kid, my brother said I ought to name it since it didn't seem quite right for a perfect stranger to be running my life." Kyle shrugged.

"Makes sense. I guess. By the way, the name fits." Boldly she reached out and touched him, and he felt as if he might explode there on the spot. "I think I'm going to like you, Al."

"Don't you think one of us is just a bit overdressed?" Kyle asked, wishing she would keep caressing him like that all night—and hoping she would hurry and get on with this dream loving that was already damn near killing him with pleasure.

Chapter Seventeen

THE GHOSTS

"I believe I have just managed to speed up a reluctant courtship," Cyrus said as he joined his Laura in the corner of the attic where they had taken their rest each night for a hundred years.

"Cyrus, what did you do? I sense from that satisfied smile on your face that you've been up to something. Tell me."

Cyrus chuckled. Knowing prim, proper Laura would have objected, he had planned and carried out his trick alone. *"I made our bedroom as it was when we were alive, my dear."*

"You used your special powers just for that?" Laura sounded incredulous, but thrilled. *"Let us spend the night there, then,"* she said breathlessly.

"We—we cannot. The room is . . . occupied."

"Cyrus Bliss, what have you done?"

Cyrus cleared his throat. *"I have helped your great-great-grandson and Miss Carey to explore the feelings they both seem so determined to ignore,"* he said, carefully choosing his words.

Laura floated to a full, standing position and glared down at him. *"Tell me, Cyrus, that you have not meddled with those dear young people's lives."*

"Only a bit, my love."

"What have you done?" From the rising tone of her voice, Cyrus could tell Laura's usually even temper was firing up.

He shrugged. *"Nothing they will not both enjoy."*

"Cyrus, I am going to that room right now if you do not explain what trick you have played!"

Reaching out as if he could grab her hand and hold her, Cyrus said in a beseeching tone, *"Sit down, Laura. I did nothing but confine them together in that room. They will be forced to talk."*

"Talk?" That came out along with an indignant-sounding snort. But she floated down to sit beside him. *"Do not play me for a fool, Cyrus! You do not think, any more than I, that those two hot-blooded youngsters will spend the night talking. You have set them up to sin in that room—just as we sinned there so long ago!"*

"We committed no sin. You were more my wife than Harry Randall's." Laura's guilt—groundless as it was, Cyrus thought—ate at him, for nothing he had said or done for more than a hundred years had wiped it from her heart.

"And by today's standards, I understand that sharing a bed without marriage is not a sin at all. Laura, we have only six more weeks to see Miss Carey wed with Randall. Can you truly fault me for giving them opportunity to explore the attraction they so obviously feel for each other?"

Laura's shoulders slumped. *"I would not see them marry only to lift this curse from us,"* she said quietly.

"Nor would I. If they are not meant to be, nothing will happen downstairs. If they are destined to be lovers, my trick will simply make it easy for them to shed the excuses they have used to avoid taking what they want."

Chapter
Eighteen

Jill's mouth was watering. Her nipples had tightened to hard, nearly painful beads, and she could already imagine feeling the heat and hardness of Kyle filling the emptiness between her legs. He looked good enough to eat, laid out on the faded quilt on the bed, watching her take off her clothes.

Big Al. She smiled. He certainly was that—twice as big as Rob, at least. And Kyle could laugh about sex in a way Rob never did! She couldn't wait to feel him inside her!

Quickly she peeled off her sweater and tights, liking the choking sound that came from his throat as he looked his fill at her naked body. For the first time Jill felt pride in the full, high breasts that Rob had hated so.

"God, you're gorgeous. If I'd have known you weren't wearing anything under those clothes, we wouldn't have wasted time eating. Come here," he muttered, holding out his arms as if in invitation.

He lay very still, legs slightly spread, a godlike statue hewn of bone and muscle, flesh and blood. More than anything, she wanted to touch him, make him burn the way she was burning for him.

As she sat on the edge of the bed, her gaze took in soft skin covering rock-hard muscle—and a massive chest sprinkled with light brown hair that narrowed around his navel, then grew denser and coarser where it cushioned his sex. She gave in to her desire, bending down and laving his navel with her tongue.

"Hey, that tickles," he rumbled, and she looked up to meet his gaze.

"Sorry."

"Don't stop, honey, I can take the heat."

His nostrils flared, as if he were inhaling her scent. She saw fiery need in forest-green eyes so dark now they appeared nearly black. He wanted her, that was obvious, yet he lay there at her mercy, giving her the power to set their pace.

She bent her head and touched a coppery nipple with her tongue, steeling herself for the moment when he would take control and force her to his stronger will. But it didn't happen. His heart beat an accelerating cadence in her ear, yet he touched her only with the intensity of his gaze.

Jill reveled in this new, heady power—power she knew was hers only at Kyle's whim. Heat pooled in her belly as she stroked satiny skin stretched taut over work-hardened pads of muscle. Her hands drifted lower, tangled in the coarse silky hair in their search for the rigid column of heat she wanted to fill her.

"Yes. Honey, don't stop," he begged as she explored velvety skin so hot it nearly burned her fingers, stretched nearly to bursting over rigid, pulsating flesh.

Where her hands had been, her lips followed, tasting and testing the musky maleness of him that made her wet with need. Seeking to break his determined passivity, she took him deeply into her mouth and suckled, swirling her tongue rhythmically against distended veins that pulsed with life.

"Enough!" The word came out of his throat as a hoarse croak, at the same time his hands came down to either side of her head. Gently he lifted her away as he sat up and cradled her trembling body against his own.

She felt his hands all over her, weighing her breasts, stroking down her body to her wet, hot core. "Please. I need you now," she murmured when he toyed with the little core of nerves that had already hardened to a throbbing nub, even before he had sought it out for his sweet torture.

Suddenly frantic with wanting him buried hard and deep inside her, she lay back, spreading her legs wide for him. "Don't make me wait. I want you inside me now."

He shifted and came down on top of her, silencing her with his mouth—and his tongue, which thrust into her mouth in the rhythm his hips beat against her aching sex. Instinctively she lifted her legs and crossed them over his broad back, opening herself farther for his piercing thrust.

"Not yet, honey." He looped his powerful arms under her knees and draped her legs over his shoulders as he slid downward, pausing along the way to lick around her navel as she had done earlier to him. "I've got to taste you, too."

His hot, moist breath fanned across her quivering mound just before he found that tingling knot of nerves and worried it gently between his teeth while his fingers plucked and tugged at her aching nipples.

She felt it coming but couldn't hold back. As she lay there trembling with the strongest climax of her life, she felt Kyle pull away for a moment. Then he was back, his breath tickling over her belly . . . against her breasts . . . across lips still tender from his kisses. He plunged his tongue deep into her throat at the same moment as he flexed his hips and joined their bodies in one long, hard thrust.

The sensations never stopped. They kept coming, intensifying with each stroke that stretched and filled her to the hilt. She felt him grip her harder and shudder just as she wilted into a quivering, incoherent heap.

Was it moments or hours later when Jill felt Kyle gently

disentangling their legs? She didn't know. She couldn't speak or move. Silently she met his softened gaze, willing him not to leave her, to stay and let the fantasy go on. When he rolled to his side and arranged her so they lay spoon fashion on the antique sleigh bed before pulling the quilt over their sated bodies, Jill relaxed and drifted off to sleep.

When sunlight bathed her face with warmth, she woke up on the floor in the fire-gutted bedroom Kyle's crew had just begun repairing. What was she doing here? she wondered. Her back felt warm, the rest of her chilled despite the old, musty quilt that covered her—and Kyle.

She rolled over—carefully because her back felt the imprint of the cold, rough plywood sheet where they apparently had spent the night. As she did so she felt him stir.

"Good morning," she said when his eyelids fluttered open, revealing green eyes that reflected her own confusion.

She watched him look around, felt his hands draw her hard against the heat of his morning erection. "It wasn't all a dream, was it?" he asked hoarsely.

Suddenly Jill remembered the doors that wouldn't open—the invitingly furnished room that bore no evidence of reconstruction, or of the destruction that fire so long ago had caused. And Kyle. The way he'd loved her, made her go up in flames brighter and hotter than anything she had ever experienced before.

"No. Some of it had to have been real," she replied softly.

A rumble of heavy engines and clattering of wheels against hard-packed dirt intruded. "The work crew will be in here—like now. If we don't get up and out of here, they're going to find us like this." Kyle untangled their legs and dragged himself up before bending and lifting Jill to her feet. Briefly Jill felt his strength and heat before he let her go and began tugging on his clothes.

"You'd better get dressed, honey. I'm going to try to get us out of here."

She watched him try the door he'd brutalized last night,

amazed when it opened easily. "Kyle," she murmured as she smoothed her bulky sweater down over her naked hips.

"Jill. I've got to get to work now. But this is just the beginning. Come home with me tonight," he said before his mouth met hers in a kiss full of erotic promises.

When she looked around the room, trying to make sense of what had happened here, Jill saw something small and shiny on the charred floor where she swore a polished walnut sleigh bed had stood last night. Carefully she stepped off the plywood sheets Kyle's crew had laid and made her way across damaged wood that creaked in protest.

When she picked up a delicate antique locket, she heard a moan from somewhere deep within Bliss House.

Chapter Nineteen

THE GHOSTS

"The locket, Cyrus. It didn't burn. She has found it."

Cyrus smiled. *"My ploy has served two purposes, then, my love. Finding your precious bauble as well as bringing those stubborn young people together."*

"They spent all night in there. And this morning Kyle appears more at ease. Look! He has spotted the photographs on the mantel." Laura floated closer to the big, good-looking brute who was her great-great-grandson.

"He does resemble your sons, Laura." Attempting diplomacy, Cyrus intentionally neglected to mention young Randall also bore an uncanny physical likeness to his love's brute of a husband—their murderer.

Laura nodded, and Cyrus watched her soft expression as she looked her fill at the descendant sent by fate to end

Harry Randall's curse. He followed her gaze to Randall's big hands, and Cyrus noticed those hands tremble as they set the old daguerreotype gently back on the mantel.

"He is feeling a closeness with the house now," Laura said later as they rested in the attic. *"Perhaps it is time for us to pay him a visit."*

"Not yet. Randall is feeling closer to Miss Carey, surely. I do not sense that he bears any love for us or Bliss House."

Laura turned and stared out the dormer window for a long time. Cyrus sensed her need to meet Kyle Randall face-to-face, but he knew it was too soon. *"My dear, we must be patient. It is our lot to lurk and learn, and only rarely to show ourselves to the mortals who hold our future in their hands."*

"If we are to bring them together we must know the secrets they so carefully keep from us." Laura was floating back and forth across the attic, as if she were a mortal pacing the floor, and her agitation disturbed Cyrus's ghostly peace.

"Could you possibly be still?"

She paused, then smiled that sweet, compliant smile that had made him love her so. *"I'm sorry. I simply thought that if we confronted Kyle, we could learn why he bears this guilt, help him exorcise it so he can come to Miss Carey without . . ."*

"Without whatever he has done that makes him who he is? Laura, the past must always shape one's present and future. Besides, we have shown ourselves to the young lady, and still she harbors secrets—secrets that obviously have affected her deeply."

Laura appeared to be considering his words, so Cyrus leaned back against the wall and sorted out his own thoughts. Why did he feel so strongly that now was not the time for Laura to reveal herself to Randall? Was it jealousy or fear for her safety? Certainly the past had clouded his reason when it came to the Randalls of Hunter's Mountain.

"How would you feel if I approached him first?" he asked when he had determined that his primary concern was fear—fear for his Laura's sanity if this descendant of hers rejected her as her own children had, after she had declared her love for him.

Chapter
Twenty

Jill paced the length of her tiny trailer, torn between telling Kyle the truth about her past and prolonging last night's tenderness. The idea of spoiling the rightness, the pleasure of what they had shared had about the same appeal as confronting that Eastern rattlesnake she'd seen stretched out in the sun along the path this morning.

Just thinking about Kyle, hard and huge inside her, made her wet and ready. And it would be hours before he would send his crew away and take her to his cabin farther up the mountain.

Instinctively she knew Kyle was a man whose sexual taste ran toward the tried and true—yet something told her he would be her willing partner in whatever bedroom games she might want to play. With two fingers she toyed with a nipple still pleasantly sore from the rasp of his beard while searching one-handed for a sexy red bra and bikini panties she had bought before leaving Atlanta.

Would he like it if she knelt at his feet and laved Big Al with her tongue? What Rob had forced her to do, Jill would do with pleasure to Kyle. She felt warm, wet heat between her legs at the thought of playing with his big, hard sex that way. She would drive him crazy for a while.

But not for too long. Just when he started to come, she would straddle him and take him inside her. Then she would rock on him, rub her nipples against the soft dark hair on his chest.

She would try every erotic trick she had ever heard of with this man who could fulfill her completely with only the magic of his magnificent body. She would revel in being a woman, bask in the feeling of sexual equality he gave her. Kyle had set her free to explore grown-up sexual needs Rob had suppressed for so long.

She felt her lips curve upward in a smile. She would say nothing, reveal none of the depravity she had shared with Rob. This time with Kyle she would walk on the wild side, take pure and sensual pleasure in being a woman. His woman.

Jill found the underwear, then set it back in the drawer. Anticipating Kyle's hunger and her own, she slipped a red silk shirt and ankle-length plaid wool skirt over her naked, sensitized flesh.

As she heard Kyle knock at the door she grabbed the scraps of wispy lace she had decided against wearing, and tucked them in her purse. When she let him in, she greeted him with a hot, wet kiss.

"Did you get any sleep?" Kyle asked as he wrapped an arm around Jill to bring her closer in the cool cab of his truck. He wanted to pull her on his lap and bury his cock inside her, but he figured that would have to wait until they got to Hunter's Mountain. Tonight he would have her again,

over and over, until he could be damn sure last night had
been real—not another sexy dream.

"Uh-huh. You must be exhausted, though."

Kyle grinned. "I may be. But Big Al is rarin' to go." He
brought her hand into his lap, and let out a groan when she
opened the zipper of his jeans and rubbed a finger over
rapidly heating bare flesh.

"He is, isn't he?"

"Yeah." The ten-minute drive up Hunter's Mountain felt
like hours, and by the time he stopped the truck, Kyle was
ready to explode. Not bothering to zip up, he got out of the
truck, practically dragging Jill along as he hurried toward
the cabin—and a bed.

Dinner could wait. He couldn't. Not even for the bed. Not
when Jill pulled up her long plaid skirt and perched on the
end of the trestle table, legs spread wide. Didn't this woman
ever wear underpants? he wondered as he shoved down his
jeans.

Out of control, Kyle sank into her wet heat, grasping her
hips to hold her as he thrust hard and fast until she screamed
his name. He let go then, collapsing on top of her as he exploded into her waiting womb.

That thought sobered him—fast. The last time he'd taken
a woman without protection, he had become a father. As if
it would help at this point, he pulled out and jerked up his
pants.

"What's wrong?"

He tried to meet Jill's confused gaze. "I didn't use a condom. God, I'm sorry."

"I'm on the Pill, mostly to regulate my periods. I don't
have any diseases. I trust you don't, either."

"No." He wondered why he felt cheated—why the hell it
should make him anything but ecstatic to learn he hadn't
gone and knocked her up in his rush to get inside her. "Come
on, honey, get up so I can fix us something to eat."

Later, as they sat in the front room by a blazing fireplace,

Kyle watched Jill's tongue dart out to capture a string of cheese as it slid off her slice of pizza.

Damn, this woman could make the simple act of eating turn his bones to jelly and his balls to stone. He guzzled down half a beer to cool his body before he could trust himself to look at her again.

"I've never felt like this before," she told him, setting down her own beer can and looking at him with shining brown eyes.

"Out of control?" Kyle knew he damn sure had never experienced feelings like this about any other woman he'd ever met.

"I guess that's as good a way to describe it as any. Maybe it's Bliss House—the ghosts—I don't know."

Kyle shrugged. "If there are ghosts, they've been there since long before I was born. They've never affected me or anyone else so far as I know, and I lived around here all my life until I left for college."

"Do you feel out of control, Kyle?"

Her voice, low and sexy, reminded him of silky caresses, erotic dreams. "Damn straight. Jill, have you started having dreams since you came to Bliss House?"

"No more than I did before. Have you?"

"Yeah. Somehow I knew how good it felt to touch you before . . . before we'd touched at all. That room where we spent last night, I'd seen before. Made love to you there another time. Hell, it's as if I'm living out a fantasy that's gone before, one so real I think I'm losing my damn mind."

"One night, I dreamed we danced together at a party in Bliss House," Jill said, her expression dreamy. "All the guests but me wore Victorian dress. I felt out of place, until you came and took me in your arms."

"Did you know me then?"

"No. You came to the house for the first time the next morning."

In the month since his first visit, Kyle realized he and Jill had been so tied up with wanting to jump each other's bones they had learned hardly anything about each other's lives before they met. "Why did you come here, Jill?" he asked as he let her hand go and reached for his beer.

"For peace. My husband died, and all that was left in Atlanta was a load of painful memories."

She must have loved the guy a lot, Kyle thought, recalling his own sense of relief when he had learned Tina had overdosed one last time and freed him from the hell that had been their marriage. "I'm sorry, honey."

"Don't be. If Rob hadn't committed suicide, I probably would have killed him."

So much for his picture of an idyllic marriage. Kyle wasn't sure he wanted to feel so pleased to know Jill wasn't grieving over some dearly departed love. "Bad marriage?"

"Bad ending. Bad beginning and middle, too, though I didn't realize it at the time. It's not something I want to talk about," she said, her gaze fixed on the empty pizza pan on the polished tree trunk that they were using as a serving table.

"No problem. My marriage was pretty much hell on earth from start to finish, too." At least Jill had no flesh-and-blood reminders of her bad judgment, Kyle thought as a picture of Alyssa flashed unbidden in his mind. He opened his mouth to tell Jill about his pathetic little girl, then changed his mind. He had no right to burden her with his personal nightmares.

Besides, Jill had given him no indication she wanted more than this magical time to explore the powerful chemistry between them. And at that moment his muscles clenched as he pictured her naked and wet for him beneath that long woolen skirt.

Maybe this time he could go slowly, indulge his fantasy of tasting every inch of her satin skin before exploding inside her like a dynamite stick. If he could hold out, maybe he could even withstand the torture of her rough, wet tongue devouring every inch of him.

Big Al twitched and expanded, and Kyle nearly laughed

out loud. When Jill was around, Al certainly had a mind of his own!

"What's so funny?"

"My buddy's trying to tell us you've turned him on again," Kyle said with a grin, taking her hand and settling it over the straining zipper of his jeans. "You game?"

Jill squeezed him playfully. "Why don't you let him loose?" she asked, before standing and unfastening her red plaid skirt.

Kyle struggled with his zipper, his attention on the erotic production she was making of unbuttoning her silky long-sleeved shirt. He gasped when it fell open, revealing the sheerest red lace bra he'd ever seen.

When she wriggled her hips, sending that skirt slithering down to the floor, he nearly choked. Sometime since they'd done each other on his kitchen table, she'd put on a tiny red triangle of lacy stuff that matched her bra.

He guessed they were panties, if one could call that enticing scrap anything as ordinary as simple underwear. That see-through G-string—and sheer black thigh-high stockings he knew would feel like silk against his back—had him more than ready to burst.

God, lady, if you only knew how you turn me on! You sure as hell don't need see-through underwear to get me hot!

He staggered to his knees, burying his cheek against that hot lace triangle. His tongue snaked out, flicking the pouting knot of nerves he found protruding between her satiny nether lips. With his teeth, he caught the tiny elastic thread that held the G-string and pulled it taut.

Her thighs, warm and soft beneath black silk, trembled as if she could barely stand. He didn't think he could stand up, either, but this time he wanted to make it last. Shakily he let her go and got to his feet, dragging her down beside him on the cooling leather of the couch.

"Do you have a bed?" she asked, her voice uneven as she tugged at the buttons of his shirt.

"In there." He managed to point an arm in the right direction but, damn it, he was so hot he knew he'd have to crawl to get there.

"Come on, big guy." She stood, breasts proudly jutting forward, and twitched her hips at him as she moved away.

He stripped down the rest of the way and followed her lead. A saint couldn't resist this woman, and Kyle knew he wasn't a saint. When he found her in the bathroom, adjusting the showerhead, he stepped inside the glass enclosure.

She still had on those clothes that were more provocative than none at all—and wet, they looked even more erotic. He nuzzled one breast through the transparent lace, then slid the cup down just enough to bare the nipple.

Bending down, he took the pebbly nub into his mouth. He pulled the nipple deeply into his mouth and began to suckle, imitating the motion of his mouth with fingers that tugged and plucked its mate.

He felt her take his cock in her hand and milk him, and he thought he'd come right then and there. But she stopped, reaching lower and gently squeezing his balls with hands slippery from the soap. He'd never been bathed like this in his life, he thought as she took the handheld showerhead and directed its warm stinging spray between his legs.

He soaped his hands and rubbed them over her water-slicked body, getting rid of the red lace as he went. She felt hot—hot from the water; but hotter, he hoped, from his touch. And he burned from hers, because she couldn't seem to keep from measuring and weighing his throbbing sex in her talented little hands.

After he rinsed her, she went to her knees. Even though he'd guessed it was coming and had steeled himself against the wild, hot burst of pleasure, he damn near came when she took him in her mouth.

His hands went down. His fingers tunneled through baby-soft wet tendrils of her short, dark hair. He wanted to tell her to stop, or to keep on until she sucked him dry, but the words came out as an unintelligible moan. When he couldn't stand up any longer, he sank onto the plastic shower seat he'd built for Dolph to use, and dragged her up to straddle his lap.

"Here?" she asked huskily.

"Why not?" He barely got the question out.

"Because I want you to remember this night for a long, long time."

There's no chance, honey, that I'll forget you in this lifetime. Still, he forced himself to rise and let her blot him head to toe with a towel while he tried to distract himself by counting tiles on the bathroom floor. Then he returned the favor, and by the time he finished, his patience had gone. Lifting her easily, he tossed her over his shoulder and carried her to his bed.

Jill lay back, still enjoying the afterglow. Not an inch of her had escaped Kyle's nimble fingers and tongue—and there wasn't an inch of his gorgeous body she hadn't explored in minutest detail. She smiled as she remembered him tracing imaginary shapes on her mound with just one big finger, lapping at it with his tongue to tease and tickle her before he moved lower to devote equal attention to her hot, wet core.

She had thought to shock him—but he'd taken the deliberately provocative lace and silk—and her deliberate seduction—in stride. Perhaps Kyle's sexual aptitude might surpass all she had ever read about or seen.

She certainly couldn't fault his skill—or his fortitude. And the equipment itself was incomparable. Her gaze drifted down his body to Big Al, who was still impressive, even while Kyle slept.

"More, honey?" he asked, and she watched one green eye crack open when she stroked his flaccid sex.

"Mmmm."

"Insatiable wench. Wake Al up and you can have him again," Kyle growled. But he reached down with one hand and turned Jill so he could reach between her legs, too. And she had to smile.

As though he was trying to memorize the feel of her, he stroked all her most private places, even slipping a finger gingerly just inside the crinkled opening of her bottom. Then he cupped her mound.

"I should go shave. I'm going to scratch you."

"It's all right. Your face feels good. Just a little rough." He hadn't commented on her lack of body hair before—was it only now beginning to register in his mind? To distract him, she leaned over and worried the tip of his penis between her lips.

She felt him rub his cheek softly against her. "You're so soft, like slick, hot satin. I love to touch you like this. My wife sometimes shaved her . . . between her legs. But when she did, she always felt like a porcupine."

"I don't shave. My late husband disliked women with hair down there, so I had it permanently removed." She blew softly where she'd been sucking, and she chuckled when Big Al began to twitch and thicken.

"Was this his idea, too?" His hand went up to toy with the short, wispy strands of her hair.

Jill jerked back. "No. It was mine. I had it done after Rob died. He never saw it. He would have had a fit."

I should have shaved my head when I was thirteen, the first time he grabbed handfuls of my hair to hold my face down on his puny little erection.

"I like to watch the light play off your hair. Sort of like a beacon, telling me it's time to come and play." Kyle's big body trembled a little when she squeezed Al again, but he lay quietly, shifting one hand up to tug at her nipple.

She felt the pressure starting to build inside her again, as though it had been months, not hours, since Kyle had coaxed her to a mind-boggling climax. Feeling bolder now that he'd acknowledged and accepted her blatant sexuality, she took him fully into her mouth and felt him swell against her throat. Could she swallow him?

She could try. As she did so she explored him with her hands, cupping his heavy testicles in her hands and feeling them grow high and tight against her lips. She let her fingers stray, dipping a fingertip, then her whole finger into the crevice between his tightly muscled buns.

She felt him twist around, shivered as his warm breath blew over her mound. She wanted his mouth on her again. Lifting one leg, she wrapped an ankle around his neck and urged him closer.

His tongue felt like wet, slippery sandpaper against her mound. It stabbed at that little knot of nerves, sending waves of fire straight through her aching body. Then he pressed hard against her with his mouth, plunging his tongue deep into the spot that ached to be filled. She swallowed again and again, wanting him so deep inside her he would never be able to get free.

As if he had read her mind, Kyle rolled to his back and pulled her on top of him. "Ride me," he said hoarsely, arching his back to nudge her legs apart.

She sank greedily onto his throbbing hardness, taking him deep—so deep she gasped. Rocking on him slowly, then faster, she felt a climax building—growing—pushing all thought but satisfaction from her heated brain.

She heard herself scream, felt her inner muscles clamp down on him. As she sank into a boneless heap in his arms, she felt him follow her over the edge.

Jill found it hard to believe. Six months ago she would have told anyone who asked that she had no use for men— for any man. She had sworn no man would get to her again. Now she could hardly wait for Kyle to finish a day's work and take her to heaven in his arms.

In bed and out, he had kept her on the edge of ecstasy since he'd taken her to his cabin that first night, five days earlier. Jill smiled. For whatever reason, her nightmares had gone away since she and Kyle had become lovers.

The work was going well—in another week the crew would have Bliss House structurally sound. Kyle had told her he would be doing the inside finish work himself, which meant they would have the days to themselves except when the plumbing and electrical subcontractors came in. Jill hummed happily as she waited for him to arrive after his workers took off for the weekend.

"Can I come in?" he called from outside her trailer.

"Sure. The door's unlocked." A little disappointed, for she had thought he would want to take her to his cozy cabin, she stood on tiptoe to share his welcoming kiss. "You want to stay here tonight?" she asked, wondering how his long muscular frame would fit into the narrow bunk that was her bed.

"I can't, honey. I've got to go to Greensboro." She thought she heard real regret in his voice, but when he didn't suggest she go with him, she began to wonder. For all she knew, he could have ten women stashed somewhere to see to his sexual pleasure.

Chapter
Twenty-One

Kyle shrugged off Dolph's litany of complaints about his two-week-long stay in Gray Hollow. "You can handle problems in the office without me, you know," he pointed out casually as he thumbed through a stack of messages on his desk.

"You've never stayed away from Alyssa this long before—not when you were within driving distance like you are on this job." Kyle watched his brother's expression as he rolled his chair over by the window and looked out at the company's heavy equipment.

Suddenly Kyle's blood began to boil. "You don't actually think Alyssa knows whether I'm ever with her, do you? Did she suddenly start talking and tell you last Sunday that she missed her daddy?"

"You know she didn't. But I believe she knows. On some level. Christ, Kyle, she is your flesh and blood."

But she should have been yours. Maybe if you hadn't been so goddamn noble, she would have been—and her mother wouldn't have poisoned her into a living death before she was born. "Drop it, Dolph. I don't need you to make me feel guilty—I do just fine at that all by myself."

"What's kept you holed up in that cabin, brother? Some fancy woman?"

Kyle grinned. "Yeah. Actually I've been having more fun than I ever remember having with a woman."

"That hot, huh?"

"Don't you remember Mom telling us never to kiss and tell?" Kyle felt uncomfortable talking about sex with the brother who would never be able to satisfy his own desires again. He often thought Dolph must realize how the subject unnerved him as Dolph goaded him into locker-room talk out of some streak of sadomasochism.

"I recall we never used to pay a lot of attention to her."

What Kyle had shared with Jill was too personal, too mind shattering to put in words, even to give his brother a vicarious thrill. "We should have. Look, Dolph, I don't intend to discuss Jill with you or anybody else."

Dolph shrugged. "Should I start pricing engagement rings for you?"

That was a joke! Kyle made a hell of a lot of money. But between carrying Dolph on his payroll at a salary big enough to finance his medical bills, and paying for Alyssa's so-called school, he couldn't afford to marry anyone. He certainly couldn't afford Jill, who was so filthy rich she could drop half a million dollars into the rat hole people called Bliss House, without batting a seductive eyelash!

"Drop it," he snapped, wishing he didn't feel he had to tiptoe around Dolph because of his injuries. "Are you feeling okay?"

"Fine. According to the urologist, that shunt's doing the trick for now. No more infection. For the moment."

"What did the neurosurgeon say?"

"I haven't had time to go and see him."

Kyle noticed Dolph's gaze waver. "Why not?"

"Doesn't seem to be much point in getting poked and prodded every three months just to hear him say I'm a lousy candidate for the surgery he keeps telling me I should have."

"Have you given it any more thought?" Part of Kyle wished Dolph would grab the chance for a more normal life, while a selfish streak in him made him want to beg his brother not to face overwhelming odds that he might die. Of course, without the surgery, Dolph's days were numbered anyhow.

Dolph nodded. "It's tempting. Some days, when I can barely drag myself out of bed, I think I'll do it. Other times, I wonder why the damn idiot keeps trying to talk me into having an operation he admits has a better chance of killing than curing me." He rubbed a hand through longish dark brown hair. "Met any ghosts up there on Hunter's Mountain?" he asked, changing the subject.

Kyle recalled the creaking floors and stuck doors in Bliss House, and the suddenly restored bedroom that just as suddenly reverted to a burned-out, half-rebuilt shell where he had awoken, sprawled on top of a plywood panel with Jill. "You'd think I was nuts if I told you," he told his brother with a grin.

"Grandpa used to tell folks he'd seen strange things at Bliss House. Remember?"

Actually Kyle didn't. He'd been just five years old when Grandpa Randall had driven his truck down Hunter's Mountain and missed a curve. But he had heard the tales from Dolph, no doubt embellished to keep the fear of the bogeyman at the forefront of his mischievous little mind. "Yeah," he said, because he knew that was what Dolph wanted to hear.

"Have you heard them moan?"

Kyle shrugged. "Could be it's the wind, blowing through the trees outside. But strange things have happened in Bliss House."

"Like what?"

"Like things you can't see or hear but you know are watching you." Kyle hesitated, then went on. "Like burned-out rooms that suddenly appear the way they must have been a hundred years ago, then turn back into what they were before. Like a woman you've never seen before, but somehow you know you've touched her, made love to her before."

"Who do you think you're kidding! It's the bottom half of me that's dead, not my brain." Dolph obviously thought Kyle had been spinning a tall tale.

"I'm not kidding, big brother. But I can't explain it either. Are you ready to go?"

Dolph shrugged. "I'll take my car. Angels' Paradise is almost halfway to Gray Hollow. No need for you to drive all the way back here. Besides, you never want to stay as long as I do."

As he drove alone along the winding secondary roads, while he sat and looked at Alyssa, and when he sped back to Gray Hollow—and Jill—Kyle silently berated himself for not being able to love his own child.

Chapter
Twenty-Two

THE GHOSTS

"I see him with a crippled man. And a little girl. She's beau-tiful. Dark hair and eyes. She is lying in a bed with rails on each side. They are in a big house somewhere not too far away from here. He's walking away." Laura opened her eyes and met Cyrus's gaze. Her expression mirrored the pain he sensed this vision caused her.

"Don't strain yourself, my love. I know how difficult it is for you to see events happening away from your view."

Laura's eyelids closed again. *"I must. Cyrus, I can feel Kyle's guilt. Strongly. It has to do with these people. Yet I cannot sense that Kyle has committed an act that justifies the pain he carries in his heart."*

Cyrus wished he could be so sure. Hard as he might try,

he tended to color all Randall men with the paintbrush Harry Randall had invented. *"Is Kyle coming here?"*

"I think so. Cyrus, he is in pain."

"I believe it is time I had a talk with young Randall. I sense he has stolen Miss Carey's heart." The thought of a Randall hurting the young woman he had come to consider as dear as his own daughter brought out Cyrus's protective instincts.

"Let me. Here in this room he has brought back to life. You will intimidate him."

Sensing Laura's need to know her own long-lost flesh and blood, Cyrus capitulated. He would let her appear—let her have her moments alone with this descendant of Harry Randall. But he would lurk nearby, unseen unless Kyle Randall said or did something to upset the woman he would always love.

Chapter
Twenty-Three

"Love?" Jill could hardly believe Maida had the nerve to ask her if she was in love with Kyle Randall. She was learning quickly that the concept of privacy hadn't reached Gray Hollow, North Carolina.

"You could do worse. He may be one of those no-account Randalls from Hunter's Mountain, but I've got to admit Kyle has done pretty good for himself."

Jill nodded. She couldn't fault Kyle—except maybe for his reluctance to talk about his family. But then, she didn't say much about hers, either. "He said he went to school there," she commented, shifting her gaze toward the old brick school building that perched on the other side of Gray Hollow.

"He did, at that. Just like every other kid who ever grew up around here. Kyle was the only boy from Gray Hollow ever to make all-state in football, though. Always was a big'un. Played at Chapel Hill, too. He's the only Randall ever to get a degree from college—come to think of it, he was one of very few to finish high school. Those Randalls weren't much for gettin' book learning, but folks say they made the best 'shine in three states."

"They made whiskey?"

"White lightning, folks call it. I remember Kyle's daddy used to bring down a bottle or two once in a while for my pa. Said it was smooth as velvet, Pa did. That was a while ago, though. The Treasury boys found the Randalls' still back, say twenty years ago. Killed Kyle's daddy and uncles when they started shootin'. Kyle couldn't have been more than ten or eleven years old at the time."

"How terrible!" No wonder Kyle didn't say much about his childhood.

"His mama sort of fell apart after that. It was Dolph, Kyle's big brother, who practically raised him."

Jill nodded. "He's told me about his brother. Says he runs the company office over in Greensboro."

"Did he tell you Dolph's in a wheelchair? While Kyle was in college, Dolph damn near got himself killed in a logging accident."

"No." Jill had the feeling there were lots of things Kyle hadn't told her, just as there were many secrets she couldn't share with him. Suddenly she felt a burst of warmth. When she turned, Kyle was stepping through the café door.

Her heart beat faster at the sight of him, hair ruffled by the late-October wind, his dark green parka collar pulled up against cheeks reddened by the cold. But when he pulled out a chair and sat down beside her, she knew something was very wrong.

"Kyle," she said, reaching over to touch his hand as he pulled off a brown leather glove. "You look as if you haven't had a wink of sleep all weekend." There was a tightness in his jaw, and the worry lines etched at the corners of his eyes alarmed her.

"I've had a lot to do. Maida, how about a cup of hot cocoa? It's getting cold outside."

Maida brought the cream-capped hot chocolate and excused herself, leaving Jill alone to watch Kyle silently drain the mug. "Come home with me?" he asked as he set it on the table and picked up his gloves.

"I have my car here." Jill had the feeling his invitation had come more from politeness than from desire to be with her tonight.

"I'll follow you, then. Pull in at Bliss House. I need to check that bedroom, anyhow—make sure the rain hasn't come through those French doors." He shrugged into his parka before picking hers up to hold for her. "We can take my truck from there."

Jill smiled. Maybe missing him—and having very nearly been caught pumping Maida for information Kyle seemed unwilling to give—had made her read more into his silence than was there. "All right," she murmured into the soft fur at the collar of her parka. "I'll run into the trailer and pick up a few things while you check the house."

Kyle wished he hadn't told Dolph about what had happened here. As he stepped into the bedroom he had described to his brother, he sensed that someone was there—closer than ever. Someone who meant him no good.

He forced aside his discomfort and crossed over to the new French doors, kneeling to be certain no water was leaking through the unfinished framework. It wasn't yet, but just to be safe he unrolled a heavy plastic tarpaulin he had brought in from his truck and tacked it securely over the wooden door frame.

Finished with that chore, Kyle stood up and glanced around. The short hairs at the back of his neck prickled, and his heartbeat accelerated. He felt a presence, but he told himself it had to be Jill, tired of waiting in the trailer, who had come inside the house.

"Jill?" he called.

No answer. "Jill! Are you out there?"

"She isn't here. My Lord! You're the living image of

Harry's brother, Dolph. I'm your great-great-grandmother, Laura Randall."

Kyle blinked his eyes. Then he blinked again. He had to be seeing things. Little ladies who had been dead a hundred years didn't just appear out of nowhere. But there she was, wearing an old-fashioned granny gown, long hair the color of his pulled into a loose knot on top of her head. "I don't believe this," he finally said, but the words came out cracked, the way they had years ago, when his voice had just begun to change.

"Tell me all about the family," the apparition begged as if they had just met at a regular, normal family reunion. *"Whose boy are you?"*

He'd never been particularly proud to admit his old man had been "Whiskey" Dolph Randall. Somehow having been the best damn bootlegger in the western North Carolina hills—until he had foolishly died in a standoff with the federal Treasury boys—wasn't an accomplishment he wanted to brag about. And it had never been a point of pride to mention his grandpa Dolph, either. From what Kyle had heard all his life, being a Randall of Hunter's Mountain was not a connection to advertise to one and all.

Still, he found himself telling this sweet-faced ghost all he could remember ever having been told about his forebears. "My brother and I are all that are left, as far as I know," he concluded, taking a deep breath to clear his head.

"Yes, I knew you must have a brother. If you had been the only one, you would have been Dolph. Harry's brother Dolph died young, so Harry named our oldest boy Dolph. He must have been your great-grandpa." Laura paused, as if she might be remembering the son she abandoned when she took up with Cyrus Bliss. *"There has always been a Dolph Randall, ever since there have been Randalls in these hills. I would love more than anything to meet him,"* she said softly.

"I don't know. Dolph doesn't get out of Greensboro much anymore." What was he doing, making excuses to a damn ghost?

"Perhaps you could bring him and your little daughter."

Kyle jerked around to meet this spook's clear blue gaze. "I didn't mention having a daughter," he spat out.

"But you do. Tell me about her."

Feeling trapped, Kyle started to bolt through the hallway door, but something or someone with the strength of steel gripped his shoulder like a vise. He whirled around, ready to attack.

"I am Cyrus Bliss. Your great-great-grandmother asked you a question, Randall. Please answer. I, too, am most interested in your reply."

"Alyssa."

"I am waiting."

"Her name is Alyssa. She's a helpless little girl. Seven years old now, but it makes no difference if she's seven or seventy. She's a vegetable, not able to see or hear or feel. All she can do on her own is breathe. Her mother destroyed her with cocaine and heroin before she was born. She requires special care, twenty-four hours a day. She will never get better. Never. Are you satisfied now, damn you?"

"We had to know. You are Miss Carey's destiny. Do not deny that you feel love for her. As you are like a son to my Laura, Jill has become as beloved as a child to both of us." Cyrus loosened his grip on Kyle's shoulder but continued to watch him closely.

"What the hell does that have to do with you forcing me to tell you what it damn near tears my heart out even to think about?"

"You two will marry. We must be certain you will not hurt her." Laura floated around Kyle. Her scrutiny made him feel like an organ grinder's monkey on display.

Marry? Hell, he had no intention of marrying Jill or anyone else. And he doubted Jill had any desire to hook up permanently with a guy whose next twenty or more years' earnings were spoken for.

"You're wrong. There's no way I'm going to take on another wife. One was more than enough. Even if I wanted to,

I couldn't marry Jill. It's all I can do to support Alyssa and Dolph."

Laura smiled. *"I get the impression, vulgar as it is to speak of, that Miss Carey is far from being a pauper."*

"Yeah, and I'm far from being a fortune hunter."

Cyrus visibly relaxed, floating into a corner by that monster wardrobe and regarding Kyle seriously. *"You will do, young man. Despite your unfortunate Randall lineage, you appear to be a decent, upstanding man. You have my blessing to court Miss Carey. Mind you, do not hurt her. I have the feeling she has been through more heartache than most."*

Kyle shook his head. This was damn unreal. He waited quietly, willing the ghosts of Bliss House to say more—but they did not. Before his eyes, their images faded. As he left the room—as fast as his feet would carry him—he thought he felt an almost motherly pat on his head.

"What took you so long in there?" Jill asked, concerned that the rain might have damaged the room Kyle had been working so hard to restore.

"Ghosts and memories."

Jill shifted on the sofa at Kyle's cabin so she could look him in the eye. "What's wrong, Kyle?" she asked again, as she had asked before down at Maida's.

He reached over to her and took her hand. "I have a lot on my mind," he admitted, "but if you don't object, I'd rather spend this evening concentrating on you."

For the first time since they'd met, Jill didn't get that instant jolt of sexual tension when they touched. "All right."

For a long time he just sat there, holding her hand. It was as though he needed to soak up the silence in his cabin. Finally he spoke.

"Have you felt the ghosts?"

Jill met his gaze. Had he encountered Laura and Cyrus? "I've felt them. Seen them. I've even talked with them."

Might as well get that out in the open, she thought, wondering if he would think she had lost her mind.

"Me, too. They believe we've come to Bliss House to save them from some curse. I thought maybe it was just me going nuts."

"No," she said softly, reaching up to stroke his cheek. "Unless both of us are." Kyle clearly was not enjoying the aftermath of his encounter with the spirits of Bliss House's infamous Victorian lovers. "When did you see them?"

"This afternoon. They seem to think they've been cursed, and that we're somehow the key to breaking the spell on them."

"I know." Jill wondered if the ghosts had been as specific with Kyle as they had been with her about exactly what had to happen between them to lift that blasted curse—but she hesitated to come right out and ask.

"They think we're going to fall in love and marry," he said, answering her unspoken question. "Ludicrous, isn't it?"

That stung Jill's ego. Worse, it stabbed at her heart. But she made herself smile. "It certainly is," she forced herself to murmur in an even tone.

Kyle lifted her chin, forcing her to meet his gaze. "Honey, I can't imagine any woman I'd rather go to bed with every night. Or one I'd be happier waking up to every morning. I wish I'd met you ten years ago."

"You'd have been a cradle robber."

"You wouldn't have thought so. I'd have skipped my college classes and come to carry your books home. And I would have driven your daddy nuts, sneaking into your room at night to talk you out of your virginity."

His comeback made her tremble. How could she tell him that at sixteen she'd married Rob—and that she hadn't been a virgin since he'd come into her home as her guardian three years before that? She couldn't—and as long as they were simply friends and lovers, she didn't have to.

Jill forced a grin. "I'd have kept a ladder by my window. You're a hot stud now—I bet every schoolgirl you used to know wanted you to be their first."

"Wish you'd been around to tell them that," he quipped

with a grin. Then he sobered. "What I'm trying to say, Jill, is that I'm an okay guy to have some fun with, but I'm not in it for the long haul of cozy cottages, kids, and lifetime commitments."

"What makes you think I want that?"

Kyle rubbed a finger along the first knuckle of her thumb. "Nothing. But the ghosts made it pretty damn clear that's what they expect."

"They don't expect it. They just hope. Kyle, they've been prisoners in Bliss House for almost a hundred years. They have some crazy notion about being freed if some member of one of their families comes to that house and falls in love with a person he or she is free to marry. When they realized you were related to Laura, they were certain you and I would be their redeemers."

Kyle looked over toward the burning embers in the fireplace. "We're free—legally. I hope I got through to them that I might as well have two wives—I would be in no worse position to go after number three."

"I'm not looking for happily-ever-after. I don't think I believe that state exists. I'm curious, though. What keeps you so locked out of a serious relationship?"

Jill watched his Adam's apple twitch as she waited for his response. "Financial obligations. Responsibilities. All I want to do tonight is forget. You up to blowing my mind, honey?" he asked, lifting his long legs off the tree-stump table and standing.

"We'll see." Jill stood and rubbed herself sensuously against him, pleased to find Big Al still wanted her even if Kyle appeared to be having his doubts. She felt that hot sexual need start flowing when Kyle scooped her up in his arms and carried her in to bed.

Was sex all she and Kyle had in common? Jill paused in her effort to scrub down an antique pitcher and bowl set she had found in the pantry off the kitchen. Funny, but Kyle had practically become her obsession in the six short weeks since he had come into her life. First he had invaded her dreams, replaced memories of horror with sweet, erotic fantasies. Now, Jill realized, most of her waking thoughts centered around him, too!

The shrill whine of a power sander reminded her Kyle was busy working just steps away, in the master bedroom that was well on the way to becoming the cozy room it must once have been for Cyrus and Laura. She had to suppress the urge to go to him, watch the play of his powerful muscles under sweat-moistened skin.

Jill forced her attention to the huge pitcher she was cleaning. As the grime soaked away, a pattern of pale green leaves and pastel-colored flowers began to emerge against a creamy background.

This bowl and pitcher set is Laura's.

Only the locket she'd found in the master bedroom and that picture of three little boys that had suddenly appeared out of nowhere to rest on the living-room mantel had carried Laura's aura. Those—and now these pieces of antique creamware. Jill scrubbed more vigorously, anxious to see the whole set as pristine as she knew Miss Laura would have kept all the things she treasured.

"It will do Laura's soul good to know you are caring for the things that meant so much to her," Cyrus said as he floated into the kitchen from the attic stairway and settled next to the tub of water Jill was using.

"I bought that pitcher and bowl set for her for Christmas back when she still lived with Harry. It was all she brought with her when she left that rickety old cabin on Hunter's Mountain. Before I installed the clawfoot tub in the water closet six months before we died, she used to fill this with hot water each evening and bring it to the bedroom so we could wash. She missed it, I think."

"Did it sit on that washstand?" As vividly as if that room had been real and not a dream, Jill pictured the graceful walnut bedroom set she and Kyle had seen that night when they had first made love.

"Yes. I should have remembered and put it there again."

"You—you're the one who . . ."

"Created a setting for you and Randall to explore the feelings neither of you can hide? Devised a way for you to be together in a way that neither of you could blame the other? Yes, my dear, I did."

"No!" Jill wanted to throttle the grinning ghost—she had sworn no man would ever manipulate her again. Then she sat back on her heels and considered not just that first night, but the ones since then. Nights with Kyle, loving him, freely giving and taking what they both wanted. Nights without guilt or nightmares or sleepless wanting.

She smiled at Cyrus. "Should I strangle you or thank you?"

"If you have to ask, child, I believe I am deserving of your thanks. That is good, considering that strangling me would be impossible, as well as futile."

"Of course. You're a ghost."

"A ghost who has your needs at heart, Miss Jill."

Suddenly Jill recalled Kyle's uneasy admission last night. "I'm surprised Kyle was willing to come back here this morning," she told Cyrus. "Your appearance yesterday must have scared him half to death."

"He did appear a bit unnerved."

Jill thought Cyrus's seemingly benevolent smile had a sort of evil undertone. "That pleased you?" she asked.

"A trifle. You may have guessed I bear little love for the Randall men, given my knowledge of the torture Harry put my Laura through before I had him sent away."

"Yes."

As though he had felt the shudder that shot through Jill's body, Cyrus gentled his tone. "This young man appears to have inherited more from Laura than from old Harry," he told Jill. "I gave him permission to court you."

Jill couldn't help grinning. The idea of Kyle Randall calling on her, bearing flowers and candy, was too ludicrous for words! More likely, he'd just lift one shapely eyebrow, smile that heated smile of his, and charm her straight into bed!

"You find the idea of being courted amusing?"

She forced a sober expression. "Not at all. It's just not done, these days. Mr. Bliss, Kyle and I have no future together. I'm sorry if that spoils your plans to leave here—but that's the way it's going to be."

"Young lady, you have given yourself to Kyle Randall! You have no choice but to lie in the bed you have made."

"This is 1997! I have all the choice in the world. So does Kyle. Making love doesn't imply that the participants have committed themselves to any more than the pleasure of the moment." As she said the words, Jill wished they weren't true—that there still was such a thing as love and happily-ever-after.

"Balderdash! You're no painted lady, and young Randall doesn't strike me as a cad. It may take him longer than most to realize his duty, considering his Randall ancestry, but I sensed honor in that boy."

Jill had sensed honor in Kyle, too. What she hadn't sensed in him was love—or any desire for commitment beyond the short time that would be theirs to slake their mutual desire. Something held him in Greensboro—something that called him back there each weekend and left him sad and taciturn when he came back to her. She wished she had the right to ask him who or what had this power over him—but she wouldn't, because if she did she would be honor bound to reveal the horror of her own unhappy past.

"Don't count on Kyle and me to break the spell for you and Laura," Jill repeated, knowing her words were falling on the ghost's deaf ears as she watched him fade away.

The image of Laura Randall settled between Kyle and the piece of heart pine fastened securely in a vise, blurring his vision and causing the hand holding the power tool to shake.

"Damn!"

"Young man, watch your tongue. Gentlemen do not swear in the presence of ladies."

"You're no lady, you're a ghost. Look what you made me do!" Kyle indicated a rough gouge in the pattern he had been carving in a long piece that was going to have been part of the baseboard in the master bedroom. "I'll have to start over now," he groused.

"I'm sorry. We do need to talk, though." Laura floated away a bit and settled on a sawhorse near the French doors.

"About what? The fact that I'm losing my mind, seeing things that don't exist?"

"Oh, Cyrus and I exist, make no mistake about that. We will exist here for a hundred years unless we break the spell your great-great-grandfather cast on us before we died."

Kyle snorted. "And how much longer will that be?" he asked.

"Another month. I want to see your brother."

"You think he'll marry Jill and break this so-called curse? Not a chance, ma'am."

"Of course not." Laura sounded indignant at the very idea that she might be seeking another living relative so she and her lover might be free of some ancient curse. *"You will be the one to marry Miss Carey."*

How could this ghost be so certain of something that was never going to happen, not in a hundred or a thousand years? Laura was beginning to annoy him! "You want to see my brother? Well, why don't you float on over to Greensboro and haunt him for a while?"

"Would that I were able to do just that! This house is Mr. Bliss's and my prison, until you and Miss Carey break the spell." With those last words, Laura faded away before Kyle's astonished gaze.

For a long time he just stood there, staring at the spot where the ghost had been. When he turned his attention back to the baseboard he had gouged, he damn near screamed. The gouge was gone, and the design completed, down to fine curving lines that connected the pattern of delicate leaves. Lines he hadn't even begun to carve.

Suddenly Kyle had to get outside. He didn't believe in ghosts! So why did he feel more spooked than he had, years ago, when a buddy had dared him to step on the porch of Bliss House?

Chapter
Twenty-Four

Kyle was damn near panting by the time he reached the stream that rambled down Hunter's Mountain toward Gray Hollow. Leaning against the trunk of an ancient oak tree, he reached out in his mind for the peace he always found in the woods he had known since childhood.

Reds and golds of autumn leaves reflected off clear water that tumbled over rounded stones of gray, beige, and gold-veined russet a few yards upstream—and a pair of slender feet. Kyle's gaze shifted upward to take in the sexiest pair of legs he'd ever seen—Jill's legs. And the body that turned him every which way but loose. Her pixie face, the one that lit up with passion when they touched.

He shook his head, trying to dispel the image he was sure must be a figment of his imagination. He had run away—from her, from the exasperating ghost of his great-great-grandmother—from Bliss House and all the promises it offered. Promises he couldn't reach out and fulfill.

Sinking cross-legged to the ground, Kyle recounted all the reasons he couldn't afford to get caught up with the ghosts' legend—or the role they had assigned him in ending some so-called curse. The very real reasons he couldn't afford to fall in love with Jill.

"Kyle?"

The melodious sound of her voice brought him back from his gloom. "Jill. What are you doing here?" It must have really been her, not a figment of his too-active imagination, wading in the stream.

"Enjoying the view." Her gaze raked him from head to toe, and he felt Big Al begin to stir. "Did you get tired of working?"

He nodded. She would think he'd lost his mind if he told her about Laura's visit—not to mention the magical transformation of the baseboard.

"You're quiet today," she observed, plopping herself down beside him and putting socks and sneakers back on. "Penny for your thoughts."

"That's about all they're worth. Actually I was thinking about you—and our ghosts."

"You've impressed Cyrus. He told me that today. No mean feat, since he makes no secret of distrusting anyone named Randall—other than his Laura, of course."

"If the legend is true, he has good reason, wouldn't you say?" Kyle forced a lightness he didn't feel into his voice as he reached over and brushed a red-gold leaf from Jill's delicate shoulder.

"I guess so. I wouldn't feel too kindly toward anyone who had burned me alive."

"Or to a man who beat his wife." Old Harry hadn't been the last Randall, Kyle knew, to take out his aggression on a woman. He had vague memories of his own father, "Whiskey" Dolph, knocking his mother around when he'd sampled too much of his own 'shine. "I don't imagine old

Cyrus thought much of Laura's boys when they turned their backs on her, either."

Jill smiled sadly, as if she understood how lousy it made Kyle feel, knowing his family had been the object of ridicule on Hunter's Mountain for over a hundred years. "You're not like Harry," she said softly.

"If I'm not, it's because of my brother making sure I grew up with at least a few values. He's the one who insisted I go to school—get a scholarship—make something of myself other than a lawless bootlegger eking out a living on this mountain."

"But it was you who had to do the actual work to get where you are today."

Kyle shrugged. "Maybe. But if it hadn't been for Dolph pushing me, and damn near killing himself as a logger so I could concentrate on school and football, I never could have done it. It was Dolph, not me, who deserved that architectural engineering degree they gave me when I left UNC."

He felt Jill's hand stroking lightly against his chest. "He must be very proud of you," she said, her voice flowing over him like sweet, warm honey.

"Laura wants to meet him."

"So have him come up here. I'd love to meet him, too."

If you do, you'll understand why I have to put his needs ahead of mine. "Dolph doesn't get out of Greensboro very often, honey," he told Jill. "Since he got hurt back when I was still in college, he's been in a wheelchair."

"I'm sorry."

"Yeah. Well, I'm sorry, too." *Sorry Dolph thought he had to do that dangerous, high-paying work so I could live the good life in Chapel Hill. Sorry Dolph pushed Tina away. And damn sorry he guilt-tripped me into marrying Tina and helping her create poor, pitiful Alyssa.* "Sorry I'm not the best of company today," he added, not wanting Jill to join him as he wallowed in regrets.

"Want to come with me this weekend to shop for furniture?"

"I'd love to, but I've got to go back to Greensboro. I'll miss you, honey."

Jill squeezed his hand. "You could take me with you. I'll bet Greensboro is loaded with antique shops where I could browse around. I've decided to use as much authentic Victorian stuff as I can, and still make the house inviting and comfortable to live in."

"Good," Kyle said, half listening as he enjoyed the feel of Jill's hand. "Maybe I can get back early Sunday and we can hit a couple of places I've seen right around here."

"Kyle, you weren't listening. I asked if I could come with you, snoop around some stores in Greensboro."

He imagined her, sharing the bed in his room . . . fixing breakfast in the kitchen where he almost never prepared a meal. Then he remembered Dolph. And Alyssa. The reasons he would never be able to consider asking Jill to share anything more than some mutual physical satisfaction. "I'd never get any work done if you were around, honey," he said in a deliberately light, dismissive tone.

"Is there someone else?"

He thought she sounded hurt. That made him mad. They had never made any promises, damn it! "A whole bunch of someone elses, Jill. The guys who work for me. Do you think my company somehow runs all by itself while I spend my time here, putting your expensive folly back together?"

"I meant a woman. Women."

"No one in particular. If there were, I wouldn't be spending my nights here in bed with you. What are you looking for, a proposal?" he asked nastily.

He watched her gaze settle on their clasped hands. "No. I'm sorry if I intruded into your private space." Her hands trembled as she unclenched them and placed them flat on the ground on either side of her hips. "I'll leave you to your own thoughts, Kyle," she said softly as she pushed herself up and walked away.

*   *   *

That night Jill's bed felt empty without Kyle beside her, even though they would hardly have fit together in the narrow trailer bunk. Jill pounded a fist into a goose-down pillow before burrowing her head into its soft depths.

I should just get into the Bronco and take myself down to Greensboro. Show Kyle he needs me as much as I need him.

Then she remembered. Once she had hurried home to Rob, sure she could win him back with her new, grown-up image. Instead, she had come close to letting him destroy her with his contempt.

She would not permit herself to get caught up in the ghosts' dreams. There would be no forever for her and Kyle, and if that meant Laura and Cyrus would languish in hell's fires for all eternity, that would have to be their problem.

Willing herself to sleep without dreaming, Jill lay in the dark, fingering the delicate locket she had found on the floor of the room where "her" ghosts had died. She tried hard not to think of the night she had found it—or of Kyle.

Tomorrow she would go into Gray Hollow. Surely Maida would know some places she might find some of the antique furniture she envisioned displaying in her new home.

"You want me to come see Bliss House? You forget, kid, I've been in that place before."

Kyle looked down at Dolph and offered a feeble grin. What the hell had he meant, asking his brother to drive up to see how the restoration of Bliss House was coming? Had his great-great-grandmother's ghost somehow bewitched him? "It looks a sight better now than it used to," he said before he could force his big mouth shut.

"If it doesn't, you'd better be prepared to give that woman her money back," Dolph said seriously as he shifted positions in his chair and locked the wheels again. "Is it the house or the woman that you really want me to see?"

"Neither. I want you to meet the goddamn ghosts." Kyle assumed Dolph would take this remark as a joke. "Did you ever think just maybe I might want to see you go somewhere except here, the house, and Angels' Paradise? Don't you ever miss your old buddies in Gray Hollow?"

Dolph's usually steady gaze shifted toward a pile of papers on Kyle's sloppy desk. "We don't have much in common anymore."

"Actually I'd like you to meet Jill. I think you'll like her."

"Never thought I'd see the day my little brother would willingly give me a shot at one of his women," Dolph said, his gaze as sad as his words were cheerful.

Dolph's uncharacteristic look of self-pity fed Kyle's guilt. "I thought I'd be generous," he replied lightly.

"Have you taken her to see Alyssa?"

Dolph couldn't have shocked Kyle more if he'd prodded him with a live electric wire. "No." The single syllable was all Kyle could manage.

"It's not Alyssa's fault she's the way she is."

Kyle felt his fists tighten and wished to hell his brother were whole so he could pound his face to a pulp. "You don't need to tell me that! I damn well know whose fault it is."

"Quit blaming yourself, Kyle."

"Myself? All I did was screw the woman you talked me into marrying. The one who must have sampled half the illegal drugs in North Carolina, trying to get you off her mind. I should blame myself for being twenty-three and horny, for going to bed with the woman the law said was my wife?" Kyle watched Dolph's expression cloud with pain, and immediately he regretted his inconsiderate outburst. "Sorry," he muttered.

"You can't blame me any more than I blame myself."

"It's not your fault, damn you. You're not the one who came in Tina night after night, knowing damn well she was too strung out to realize it wasn't *you* she was in bed with. You're not the one who neglected to figure out she might have forgotten about the one kind of pill she *should* have been taking. And it's not your kid who'll never do anything but lie there, not hearing or seeing or thinking." Kyle slammed a fist into the corner of his desk, welcoming the sharp pain.

"I know."

"Look, I'm lousy company. I'm going back to Hunter's Mountain. Maybe I'll be able to get some of these proposals finished this weekend," Kyle said, gathering up a handful of blueprints and materials estimates before he strode out the door.

Dolph watched the fumes from Kyle's truck's exhaust pipe swirl away in the chilly November air. He sensed his brother was close to the breaking point.

Tina.

Kyle might remember her with bitterness, but to Dolph she would always be the bright, laughing girl who had loved him. He wouldn't turn his back on her daughter. He couldn't. He couldn't let Kyle do it, either.

By the time Dolph got to the house he shared with Kyle, his arms and upper back ached. Hammers pounded in his head. Every day it got harder to pull himself out of bed and accomplish the tasks he set out to do. Popping a couple of pain pills, he opened the textbook on the table and forced himself to study.

Two hours later he closed the book and wheeled slowly into his bedroom. As he had done each night for the past eleven years, Dolph stripped off his shirt and unfastened his belt and pants. Grabbing one useless leg with both hands, he crossed it over the other and slipped off shoe and sock before repeating the procedure with the other foot.

Not too long ago he had been able to swing himself easily from his chair onto the bed, using the elaborate rigging Kyle had built. Now his shoulders trembled with the strain of holding up his body long enough for the loose pants he wore to slide down. And he couldn't hold on long enough to get himself aligned straight on the bed.

He raised himself up on his arms and stared dispassionately at his wasted legs—at the plastic tubing that snaked

from an artificial hole in his lower abdomen to a flat plastic
bag strapped to the outside of his left thigh. With clinical de-
tachment he unfastened the bag and hung it from the hook
on the side of the bed.

*You could regain control of your bladder. Possibly even
recover some sexual function. At the very least you would
be free of the cramping pain in your upper back.* Dr.
Granger's words taunted Dolph, as they did several times
each day.

Part of Dolph wanted to jump at the neurosurgeon's offer
to operate. But he couldn't risk dying just yet—not when
Kyle held so much bitterness. Someone had to be there to
love Alyssa.

Granger's assessment rang in his ears. *You've got a fifty-
fifty chance of coming through it.*

"Not good enough," Dolph murmured as he took one last
look at his thin, shriveled legs and the limp blob of flesh that
made a mockery of sex organs.

He lay back across the bed and burrowed his head into the
pillow. Jumbled pictures came to him, of himself and Alyssa
and Kyle, and the faceless woman he had a feeling his
brother loved as much as he himself had once loved Tina.
He wondered about going back to Gray Hollow and that old
haunted house on the rise to Hunter's Mountain where he
had a feeling there were spirits that could alter all their lives.

He would go. Next weekend. Somehow he would call up
the endurance to make that trek back into the past. Now
Dolph forced all the thoughts that troubled him from his
mind and went to sleep.

Kyle opened one eye and regarded the telephone with disgust. It couldn't be much later than four o'clock, he figured
as he snatched up the receiver and mumbled a sleepy,
"Hello."

After a minute he hung up and shifted his gaze to Jill.
Sleeping, she looked almost childlike, curled up like a kitten
under the brightly colored quilt he had bought a few years

back at a craft show down in Gray Hollow. He watched sooty eyelashes flutter against her cheek before the lids came open to reveal sleepy, sexy brown eyes.

"Good morning."

I'd like to wake up and find you next to me for the rest of my life. But Kyle couldn't say that out loud. He didn't have the right.

Instead he grinned and lowered his head until his lips almost met hers. "Morning, honey," he whispered as he sank down next to her and cradled her in his arms.

"Who was that?" she asked, snaking one leg over his and rubbing his calf with a dainty foot.

"Dolph. He's going to come up here today. Wants to see Bliss House and meet our ghosts, I guess." Kyle figured Dolph wanted to meet Jill, too, but voicing this would make this pleasant interlude much too serious—too much as if it was a prelude to something a hell of a lot more permanent than it could ever be.

"I'm anxious to meet him." Jill concluded that sleepy comment with a gentle nip at Kyle's shoulder and a sweep down his rapidly awakening body with her talented fingers. "Kyle, I bought some furniture while you were gone. An old brass bed. I also got a couple of those huge Victorian wardrobes I thought I'd use to show off the accessories I'm going to be putting in my mail-order catalog."

"What kind of stuff are you going to sell?"

"Country crafts. Quilts, afghans, handmade comforters and pillows. Fancy bedspreads and such. Paintings and sculpture if I find some I think will sell. That sort of thing."

Gently he pried her teasing fingers from around Big Al. "I might be able to drum up some business for you," he said, thinking how nicely the mail-order business she planned to start would mesh with the restoration work that made up a large portion of his contracting business. "But we've got to get up now and get on down to Bliss House if I'm going to finish up your haunted house on schedule."

She pouted, and he wished he could say to hell with his

schedule—to hell with everything but rolling over and burying himself inside this woman who turned him inside out.
"Come on, sleepyhead," he coaxed as he untangled himself
from her and the covers and stumbled out of bed.

Chapter
Twenty-Five

THE GHOSTS

"Come on, Cyrus. Help. Kyle's brother will be here soon."

Amused, Cyrus watched Laura flit around the parlor that looked very much as it had a hundred years ago, blowing sawdust residue off baseboards.

"Cyrus! Come over here and uncover this couch."

"It looks better with that cloth draped over it." Cyrus supposed the hideous monstrosity his late wife had bought was still here because it was so damned ugly none of his relatives had wanted it—and because if they had tried to sell it, no one would have been fool enough to buy. He floated over, though, and lifted the dustcover to reveal the couch in all its puce brocade-covered ugliness.

Laura laughed. *"You're right,"* she said. *"I had forgotten just how unattractive that sofa is. But Kyle's brother will need somewhere to sit. Miss Carey mentioned yesterday that she had bought some new furniture. I do so hope she will not be filling your lovely home with oddly shaped glass-and-metal tables and chairs like the ones we saw in that magazine."*

"Our home, my love."

He watched her expression sadden. *"No. Not mine. I never had the right to be mistress here."*

"But you have been. For a hundred years now. My dear, this is certainly your home as much as it has ever been mine."

"I'm sorry, Cyrus. Today is not a day for sad memories, but for joy. I only wish fate had brought one of your children's children here for you."

Perhaps, Cyrus thought, it was better that only Laura's descendants would be here today, so that he could see his love's goodness overshadowing the evil that had come to Kyle—and, he hoped, his brother as well—from that devil Harry Randall.

"I am content for you to see what changes time has made in your kin, my dear. Now cease your fretting. The young man will see our home as his brother has restored it."

"You could . . ."

"Conjure up the furnishings?"

"Yes. The way you did when you forced Miss Carey and Kyle to spend the night together in our room!"

Cyrus laughed. *"I think not. Your great-great-grandson still thinks he had some strange hallucination that night—although I believe Miss Carey accepts that we made magic for them in that room."*

"We, Cyrus? I never would have condoned that plan. Why, you practically forced them into each other's arms."

"They are still together, are they not? I feel, with Randall's brother coming here, that he and Miss Carey are close to making the decision which will set us free. Come now, Laura, rest with me and dream of a time not far away, a time for us to be together again." Cyrus floated across the room and ushered Laura up the attic stairs.

Chapter Twenty-Six

Jill felt rather than saw her ghostly boarders leave the parlor as she and Kyle walked in. "What time will Dolph get here?" she asked as she bent to pick the grimy dustcover off the floor.

"I'm not sure. My God! That's the ugliest damn couch I ever saw!" Kyle exclaimed, coming dead still to stare at the ornate carved rosewood piece with its bilious brocade upholstery.

"Maybe that's why I had that nightmare." Jill doubted this, but those faded magenta cabbage roses embossed on sickly yellow-green plush certainly *could* dredge up horrifying thoughts in anyone! "I wonder if Laura came in here and pulled this cover off."

"Jill, I'd rather not think about my long-departed relative or her ghostly lover, if you don't mind."

Playfully Jill punched Kyle's arm. "Don't tell me a big,

strong man like you is afraid of two harmless spirits," she teased.

"Spooked would be a better word."

Jill loved the way one corner of Kyle's mouth turned up in a quirky grin. She imagined him wearing an expression much like that when he had been a carefree boy, playing a trick on a friend—or the brother she was going to meet later today. "Don't we have work to do?" she asked.

"Yeah. I thought I'd start rebuilding the mantel for the fireplace in the back parlor. Want to help?"

"Sure." Watching Kyle work magic on unfinished pieces of wood fascinated Jill. Lately he had been letting her sand the wood he had already carved while he shaped other pieces and re-created designs to replace old sections damaged beyond repair.

She followed him through the archway made of newly stained, carved heart pine, into the back parlor she had seen in a dream—the dream where she had danced with Kyle before they ever met. More each day, Jill believed Bliss House had been her fate, that Kyle had been destined to be her lover long before either of them had been born.

She watched him pry off a water-warped, dusty board from above the newly cleaned fireplace and set it on the floor. Lightly he touched it, as if feeling every groove and crevice in the ancient wood. Then he stretched a steel tape measure from end to end and side to side, noting measurements before setting the ruined shelf aside.

"Need some help?"

He grinned as he looked up from his task of choosing a board from a stack of lumber in the corner. "You can steady the end of this while I cut it," he told her, lifting up an eight-foot length of rough wood and hauling it easily to the table saw he had set up in the middle of the floor.

As he cut the board to the required dimensions Jill heard a car horn over the buzzing of the saw. "Kyle," she yelled.

"Yeah, honey?" His voice rumbled over the harsh sound of metal grinding through wood.

"Someone's here."

Kyle finished the cut he had started and shut off the saw. "It's probably Dolph. I'd better help him in."

Jill followed him, running her fingers through her hair after brushing them over her jeans and sweatshirt to get rid of what sawdust and dirt she could. At the edge of the porch she stopped and stared at the makeshift ramp Kyle had tossed together. She would have gone out to the car if she hadn't sensed that Dolph might not want a stranger to observe him struggle into the wheelchair Kyle had told her was a permanent fixture in his life.

"You've made this place look brand-new."

"Thanks. The inside still has a way to go."

Kyle felt his brother let out his breath in a whistle. "She's a looker," Dolph said, his voice full of masculine appreciation Kyle doubted he was directing toward Bliss House.

He glanced up to see Jill, her delectable curves contrasting with a hefty square porch column that halfway hid her from view. "Yeah," Kyle replied before turning back to the task of getting Dolph out of the damn little compact car he insisted on driving. "You ought to let me order you that van with the hydraulic lift," he muttered as he wrestled with his brother's still-considerable weight. When he caught his left elbow on the damn hand control, he had to choke back a curse.

"No." Dolph tightened his grip on Kyle's shoulders as Kyle pulled him as gently as possible through the car's small front door.

Kyle set him in his chair and reached back into the car for the red-and-black-checkered lap robe he figured Dolph had started using more to hide his wasted lower body than to keep it warm. "We're set to roll," he said, going behind the wheelchair so he could push it up to Bliss House. "You ready to meet some ghosts?"

"Sure. I'm more ready to meet the lady who thinks she wants to live in a haunted house. You know, the trip from

Greensboro seemed a hell of a lot longer than I'd remembered it."

"Pretty rough drive?" Kyle maneuvered the chair over ground hardened by the first hard freeze of the season.

"It was for me."

Aligning the chair with the boards he had set up earlier, Kyle pushed Dolph's chair up onto the porch. "Jill, this is my brother, Dolph. Dolph, Jill Carey," he said, his mind more on Dolph's obviously increasing weakness than on small talk.

"I'm glad to meet you." Jill's husky voice intruded on Kyle's thoughts, and he looked on with approval while she bent and shook his brother's hand. "Come on inside, it's cold out here," she said as she straightened up and hurried to open the door.

"Well, little brother, when am I going to meet these ghosts of yours?" Dolph asked after they had toured the house and settled in to talk in the finished but nearly bare front parlor. "Jill, I think Kyle has lost his mind. What about you?"

She leaned against the back of the monstrosity of a sofa Kyle had decided was going to do a permanent number on his aching backside. "If he's crazy, then I am, too. Bliss House does have ghosts. I've seen and talked to them. They want Kyle and me to get together, you know." She aimed a teasing grin at Kyle before sipping the hot chocolate she had made in the trailer and brought over in a thermos.

"So he said." Dolph glanced around the room. "Kyle, you've outdone yourself. This place is a far cry from the tumbledown pile of wood and stone that I remember sneaking into back when I was a kid. I'd have never thought it could look this good."

"I never knew you were one of my own kin. You should have been ashamed, young man, breaking into someone's private home the way you did!" Kyle jumped when he heard that familiar voice, then shifted his gaze from Dolph to the door that opened into the master bedroom. There was Laura, with Cyrus at her side.

Kyle watched his brother's mouth drop open and his dark

eyes widen. He was certain Dolph hadn't believed, any more than he had, that the ghosts of Laura and Cyrus had really haunted Bliss House for nearly a hundred years. Perversely he hoped Dolph would lose as many hours' sleep as he himself had when he was forced to acknowledge the spirits' presence.

"Won't you join us?" Jill asked as if to fill the sudden silence.

The ghosts floated into the parlor. Noting Cyrus's stiff white collar and the patterned vest he wore under a black suit made of some sort of shiny material, Kyle felt grateful he had been born in an age when it was okay for men to be comfortable. Laura, though, looked pretty as a picture in a lacy white blouse and a floor-length dark blue skirt that reminded him of the delightful secrets Jill had hidden under a certain long red plaid skirt not long ago.

"This is my brother, Dolph," Kyle said, not quite sure how one went about introducing ghosts. He relaxed a bit and let himself enjoy Dolph's obvious disbelief.

Laura glided closer to Dolph's wheelchair. *"You look exactly like my eldest son,"* she told him, and Kyle could see her eyelids flutter as if she were holding back tears. *"I'm so happy you came so I could meet you. Tell me about yourself."*

After Dolph got over the shock of meeting disembodied spirits, he warmed to telling tales Kyle remembered having heard many times. Caught up in what had become, impossibly, a macabre family reunion, Kyle sat back and watched Jill enjoy the show.

"I've never married. Didn't have much to offer a woman before, I guess—but since I lost the fight with that pine tree, I've had nothing at all. Kyle married, though. Beautiful woman. She gave him a beautiful little girl before she died."

Jill's mouth dropped open, and her beautiful dark eyes glistened with tears. Damn! If Kyle hadn't constantly wished Dolph were well and whole, he certainly would have wished it now! He would like nothing better than to pound his fist into his brother's face.

Yes, he should have told Jill about Alyssa—but their time

had been so precious, too happy to spoil by talking about his damaged child. Still Dolph should have kept his damn mouth shut!

"And where do you keep this child?" Jill's smile looked forced, and her usually mellow voice took on a brittle tone.

"She lives at a school called Angels' Paradise," he said before Dolph could jump in and supply an answer.

"My parents stuffed me into a boarding school, too, before they forgot I existed. Excuse me, Dolph—Miss Laura and Mr. Bliss. I don't want to disturb your reunion, but I've suddenly developed a rather nasty headache." Jill stood up and began a stiff-legged trek toward the front door.

"Thanks a hell of a lot," Kyle said to Dolph as he watched Jill leave.

"I believe you boys need some time alone. We will take our leave now as well," Cyrus murmured, extending a ghostly hand to Laura.

Kyle rose politely, and he thought he felt a slight breeze touch his cheek when Laura floated up beside him. *"I understand. Miss Carey may be angry now. When she returns, I shall speak to her,"* Laura promised. Then she disappeared.

"I can't believe you can sleep with a woman and not mention someone as important as Alyssa should be to you," Dolph spat out as Kyle pushed the wheelchair roughly toward the car.

"Believe it. Talking about Alyssa, and the way she has existed and will continue to exist like a vegetable in that warehouse full of a hundred other unfortunate kids, is not conducive to making love. It's not conducive to anything—except making me want to shoot myself for ever having thought I should take advantage of being married and get my rocks off by screwing my doped-up shell of a wife."

"Kyle, I thought Tina had quit the drugs." Dolph managed to lever himself out of the chair and into the car by himself, so Kyle folded the wheelchair and slid it behind the front seat.

Suddenly he wanted to lash out at Dolph, make him assume at least some of the guilt for Tina's deterioration. "I believe she did lay off them for a while, back when she thought you'd changed your mind and were willing to marry her. Before you decided she would be better off with me even though you knew she still loved you—all because you figured she needed a guy with a functioning dick. Look in the mirror if you've got to blame somebody for what spoiled, selfish Tina did all by herself."

"You shouldn't hate your daughter." Dolph's voice rang with conviction, but he sounded tired, so tired Kyle knew he shouldn't attempt driving back to Greensboro tonight.

"I don't hate her. Look, I've got to try to make this right with Jill. Go on up to the cabin. I'll join you in a little while."

Kyle hated like hell making Dolph feel worse, but damn it, he didn't need his brother acting like a second conscience. It wasn't as if Kyle didn't condemn himself every day for having helped Tina create a child like Alyssa.

"Jill?" he called out when she didn't respond to his knock on the metal trailer door.

"Go away." She sounded as if she had been crying, but Kyle got the message loud and clear.

"We need to talk," he yelled through the door.

She sounded terribly sad when she called back, "We needed to talk long before now. Please go."

Leaves crackled under Kyle's heavy footsteps, their sound muted by the thin walls of the trailer. Jill knew she should be glad he had taken her at her word and left, but her heart ached.

"You have a way of picking winners," she muttered to the tear-streaked, mottled face that stared back at her from the mirrored closet door. First a pervert who had loved her only as long as she remained an adolescent, now a man she couldn't help likening to the father she had rarely seen.

How could Kyle, whose concern for his crippled brother showed how deeply he could care, abandon a helpless child to the custody of strangers at some fancy boarding school?

Even Grandmother had been kind enough to take her in, let her have her own room in that mausoleum the old woman had called home!

Before lying down, Jill noisily blew her nose into a tissue already decimated by the tears she had just wiped away. As she lay in bed every fiber in her body called out for Kyle's warmth to drive out the chilling pain. Tormented, she couldn't stop her mind from arguing with her heart.

You have your secrets, too.

Jill tried to shove that guilty thought to the back of her mind. *My secrets aren't as real—as lasting—as the existence of a child.*

Really? her conscience prodded.

Burrowing her head deeper into the down pillow, she curled into a tight ball on the bed. But she couldn't sleep. An image of a girl, sad-faced and lonely, with forest-green eyes and hair the muted honey color of Kyle's, stared out the window of an impersonal dorm room toward a frigid, winter scene.

Jill recognized that room. It had been her prison from the day she had graduated from the care of a no-nonsense, stiff-necked nanny at the big house her parents visited between their treks all over the world, to the luxuriously sterile environment of Oak Hill School for Young Ladies. How she had rejoiced that day her grandmother had arrived in her ancient, chauffeur-driven Rolls and taken her away!

"Damn him!" Never in a hundred years would Jill have figured Kyle to be the kind of bastard who would consign his own flesh and blood to the sterile upbringing her parents had forced on her. Nothing about him had smacked of that kind of selfishness. He didn't even have their excuse—that they were rearing her the way they themselves had been.

No, Kyle had jerked himself up out of poverty. He had lived on Hunter's Mountain and gone to that quaint brick schoolhouse in Gray Hollow. If Maida had been telling her the truth, he had been the first of his family to earn a college degree.

Jill couldn't figure Kyle out. Neither his deliberate omission of the fact that he had a child nor his rejection of the little girl made sense.

It made her furious that she still wanted and loved him in spite of it all.

Now that he knew he had blown whatever he and Jill had going between them, Kyle finally admitted to himself that he loved her. He must have some latent streak of masochism, he decided as he finally quit staring up toward the peak of Hunter's Mountain, got out of his truck, and stomped into the cabin. Seeing Dolph there in the small front room, still awake, reminded him of why he would be sleeping alone tonight.

Tonight, hell. More likely forever! On that miserable prediction, Kyle scowled.

"I take it your lady wasn't in the mood for explanations," Dolph commented.

"No. I see you managed to get in here all right." His voice lacked emotion, but Dolph could see pain in Kyle's eyes as his gaze settled on the hand rims of the wheelchair.

Dolph felt a pang of conscience. Maybe he shouldn't have mentioned Alyssa, knowing as he did how difficult it was for his brother to talk—even to think—about her. "Yeah. Look, I'm sorry if I screwed things up for you with Jill."

"Right now she's mad as hell."

"Wouldn't talk to you, huh?"

"No." Kyle sat down on the leather lounge chair and stretched his legs out on a stump he had polished and made into a rustic coffee table.

Dolph wondered for a minute whether his presence might be the reason Kyle hadn't brought Jill to the cabin. He had caught whiffs of her sexy perfume, and seen small signs of her presence—like that silky pair of thigh-high stockings that had damn near reached out off the towel rack and strangled him when he'd wheeled himself into the bathroom.

"I could have made it back to Greensboro tonight," he

said, hating the fact that every day it became more of an effort for him to go through the motions of living.

"She wouldn't be here anyhow," Kyle muttered. "She wouldn't even let me inside her trailer."

"And you care. Right?"

"Yeah. More than I thought I would. Jill's special."

Dolph shifted in the chair, trying to ease the stabbing pains in his back that kept worsening each day. "How about helping me lie down on that sofa?" he asked, resenting the hell out of being so helpless that he couldn't even lever his body out of the chair by himself.

When he had settled, he found his conscience pricking him as much as his damn useless spine had been hurting when he was sitting up. "You've got to stop feeling guilty, Kyle," he said quietly.

"I damn well am guilty." Kyle rubbed a hand through his hair, as if he ached, too.

"Of what? Trying to make a go of marriage with a woman you didn't love? Who couldn't love you or anybody else, considering the shape she was in? Alyssa would be the way she is, no matter what man had gotten Tina pregnant."

"But I can't love Alyssa. No matter how hard I try. Damnit, I can't even tell the woman I'm sleeping with why I can't give her more than a few tumbles in bed. That I gave up that right because one night, eight years ago, I fucked up royally and made a defective baby with the strung-out dope addict who happened to be my wife."

Dolph's own guilt dulled the ever-present agony in his spine. "You were twenty-three years old, Kyle. No one can say you didn't try to straighten Tina out."

"Not hard enough. Damn it, she died calling out your name!"

"What?"

Kyle punched a fist into his thigh, not flinching any more than Dolph would have if he smacked his own deadened limbs. "I didn't mean that," he said, his eyes suspiciously bright as he regarded his brother.

Suddenly Dolph knew. For years Kyle had focused his resentment on Tina—and Alyssa—instead of where it belonged. "Yes, you did. Damn you, Kyle, I may be crippled, but there's not shit wrong with my brain. You married her for me, didn't you?"

"I—I thought you wanted that."

For long minutes Dolph stared at Kyle, letting himself recall all the times after the accident when he had pushed Tina away. Not just in the hospital, but afterward when she had followed him to Greensboro. He forced himself to remember that night she had teased him into bed and had cried with him when he hadn't been able to get it up. How she had sworn it didn't matter, that she needed *him*, not sex.

The next morning, not able to face Tina after that humiliating scene, he *had* sent her away. And when she kept coming back, he *had* thrown her together with Kyle. Maybe he *had* used his young brother's guilt to encourage him to marry the woman he himself could no longer satisfy.

"You gave up so goddamn much for me."

Kyle's gut-wrenching statement brought Dolph back from the past. Was that what Kyle thought? "Shit. I didn't join that logging crew for you. That job paid big bucks, bucks I wanted for *me*. I pictured myself breaking out of the Randall mold, getting off this goddamn mountain and in a cushy place somewhere far away. I just was too lazy to do it your way, hitting the books and getting my bones crunched playing football."

Dolph took in Kyle's disbelieving stare. "I know. I've used you, played on whatever misplaced guilt you've felt because I'm stuck in a wheelchair while you're healthy and whole."

"No." Kyle's denial came from somewhere deep down in his throat.

"Yeah. I even tossed away a woman who loved me, because every time I looked at her, I resented like hell that I couldn't get so much as a hint of a hard-on. Destroyed her, if what you say is true. All because I got careless one too many times and lost a wrestling match with a goddamn fucking pine tree."

Kyle met and held Dolph's gaze. "Doesn't matter. You're my brother. The only family I've got left, if you don't count the ghost of our great-great-grandma down at Bliss House. I want to take care of you."

Dolph winced. Ever since he had finished college, Kyle had been doing a pretty good job sheltering Dolph from the realities of living. His brother had every reason to believe he would be taking care of him the rest of his miserable life—which wouldn't be too long if he didn't risk the tricky spinal-fusion operation.

"You know, what I want more than anything, except for knowing Alyssa will always have someone to love her, is to be able to take care of myself," he said, hating the choked-up sound of words he had kept bottled up inside for years. "Get away from here, go somewhere warm, use the damn degree I'm about to get . . ."

"Degree?" Kyle sat up straighter, and his expression revealed his shock.

Dolph shrugged. "Between the classes I took to keep the shrink off my back while I was in rehab and the ones I've been taking at the college in Greensboro, I've managed to collect enough credits. Shocked me, too, when they told me I'd be getting my own sheepskin at the end of this semester."

"What?"

"You think when you're working out of town I spend nights in front of a TV set? Stare at the four walls of my room, maybe? You know damn well I'm not passing my nights curled up with some sexy woman like Jill."

"I doubt I'll be doing that anymore," Kyle said sadly, but Dolph could tell his brother was trying to picture him—good old Dolph, all brawn and no brains—managing to earn a college degree. "What's your major—finance?"

"Social work."

"For God's sake, why?"

Dolph shrugged. "At first I signed up for classes in buildings I could get around in without much hassle." That had been his only reason, then—but soon he had become deeply interested in learning to help others—particularly children whose lives had been disrupted. "Hell, pretty soon I got to thinking I'll never have kids of my own—I might as well learn to help other folks' problem kids."

"You could."

"Yeah, and pigs can fly. I may eventually have that damn surgery, but if I do, I won't be expecting miracles. Tell you what, Kyle, if I ever find a woman dumb enough to marry me and she's hell-bent on having a kid, I'll get you to donate the sperm." Dolph shot his brother a self-deprecating grin.

"I already did that once. In a manner of speaking."

"Yeah. I fucked up with Tina. If there's ever a next time, I'll ask you to do the deed in the quiet, peaceful solitude of a doctor's office. Should cause you a lot less grief."

"Yeah." Kyle unfolded himself from the lounge chair and paced across the room. "I don't know how to explain Alyssa to Jill," he said as he stared out into the cold, dark night.

"You could take her to Angels' Paradise, let her meet your daughter, and draw her own conclusions," Dolph suggested, but as he expected, Kyle did not reply.

Jill's Bronco was gone, Kyle noticed when he parked his truck in front of Bliss House the next morning. He found himself listening for her every few minutes as he finished rebuilding the mantel they had started yesterday. While he checked with the electrical subcontractor who was hooking up the new kitchen appliances, Kyle thought he heard her voice. But it was only the wind in the trees.

"What a huge icebox!" Laura exclaimed as she floated into Kyle's field of vision after the electricians had left. He couldn't help chuckling when she opened one door of the white side-by-side refrigerator and gazed, wide-eyed, inside.

"I can feel the cold. But I don't see any ice."

"That's because there isn't any, except what the icemaker will spit out after a while."

"This box makes its own ice? But how?"

Kyle felt as if he had stepped back in time, watching his

ghostly grandma ogling the ordinary refrigerator as though it were magic. "It's electric. The motor chills a gas that circulates through coils inside the refrigerator walls."

"Oh, my. How I would have loved to have had a modern invention like this!"

"They've been around a long time. Now this is relatively new." He indicated the microwave oven whose digital clock indicated it was nearly time for him to go for the day, and popped open the door so Laura could peer inside.

"Looks like a newfangled bread box to me," she said, apparently unimpressed by the appliance Kyle considered essential. He figured he probably would starve if he ever had to do without one.

Turning on the faucet at the sink the plumbers had just connected, Kyle poured some water into a glass mug and showed Laura how, in just a few seconds, the microwave could make the water boil. Then he started to gather his tools.

"Don't go."

He didn't want to leave, not without seeing Jill, but he felt he had no choice. Yesterday he had been Jill's lover, free to come and go from Bliss House at his whim. Today he was just her building contractor, allowed in the house only when on the job.

"It's getting late, Miss Laura," he said sadly, still listening for the sound of car tires crunching along on the gravel drive. "Jill obviously doesn't want to see me. If she did she would have stayed here instead of gallivanting off to God-only-knows where."

"She loves you. She will come back, I know. If she comes to talk with me, I will try to help her understand."

Chapter
Twenty-Seven

After a day of driving aimlessly through the mountains, Jill was still as confused as she had been when she had sent Kyle away. She had tried all day to tell herself she had over-reacted, that he had been under no obligation to tell her about his child.

She had even tried to excuse his consigning his daughter to a lonely existence in some boarding school. After all, she had told herself, he had a business to run and no wife to look after the child. Perhaps he had made the only rational decision he could, to see to the girl's safety and care.

Still her hurt feelings wouldn't go away, but she would bet there were pieces missing from the puzzle of Kyle's apparently uncaring behavior. She sensed that he had more secrets—secrets she knew she had to learn, or she was going to go slowly, quietly insane.

Tired and hungry, she pulled into Maida's parking lot and

went inside. It was too late for lunch, yet too early for dinner. Jill hoped she would be the only customer so she and the gregarious café owner would have a chance to talk.

"Now, you eat every bite of my delicious chicken fricassee," Maida urged as she set the steaming plate down in front of Jill. "You're just lucky it's blustery cold today. If the weather had stayed nice, this would have been gone hours ago."

Jill's mouth watered as the delicious aroma of chicken, celery, and carrots wafted from the plate. "I guess I'm lucky. Do you have time to keep me company for a while?"

Maida grinned as she fit herself into the booth across from Jill. "You know I don't miss a chance to gossip," she said with a twinkle in her eyes. "So how is your haunted house coming? Or should I be asking how you're enjoying your nights with that good-looking son of a gun you hired to fix it up?"

Suddenly Jill felt as though she were about to violate Kyle's privacy. What they had shared before his brother's shocking revelation had been too mind-boggling, too personal to discuss—even as bait to tempt revelations from Gray Hollow's answer to the *National Enquirer.* "The house is looking better every day," she said evasively as she speared a chunk of chicken with her fork and brought it to her lips.

A sudden gust of cold air drew her attention to the front of the café. *Dolph.* Obviously Maida recognized him, too, because she hurried over to help him close the door, then greeted him with an effusive hug. Jill watched him maneuver his chair between tables, straight toward her booth by the back window.

"Nice view, isn't it?" he asked as he locked the wheels of the chair and began to work supple brown leather gloves off his fingers.

Uncomfortable, she looked around for Maida. When she didn't spot the café owner, she met Dolph's gaze. "The fall colors are almost gone," she replied, glancing out the window at a scene nearly as stark as the look on Dolph's thin, pain-lined face.

She imagined his perfectly chiseled features had once charmed at least half the girls in this tiny community. "I thought you had gone back to Greensboro," she commented.

"Kyle thought I was too tired to make the trip home yesterday. I disagreed, but my body didn't—so I spent the night at his cabin. First time I've been back here in years," he told her with a sad-looking smile. "Couldn't leave without a taste of Maida's cooking."

Jill sensed that it was more her Bronco in the parking lot than the prospect of a home-cooked meal that had brought Dolph Randall to Maida's, but she politely held her tongue. One part of her wanted to lash out at Dolph—take a piece off him, the way his revelation had cut short her loving interlude with Kyle.

Another, kinder voice told her to go easy on Kyle's debilitated brother.

"So you're on your way back home tonight?" she asked.

Dolph nodded. "Should have left hours ago. Would have if I could have gotten myself off that couch and moving around any earlier than I did."

"I see you made it."

"Yeah. Don't shut out my brother, Jill." He struggled to free his arms from the navy nylon parka he was wearing, but Jill sensed that he wouldn't want her to get up and help him. "He cares for you."

"If you'd known he hadn't told me he had a little girl, you wouldn't have said a word. Would you?" she asked pointedly.

"No." Dolph draped his parka across the empty booth where Maida had been sitting.

The monosyllabic reply held a wealth of regret, Jill thought as she mentally contrasted this quiet, darkly handsome man with the big, jovial guy she loved. The silence stretched out until she began to feel as though Dolph were mentally stripping *her* of her secrets, the way he had inadvertently done with Kyle so recently.

"Would you care to enlighten me as to why a man who you say cares for me would neglect to tell me about something so important as having a child?" she finally asked.

"He had his reasons. You should let him explain them to you."

What could Kyle possibly tell me that would excuse his keeping such a vital part of himself secret? Especially if he really cares? Jill couldn't imagine, yet she wanted desperately to hear something—anything—that could justify her excusing Kyle's silence.

"You're here," she pointed out to Dolph. "Since you're the one who let the cat out of the bag, so to speak, you might as well tell all."

Dolph shook his head. "It's not my place. All I will tell you is that Kyle has good reason for not saying much about his late wife—or his daughter."

"I—I don't know. I have pretty strong feelings about any parents who care so little for their children that they hide them away in fancy boarding schools. My mother and father did that with me. But at least they didn't deliberately avoid telling their friends I existed—so far as I know." Jill met Dolph's gaze and appreciated the gentle sympathy of his expression.

His deep green eyes reminded her so much of Kyle's, she nearly broke down in tears. She had a feeling he was about to say more when Maida hurried to the table with another plate of chicken.

"Here's some lunch for you, Dolph. Eat up. You need to put some meat on those bones of yours," Maida said, ending the poignant silence.

Jill watched while Dolph ate less than half of the generous portion she knew Kyle would have wolfed down—before ordering a second helping. "You say Kyle will be able to make me understand, Dolph. Tell me. Save Kyle the trouble of opening up some old wound and making it bleed," she coaxed after he had set his fork down across the half-full plate.

He appeared to consider her words. "I could take you to see Alyssa," he finally said.

She could feel the love in Dolph's voice. Kyle might not care for his child—but Jill sensed that his brother did. "Her school is near here?" she asked, recalling that her own parents had chosen a place five hundred miles away from home.

"About halfway between here and Greensboro. I plan to stop by on my way home. Want to follow me?"

"Thanks, but I don't think so. I wouldn't feel right, going behind Kyle's back to meet his little girl. If I decide to speak to him again, and if we ever get to the point in our—our relationship—where he thinks Alyssa and I should meet, he will have to be the one to do the introductions."

"You're right. I should be leaving now if I'm going to make it back to Greensboro before dark. Give Kyle a chance, Jill. He was wrong not to let you know about Alyssa, but he's not a monster. He's doing the best he can by her."

As Jill watched Dolph's compact car disappear into the mist, she mulled over his words. She wanted to head up Hunter's Mountain, to feel Kyle's strong arms encircle her with the warmth she had come so quickly to rely on. She wanted to make him love her as much as she loved him. And she needed to hear him tell her why he had kept her closed off from what should be the most important person in his life.

If Kyle shared his darkest secrets, though, she would feel honor bound to tell him hers. She had this awful feeling that while their fragile new relationship might survive his revelations, it would shatter into a million pieces when she unveiled the demons of her past. Suddenly she needed to talk to Laura.

* * *

Bliss House practically glowed with light from the newly installed fixtures, Jill noticed as she hurried up onto the porch and fit her key into the front door Kyle had planed and sanded just last week. Shards of rainbow colors reflected off beveled panes of glass at each side of the doorway. What just two months ago had been a sad derelict was well on its way to becoming the showplace it must have been when Laura had lived here with Cyrus.

Inside, wide plank floors gleamed from wax Jill had rubbed into them. Normally she would have knelt and savored the feel of the smooth, aged wood—but tonight she had more urgent business.

"Laura?" she said softly.

"Jill. Come into the kitchen."

She followed the sound of the ghost's excited-sounding voice and found Laura hovering in front of the side-by-side refrigerator's open door, gaping at the icemaker as it dumped cubes into the hopper. "Would you like some ice?" Jill asked, smiling.

"This is truly amazing. Lights coming on at the touch of a button. An icebox that makes its own ice, and that little box over there that can make water boil while the cup it is in stays cool! Were it not that Cyrus and I are prisoners, I could stay forever, observing what men of genius have invented since we died."

"Sounds like you've been checking out the kitchen, Miss Laura," Jill teased.

"Kyle showed me how that magic box works. And how to turn on the lights. Mr. Bliss has been exploring, and marveling at my great-great-grandson's magic."

Jill pulled out an old oak straight-backed chair and sat down at the kitchen table. "Speaking of magic, Miss Laura, do you have magical powers?" she asked, suddenly reminded of why she had hurried home. "Other than being able to appear and disappear whenever you feel like it?"

"No, child. Whatever makes you ask that?"

"Just a feeling. A feeling you could tell me why Kyle keeps his daughter some deep, dark secret."

Laura shook her head. *"Sometimes I picture things, people, away from Bliss House. I saw a child in my mind and I may have mentioned her to him."*

"Tell me about her." Restless, Jill stood up and walked over to close the freezer door.

"She is pretty. Delicate looking. I saw her sleeping, her dark hair spread out on a pure white pillowcase." Laura paused, lifting a hand to rub at the corner of her eyes where Jill thought she saw tears threatening to spill.

"And . . ."

"That is all I saw. Kyle told me more, but it is not my way to carry tales. You must ask him, my dear, if you want to know more about this shadow-child of his." With that pronouncement, Laura began to fade away.

Shadow-child? Yes, Jill thought, Miss Laura was right about that. Speaking of the child drove the ghost of her many-times-great-grandmother practically to tears. Dolph, when he discussed her, got a sad, wistful look in his eyes. Yet the little girl's name apparently never crossed her father's lips.

Well, it was time for her to find out whether Kyle cared enough for her to bring his little girl out into the sunshine! Jill hurried back to the Bronco. As she drove along the winding road up Hunter's Mountain, she hoped she would gain a love, not lose a lover. When she got to Kyle's cabin, though, he wasn't there.

She's not back yet. For a long time Kyle stared at the spot where Jill always parked her Bronco. Then he shifted his gaze to her darkened trailer, the softly lit windows of the haunted house. Had he lost Jill only to finally figure out that what he felt for her was love?

"Damn it to hell!" *I should have knocked that door down last night, made her listen.*

He glanced at his watch. Where the hell could she be? It

was ten o'clock at night, and nothing he knew of for miles around here stayed open much past eight. For a minute he panicked, imagining her stranded on some treacherous mountain road . . . lying hurt at the bottom of any of a thousand steep drop-offs that dotted the narrow highways carved into the side of stark, granite mountains.

First he saw headlights, then an outline of her Bronco bouncing up the drive, and he let out the breath he finally realized he had been holding painfully in his lungs. Not wanting her to get inside and lock him out again, Kyle got out of his pickup and ran to open Jill's car door.

"Better late than never," he murmured as he curled a hand around her upper arm. "You may be mad as hell at me, but you *are* going to listen. What we've got together is too damn good to throw away because—"

"Because you're such a selfish ass you forgot you had a child? Or was it just that you neglected to mention your own daughter—"

"Damnit, Jill, I didn't neglect mentioning her. And there's no way in hell I could forget her. Think, honey. The time we've spent together out of bed we've spent working on or talking about that damn house over there. Come on, let's go inside." He half guided, half dragged her onto the porch and into the now half-furnished front parlor of Bliss House.

He tried to pull her down beside him on the couch, but she jerked away and took a seat on the edge of the uneven granite hearth. The look she gave him could have frozen hell, but thankfully she had stayed. Apparently she had resigned herself to hearing what he had to say.

"I think I mentioned I was married. That my wife died." Kyle made himself meet Jill's accusing gaze.

"Yes. You did say that." Her tone was grudging.

"It was a long time ago, right after I finished college. And it wasn't what I'd hoped marriage would be. Tina had . . . problems. Serious problems. I don't guess I helped her with them—at least not the way I should have. She died a little more than seven years ago."

Jill raised an eyebrow but kept regarding Kyle with that cool, doubtful expression. "But before she died she had a baby?" she prodded.

"Yes."

"A baby you dumped into some high-priced boarding school the minute she was old enough, as though she was a troublesome puppy?"

Kyle barely resisted an urge to get up and put a fist through one of the walls he had just restored. Instead he clenched his fists and tried to bite back the words that threatened to ruin any chance he might still have with Jill.

"No. I'd have given anything not to have had to place her at Angels' Paradise. But I couldn't give her the care she needs."

"Why is it so hard for you to talk about Alyssa, Kyle?" Jill's expression had softened, and Kyle thought her brittle tone had mellowed a bit. Still, he could barely stand to think about his daughter, let alone talk about her "limitations," as the workers at Angels' Paradise so euphemistically described the conditions of all their "students."

"Kyle?"

"It hurts. That's why I don't talk about her . . . or think about her any more than I have to. Jill, my little girl is handicapped. Severely handicapped."

He watched Jill's expression register first surprise, then sympathy, before she got up and sank on her knees in front of him, cradling his left hand between her palms. "I'm sorry. Surely you didn't believe that would . . ."

"Turn you off? Make you run as far and as fast as you could away from me? No, honey, I didn't." Kyle ran his fingers through the fine, silky tendrils of her hair and wished to hell he could just let her think that so he wouldn't have to go on.

"Then, why? I sense you care for Alyssa. Yet it seems you do your best to shut her out of your heart. You haven't even called her by name."

Jill was right. He hadn't. Kyle suddenly realized that

more and more he had been avoiding thinking, let alone talking, about his imperfect child. He seldom thought, let alone said, Alyssa's name. Had he been distancing himself on purpose, trying to forget?

"Alyssa. Her name's Alyssa," he choked out, hardly recognizing the tortured sound of his own voice. While he could, he went on, coldly reciting the flaws that condemned his little girl to an existence he could not equate with life.

He felt Jill's work-roughened hands wiping tears from his cheeks, lending comfort with each feathery touch. When he lifted her chin off his thigh so he could see her face, he realized she was crying, too. "Honey, don't cry," he murmured, sorry she had demanded he share the burden he had helped create—the evidence of his guilt that he would have to face each week of the rest of his life.

"That's why I didn't tell you. Wouldn't have told you at all if Dolph hadn't opened his big mouth."

Jill sat back on her heels and regarded Kyle with what appeared to be disbelief. "You would never have said anything? Ever?"

Had Jill fallen in love with him, too? Had she only acted as if she wanted a casual affair because she had thought that was all he was offering? As he looked down at her trembling lower lip and downcast eyes, Kyle felt like the world's biggest bastard.

"I don't have the right to ask you to share my troubles, honey. Because of Alyssa and Dolph. They're the reasons I told you about, the responsibilities I can't turn my back on to make a life with you—no matter what our ghosts may think."

Jill smiled, and Kyle wondered if she was remembering that night—the first night Laura and Cyrus had appeared to him and scared him damn near out of his skin, telling him he would be the one to break some evil spell that had kept them imprisoned in Bliss House for a hundred years. The night he had told Jill that if liberating those ghosts required a lifetime commitment, he wouldn't be the one to set them free.

He would never forget the way she had loved him later, or how good he had felt waking up with her snuggled warmly against him under the quilt on his bed.

"What if I gave you the right?" she asked softly, lifting her head off his thigh and meeting his gaze.

"Honey, I couldn't take it." Kyle reached down and pulled Jill up beside him on the couch. Turning to her and holding both her hands, he recited the dollars-and-cents facts of Alyssa and Dolph's care, financial responsibilities that held him prisoner as surely as if they were steel prison bars.

Jill could feel Kyle's tension in the slight unsteadiness of his hands, could see it in the tight set of his jaw. She had a feeling the staggering details he had just revealed with clinical precision were only the tip of the iceberg, that what really drove and tortured him went far deeper. Working one hand free of his grip, she raised it to caress his cheek.

The way he turned his head, the soft, caring touch of his lips on her fingers, made her wonder. Did he want more from her, yet feel he couldn't ask? "Kyle, if you could, would you . . . ?" she asked before she could bite back the words that sounded plaintive even to her own ears.

He nuzzled her fingers, then drew one gently into his mouth and suckled it. "Yeah. I would. You've gotten to me, honey, not just to Big Al."

Jill smiled. "You've gotten to me, too." *I love you, more than I ever dreamed I could love a man. But I've got a feeling that you'd bolt like an escaped convict if I told you.* "Thank you for telling me about Alyssa. I'm sorry I jumped to the wrong conclusions."

"It's going to be damn hard to let you go."

And it's going to be hell to watch you walk away. Jill shoved that heart-wrenching thought to the back of her mind and forced a smile. "Let's not think of that tonight," she said softly. "Take me to the cabin."

Later, as they lay entwined in his bed, Jill listened to Kyle's steady heartbeat against her ear. He made her feel complete, whole—clean and new and so full of love she thought she could conquer the world.

Here, now, she believed he would understand and accept her revelation of the sordid secrets of her life with Rob. Tomorrow, next week—anytime she might face him without the gentling afterglow of lovemaking—Jill feared her past would destroy his fragile feelings for her.

"Honey?"

He sounded so sexy when he was half-asleep! "Mmmm?" she replied, flicking his flat, pebbly nipple with her tongue.

"Stop that! It's Saturday morning, and I've got to drive down to see Alyssa. It won't be any picnic, and I feel guilty as hell for asking, but I'd like you to go with me. We can go to my place in Greensboro afterward, maybe hit a club or two if you'd like."

"All right." While they drove maybe she could whip up the courage to say what she had to say—and he would have to accept—if they were to have a chance for a future after the completion of Bliss House. Jill tried to suppress a shudder as she climbed out of bed and began to dress.

Chapter
Twenty-Eight

THE GHOSTS

"They're both there, at that place where his daughter lives."
Cyrus hoped Laura wasn't getting her hopes up for naught. *"Do not stress yourself, my love. What will be, will be."* Seeing the couple last night, watching Jill's anger turn to gentle understanding as young Randall related the facts of his child's tragic affliction, had convinced Cyrus they must back off—let nature take its course in the relationship of Laura's great-great-grandson and the wanton young woman who was restoring his home.

"Come sit by me." Laura patted the edge of the kitchen table where she had perched. *"I long for you to touch me again, hold me in your arms."*

"You know that may never be." Cyrus floated to the table

and rested just above its gleaming surface. *"There are but three more weeks."*

"Kyle and Miss Carey are in love. With luck, even now she may be carrying his child. No matter how shamed he feels not to have amassed a fortune to bring her, I do not believe my grandson would allow her to bear a bastard."

Cyrus winced. *"You would have borne my bastard if Harry Randall hadn't foully murdered us. I believe the means of preventing untimely pregnancies are quite advanced now, my dear."*

Laura's image faded until Cyrus could see clear through her. He hated seeing her wilt, as if all hope had been sucked from her soul.

Cyrus sighed before he spoke. *"Leave the young people alone, Laura. You cannot mold their futures. Exhausting yourself to observe them in some faraway place serves no purpose. Come. Let us explore more of the modern wonders the workers have brought to our old house."*

Chapter
Twenty-Nine

Coward!

Jill silently cursed herself for having avoided the subject she dreaded most. Instead, as they drove to Angels' Paradise, she had let Kyle lead her into an innocuous conversation. She had gotten downright enthusiastic about a gazebo he suggested might house the Jacuzzi and shower she wanted—but had decided wouldn't match the era or decor of the house itself.

Now certainly wasn't the time for revelations, she realized when Kyle pulled his truck to a stop in front of an ivy-covered red-brick building. A white wrought-iron angel perched at the side of the door held a discreet sign that welcomed visitors to Angels' Paradise.

She felt Kyle's hand tremble when he helped her out of the truck cab. "I've never brought anyone here before," he muttered, as though he had decided—too late—that she had no business in this part of his life.

"Do you want me to wait out here?"

"No. Come on." He practically dragged her up the few stairs and through the door. Then he turned, as if he had suddenly changed his mind. "You don't have to do this, honey. I'd like you to go with me, but—"

"It's okay, Kyle. I want to meet Alyssa."

The choked-up sound he made sent a chill down Jill's spine, but she made herself smile as she took his hand. "I'm here to visit Alyssa," he told the gray-haired lady at the antique desk in the foyer.

"My! Alyssa's a popular young lady today. You two go right on up. But, of course, Mr. Randall, you know the way." Jill met the woman's gaze and decided that her cheery monologue did a lousy job of masking the pitying look in her faded blue eyes.

She felt Kyle step back, pulling her along toward a cage-style elevator not too different from the one she had loved playing with as a child at her grandmother's house. That thought served as another reminder that it would soon be time for her to make her own painful confessions.

"This used to be a private home, didn't it?" she asked to fill the silence that suddenly had become too much to bear.

"Years ago, I guess. Dolph must already be here. Jill, if seeing my . . . Alyssa . . . is too much for you, we'll go. Like I told you, she won't know whether we're with her or not."

Touched, Jill squeezed Kyle's hand. "I'll be all right," she told him as they stepped off the wheezing contraption and started down a long, wide hallway. "Does your brother come here every Saturday, too?"

"Yeah. This way," he said as he pushed open a swinging door, stepping back to let her into a sun-filled room where high-railed beds lined both walls. She felt his hand at her back as he joined her. "They say the attendants can take better care of them in one big room like this," he muttered.

Jill searched among the seven children of various sizes

for a seven-year-old girl she could identify as Kyle's. Some lay unmoving, others twitched beneath brightly colored blankets, while one strained against some kind of restraints while making guttural, animal sounds that tore at Jill's soul. She wondered how the two women who hurried to the disturbed child's bed stood working here, in this place devoid of hope.

One of the women looked up and smiled at Kyle. "Sorry. Brendon's fussy today," she said apologetically. "Alyssa's in the visiting room with your brother. You and your friend can go on back there." She gestured toward a glassed-in partition at the back of the ward.

Jill would have recognized Alyssa anywhere. The child looked just as she had imagined, except for hair that was glossy black instead of dark blond like her father's.

While Kyle had told her what to expect when she saw his daughter, such knowledge paled before the reality of this beautiful little girl who lay on her side with her knees drawn to her chest, one hand curled into a loose fist while the other lay relaxed against Dolph's much bigger palm.

Dolph brushed Alyssa's cheek, drawing Jill's attention to the child's dark green eyes—eyes that would have been like Kyle's but for that unseeing stare. During the hour they spent in that tiny room, Jill saw Alyssa move only once—to loosen a fist, then tighten it nearly imperceptibly around Kyle's outstretched finger after Dolph had left.

"You still game to go to Greensboro?" Kyle wouldn't blame Jill if she chose to run as fast as she could away from him and the child who would never develop past infancy.

"Yes. If you are."

He reached out and stroked the satiny smoothness of her arm as he pulled out onto the highway. "Other than Dolph, you're the only person I've ever taken to visit her—Alyssa," he blurted, needing to know how seeing his daughter had affected Jill—and her feelings for him.

"Thank you. She's beautiful."

"She looks like her mother."

"Her eyes are like yours," Jill pointed out quietly.

"Except that I can see." Kyle couldn't keep the bitterness out of his reply.

"Sweetheart, I believe Alyssa knows you—knows when you're there. Didn't you notice how she clenched your fingers when you took her hand to say good-bye?"

"That was just a reflex action. Dolph had held her hand for a long time, in case you didn't notice. When he left, it just took a few minutes for her fingers to retract into a fist. My finger happened to be in the way at the time, so it got a squeeze."

Kyle hated bursting Jill's bubble, but he was long past reading miracles into each small motion Alyssa made.

Jill twisted around so she nearly faced him across the stickshift of his truck. "Maybe. Kyle, no one would deny it's tragic that Alyssa can't express her feelings, that a beautiful child should have to live so impaired. Think about her for a minute, though. *You* hurt for what she can't do. *She* doesn't, because she can't miss what she has never known."

That made sense, Kyle thought—a lot more sense than the mumbo jumbo the shrinks and social workers and well-meaning church people had tossed his way over the years as he agonized over his child's plight. "I guess you're right about that," he told her as he pulled up in front of his company building on the outskirts of Greensboro. "I need to grab some papers, honey. I'll be right out."

It took him less than a minute to gather up the stack of blueprints and catalogs he had asked Dolph to leave on the corner of his desk, but Kyle missed Jill even for that short time. Yeah, she kept him hot and horny, but she was a lot more to him than just a talented bed partner!

She had a way of making him feel good, helping him cast aside the guilt that had driven him so long. Before he started the pickup, he reached impulsively across the seat and drew her into his arms.

"You're good for me," he murmured when he had to come up for air. "Where do you want to go tonight?"

Jill met his gaze. "To bed." Her voice reminded him of honey, smooth and sweet and sexy as hell.

"Want me to feed you first?"

He thought he felt her hesitate. "We've still got some talking to do."

"Before . . . ?"

"After. Definitely after." She lightly squeezed him through the heavy denim of his jeans and damn near made him jump out of his skin. "Maybe we could order a pizza, sit up in bed, and eat it while we talk."

Kyle chuckled. After the ordeal of seeing Alyssa, he craved some fun—and he loved Jill for understanding and feeding that need. "If we're naked in a bed together, we won't be talking, honey."

Reluctantly he lifted her talented hand off his swelling cock and set it firmly against his thigh. "Save that for later," he told her as he started the engine. "Otherwise, I'll get so hot I'll forget about driving and get us both killed."

He wished he'd had sense enough to buy a house closer to his company headquarters. He cursed himself for coming here instead of rushing to Hunter's Mountain and the big bed in his cabin. He prayed that Dolph had gone anywhere else but home when he had left them at Angels' Paradise, and felt guilty for the selfish wish.

Most of all, Kyle silently swore at the fickle gods who had brought him the woman of his dreams, too late for them to have a life together.

"Bedroom's through that door," Kyle whispered as he flipped on the light in the tiny foyer of the house he had told her he shared with Dolph. "First one naked gets to be on top."

Jill laughed. "You're so bad!" But she loved the way he made sex an adventure. And she was glad Kyle's brother wasn't home. "I want a shower first."

"How about making it in the spa?" he asked, scooping her effortlessly into his arms and nuzzling her breasts through the soft, loosely knit black sweater she'd unbuttoned but hadn't had the chance to shed.

She poked him in the ribs, eliciting a yelp of protest. "Beast! Can't you wait?"

"Not for long, honey. Big Al's damn near bustin' out my zipper now. Feel him?" He lowered her backside until it nudged the rock-hard bulge in his jeans.

"Uh-huh. Oh, I like this spa." Kyle strode into a small room lined with the same kind of redwood boards that surrounded a bubbling, forest-green whirlpool just big enough for two. As soon as he lowered her feet to the floor, she pulled her sweater off and stepped out of her shoes, then shucked off her jeans and panties.

"I won! I won!"

"Naw, sweetie, I'm the winner. I get to enjoy watching you while I take my time with these." He made a production of raking her from head to toe with a heated gaze as he slowly shrugged out of his green plaid shirt and slipped off his loafers.

She longed to tackle the buttons under his bulging fly—but he beat her to it. "Hey, what do you think? Could I make it as a stripper at one of those working girls' bars?" he asked.

"Don't know," she lied. Jill couldn't vouch for other women, but *she* would damn sure pay well to look at Kyle's hard, work-honed body and drool over his impressive pal, Big Al. She already felt hot, wet, and ready—and he hadn't even touched her, or finished taking off his clothes. "Can you do it to music?"

"Baby—I mean Jill—I can do it any way you want it." He shoved down his jeans with more haste than finesse, then bent to pull down his socks. Stripped down now to tiny black briefs, he moved closer, just out of her reach, before hooking his finger into the waistband and deliberately pushing them down.

"We can, can't we?" Jill licked her lips as she watched Big Al spring free of the restraining cloth. "Is that for me?"

Kyle grinned. "Yeah. Don't see anybody else in here who might have caught Al's eye."

"Can I have him now?" She came closer and rubbed an inquisitive finger along his impressive length. A little demon inside her made her turn her back on him, climb onto the low platform that surrounded the hot tub, and bend over, gripping the edge of the tub for support. "Like this?"

"Any way you want, you've got it." He nipped playfully at the back of her neck as he nudged her legs farther apart and positioned himself between them. She felt his fingers slip inside her, and she gave them a welcoming squeeze.

"Oh, God," he growled, withdrawing his fingers and bathing her cleft with her own slick, wet heat.

"Now!" She sounded fierce as she uttered that terse command.

Velvety smooth, hard as steel, he found his mark. His big hands grasped her hips, holding her still while he sank slowly into her aching body. She wanted to scream, because when he was just inches inside her he stopped moving, rolling his hips to taunt and tease her.

"Kyle!"

"Want more, honey?"

"Yes. I want all of you. Now!"

He pulled her back as he thrust forward, stretching and filling the emptiness inside her. Again his body stilled, and she retaliated by clenching her muscles as hard as she could around his huge, hard penis.

"God, honey. Do that much more and it'll be all over but the shouting." She loved the way he growled when they made love. He moved once, pulling out the tiniest bit and slamming back, changing the angle just enough so the big blunt head of him made contact with the spot that sent her flying into oblivion.

"Found that button, honey, didn't I?" He was pumping hard and fast now, in time to the wild contractions of her own body. And when he buried himself inside her one last time, she felt the hot, wet burst that accompanied his triumphant shout.

It took several minutes for her to recover enough to crawl into the hot tub and straddle Kyle's lap.

"Al's beat."

"But you said first one naked got to be on top." Jill pretended to pout, but her grin and sassy gaze told Kyle she was teasing. She tangled her fingers in the nest of coarse curls that cushioned his wrung-out buddy and raked him lightly with her nails. "I'll bet I can wake Al up."

"God, honey, you'll kill me yet."

She grinned as she took him in her hand and rubbed him lightly against her soft, pink cleft. "Don't want to do that," she said. "You make me feel too good."

The water swirled around them, cloaking them in foam. Every once in a while bubbles would burst, giving him a fleeting vision of pebbly rose-colored nipples. Lowering his head, he took one in his mouth, only to come up sputtering when a wave got him smack in the face.

She laughed, a welcome, tinkling sound that made him forget his stinging nostrils.

"Think that's funny, do you? I'll show you funny." Grabbing her shoulders, he dunked her briefly below the churning bubbles.

"Bully!" Her hands tangled in his hair, and she tugged him forward. He let himself go limp to take the headfirst tumble, then righted himself and grabbed her waist. "Kyle, stop!" she cried when he lifted her high in the air, as if to toss her beneath the foam.

Instead he held her there long enough to taste her honey, then began slowly to bring her down. "Wrap your legs around me," he said, and when she complied the satiny feel of her sliding along his chest made Big Al forget it had been just minutes since he had come inside her hot, slick sheath.

"I've got something for you," he said as he lowered them

to the built-in seat and brought her down hard on his renewed erection. "Feel good?"

"Mmmm." Her fingers tweaked his nipples. "Kyle, I'm turning into a prune. And I'm getting hungry."

"For this?" He flexed his hips and sank deeper inside her.

"Uh-huh." He damn near came again when he felt her muscles tighten like a velvet fist around his cock, and he wanted this to last, so he lifted her off him and stood, picking her up and setting her out of the tub. So hot he could barely move, he followed her, grabbing some towels off the rack on the way to the bedroom.

"I'll dry you off," he told her, wrapping one big towel around her waist and dragging her up against his dripping body. She rubbed her flat belly sensuously against him, damn near driving him crazy before he got them reasonably dry. Tossing the towels onto the floor, he flopped onto the bed. "Come here," he said, the words coming between gasps for air that suddenly had become scarce.

"I love looking at you." Jill stared straight at his throbbing erection while he watched her tongue dart out of her mouth and wet her smiling lips. He wondered how much he could take when she knelt between his legs and lapped up beads of water the towel must have missed.

Not much! She was making his insides churn and boil, and he wasn't ready to come alone. Letting out a groan that was part regret, part agony, Kyle grabbed her shoulders and dragged her up his body. At the same time he flexed his hips and sank into her as his tongue plunged into her mouth to savor the taste of her and him, and the heat they made together.

He arched his back and began to move, slowly at first, then faster and harder as he felt her milking him and her nails biting hard into his shoulders. When he absorbed her gasp of pleasure deep in his throat, he slammed into her again once, twice . . . and one last time before he exploded again into her hot, giving heat.

*   *   *

How long had they slept like this? Jill wondered, taking in a room that was as dark now as it had been bright when she and Kyle had come to bed. She could barely make out the outline of his body, sprawled out in sleep under a quilted comforter he had pulled over both of them after they had made love.

Gently she turned his left hand over and pressed the button that lit his watch. *Eight o'clock?* They had slept the afternoon away, and she hadn't told him about herself and Rob—or that little girl whose death would forever be on her conscience.

Some things are best spoken of in the dark of night, she told herself as she untangled herself from the coverlet and propped her back against the headboard. "Kyle?" she said softly, willing herself not to touch him and begin another hot, sweet session of lovemaking that would distract her from her purpose.

"Come here," he grumbled, still mostly asleep.

She caught the hand that would have pulled her back into his arms. "It's time for that talk. And I can't think when you're so close."

He reached for the lamp on the nightstand. "Okay. I'll call for that pizza."

You probably won't want to eat it after you've heard what I have to say. And I don't imagine you'll ever want to be with me again.

"All right." Jill would have rather sat there in the dark like the coward she was, not having to see Kyle's expression turn from lust to disgust when—

"What do you want on it?"

"What?"

"The pizza. What do you like on it?"

"I don't care. Whatever you want." Jill's gaze dropped from Kyle's sleepy, sexy face to his massive chest and lower. She wanted to memorize every inch of him, burn it into her soul so that when he left her she would be able to relive their loving times in her memory.

"What's the matter?" he asked after he had called in their pizza order. Kyle rolled over, settling some pillows against the headboard before leaning back and settling in next to Jill. "Honey?"

Haltingly, Jill began her story. When the pizza arrived, she had just reached the part where she had gone to live in her grandmother's Atlanta mansion. After they ate it, she told Kyle about her life with Rob, and about the guilt she would always feel for her part in causing an innocent child to die.

Chapter
Thirty

Kyle smashed the heavy cardboard pizza box and tossed it hard into the wall. "If that bastard were still alive, I'd murder him with my bare hands," he muttered, his voice as gentle as his guts were churning. His hands clenched into fists around a piece of the sheet that had settled in his lap.

The sight of Jill huddled against the headboard as far from him as she could get, her face buried in her hands, her shoulders heaving with each choked-out sob, brought tears to Kyle's eyes. The thought of her, hardly older than Alyssa, reaching out for the twisted parody that that—that fucking pervert—had offered as love, made him want to strike out and break something apart.

A sudden, tearing sound interrupted Kyle's furious thoughts. Loosening his fists from the sheet, he realized he had ripped it the way he wished he could rip out Rob Carey's throat.

Unlike Rob, Jill was alive. Her choked sobs quieted, leaving the room silent except for the raspy cadence of her breathing. Her tear-stained gaze focused on trembling hands clutched together in her lap. As Kyle looked at her he wondered how she had found the strength to endure the life she had recounted in that flat, hopeless voice.

"Honey?" he said softly, unclenching a fist from the ruined sheet and reaching out to touch her cheek. The tortured look in her eyes when she turned her face toward him nearly did him in.

"You don't have to touch me, Kyle." She sounded small, hopeless, as he imagined her having been when her world had come crashing down around her not so long ago. "I know you can't possibly want . . . "

He swiveled around on the bed to face her and grasped both her hands. "I want to touch you. Hold you. I wish to hell I had the right to love you the way you deserve to be loved. Jill, you didn't do anything to feel guilty about."

She shook her head, hard, as though denying the truth of his words.

"Why would what you told me turn me off? I'm not him, Jill. I'm the same guy I was this afternoon when we made love." How strong she must be, to have survived such cruelty and remained the sensual, loving woman she so clearly was. "And you're the same sexy, sexy lady," he added, sliding closer and draping his arm around her shoulders.

"You—you mean that what I told you doesn't bother you?"

"Damn straight it bothers me, honey. I'd like to raise that bastard out of his grave just so I could kill him again. And I'd love to hold you, protect you, promise you a hundred forevers where no one like him could ever hurt you again."

"It makes me feel so dirty . . . I let him . . . I played his little games, and . . . damn it, Kyle, I enjoyed them. I'm no better than he was. If I'd—"

"How could you have known when you were just a kid that this guy you trusted had a bunch of screws loose in his perverted head?" Kyle grasped her shoulders and willed her to meet his gaze.

Jill shuddered. "I should have told my grandmother. Or my teachers. Or one of the maids. But no! Rob told me what we did together was just for us to know, and I believed him. Believed what he taught me to do was right. For years I did everything I could to hold him, make him keep wanting me. Goddamnit, Kyle, I was as much a pervert as he was."

New tears caught the light as they flowed down Jill's pale cheeks. Kyle brushed them away with his thumbs. "You're no pervert. And you're no child, either. You're the sexiest woman I've ever known."

"I'm dirty. Used. Kyle, you must not have heard me. I haven't been clean since I was thirteen years old. And I caused a poor homeless little girl to die, as surely as if I had been the one to put that gun to her head and pull the trigger."

He pulled her rigid body tightly against him and stroked her until he felt her begin to relax. "Hush. Just let me hold you," he murmured as he lay back and pulled her half on top of him. "Go to sleep."

Eventually Jill slept while Kyle lay awake, staring at the patterns the streetlights cast through the window onto the bedroom ceiling. Her tragedy and misplaced guilt had brought Jill to Bliss House—and to him. His own real guilt, and the tragedies he had caused, would soon make him walk away.

The sound of Dolph's car pulling into the driveway, and later of his brother struggling to get inside the house and to his room, punctuated Kyle's silent regrets for a past he couldn't change—and a future he couldn't claim.

The smell of freshly brewed coffee drew Jill out of bed and into the living area of Kyle's small house. Kyle, she supposed, must still be with his brother, since he had left her still half-asleep in his bed after Dolph's cry for help had awakened them a few minutes earlier.

Curiosity drew her to the desk—more specifically to a

framed studio portrait of the woman who had to have been Alyssa's mother. Jill sighed. Kyle and this woman may have had problems—as he had said—but they certainly made a stunning couple! The woman looked young—as if she was still a schoolgirl when the picture had been taken. Jill shuddered.

Fool. He's not Rob. She set the picture back on the desk and turned away to find Dolph in the doorway, observing her every move.

"That was Tina," he said, and she thought she heard a catch in his mellow voice.

"I could tell. Alyssa looks like her." Why did it hurt so, she wondered, to realize a picture of Kyle's dead wife still occupied a place of honor on his desk?

Kyle came up behind his brother and gave him a push through the doorway. "Yeah. She does." He sounded as bleak as the November day. "Come on, coffee's ready," he told them, as though intent on getting away from a past too sad to recall.

While Kyle fried bacon and scrambled eggs Jill sat across from Dolph at the kitchen table. He looked tired—much too weary to have just gotten out of bed. In the short time since she had first met Dolph, his condition had obviously deteriorated.

Dark circles lined Kyle's eyes, too, and Jill guiltily figured he must have spent the night digesting the horror that had been her life. He hadn't shown it if disgust had begun to set in, though.

Jill felt the corners of her lips curve upward in a smile. Before he had gone to Dolph, Kyle had kissed her awake with fervor that said much of need and passion and nothing of disdain. Still, she couldn't believe he wouldn't eventually recoil from her because of her life with Rob.

"What?" She had been so deep in thought, she hadn't caught Dolph's words.

"I asked if you enjoyed your visit with Alyssa," he repeated, his gaze steady as it met hers.

Jill hesitated. Enjoyment was not a word she would use to describe her feelings when she had looked at, and touched, Kyle's daughter. "I—I'm glad Kyle asked me to go meet her," she finally replied.

"What did you think of her?"

Jill glanced over at Kyle. From his tightly set jaw to the fist that clenched a spatula as though intent on shattering the tough wood handle, she could see he didn't care for Dolph's line of questioning. But then, neither did she. "She's beautiful. Seeing Alyssa made me want to curse the God who doomed her to such a life."

"God didn't doom her. Her mother did," Kyle snapped, slamming down the spatula and turning to face them. "Dolph, can't you talk about a goddamn thing but Alyssa—or Tina?"

"Sorry, Kyle. Jill, I'm sorry if I embarrassed you."

Jill met Dolph's gaze. "It's all right." He looked so tired, so pained, she couldn't be angry with him, not even when she knew he'd hit one of Kyle's emotional sore spots. "I didn't hear you come in last night," she said. Perhaps a change of topic would improve the atmosphere.

"I had studying to do," Dolph said shortly.

"My big brother's about to get his college degree," Kyle explained as he set down a platter of bacon and eggs on the table.

Jill smiled at Kyle when he sat down beside her. As they ate they kept the conversation casual. Still, Jill felt the friction between Kyle and Dolph. She couldn't help commenting on it as she and Kyle drove back to Bliss House.

"You and Dolph must have had words this morning," she said, drawing the collar of her parka around her neck.

Kyle cleared his throat. "I rode him pretty hard, told him he ought to have some surgery the doctor's been recommending to him for a couple of years now. Damn it, he's getting so bad, I'm afraid to leave him alone in the house anymore."

"What?"

"I had to help him out of bed this morning. He was too weak to pull himself up and into his chair."

"And the surgery would help?"

"Yeah. My dumb brother's been putting off having it because it's risky—now he's stalling until after he finishes this semester's exams. When they're over, I'm certain he will find some other excuse."

Jill murmured sympathetically. "Why?"

"Because he's afraid that if he's not around, Alyssa won't have anyone who really cares for her."

"Meaning you don't? Or he doesn't think you do?"

"I suppose so," Kyle replied brusquely.

"Kyle, are you still so tied up with memories of Alyssa's mother, you can't be rational about her? You were pretty tough on Dolph when he asked me about—"

"About how you tolerated seeing her lying there, saying nothing, doing nothing, alive but not really alive? I just didn't want him putting you on the spot like that."

Jill had a feeling Kyle's anger had far deeper roots. "You're having trouble with what *I* am, aren't you?" she asked, afraid to know but more afraid to bury her fears inside her.

He took his right hand off the steering wheel and reached out to her. "No, honey. I'm having trouble with what *I* am, what I've done. What say we test out the fireplace in the parlor at your haunted house, and I'll try to keep my hands off you long enough to tell you my own deep, dark secrets?"

What was Kyle building up to tell her? Jill wavered between eagerness to hear and fear that his confession would end whatever small chance they had for a future together. As she watched him kneel before the hearth, lighting a cozy fire, she realized again how much she had come to love him.

She had heard some of it before—from Maida and from Kyle himself—but when he put it all together, Jill could feel Kyle's anguish. From the look on his face, he felt as deeply today as he must have twelve years earlier, when he got the call that Dolph lay near death in a Greensboro hospital.

"He was just six years older than me, but he practically raised me. Like I told you, he was the one who persuaded me to go to UNC, make something out of myself instead of eking out a living making white lightning up on Hunter's Mountain. Dolph says he took that logging job to get *himself* off the mountain—but I know he did it for me."

Jill rubbed her thumb across Kyle's palm. "But Maida told me you had a full scholarship."

"Yeah, I did—but every week Dolph would send me a twenty or a fifty, spending money so I wouldn't be stuck in the dorm, he used to say."

"Oh. Go on."

"So there I was, having the time of my life, while my brother crippled himself so I could party with the rich boys at Chapel Hill. I'll never forget the way he looked, lying in that bed with tubes coming out of everywhere. Or how he sent Tina away the day the doctors told him just how bad off he was going to be."

"Your *wife* Tina?"

"Yeah. That Tina. They had been planning to get married after Dolph saw me through school. But Dolph couldn't stand the sight of her after the doctors told him he'd never be able to make love to her again."

What kind of man would marry his brother's fiancée? Jill started to ask, then closed her mouth as Kyle continued.

"Dolph got out of rehab about six months before I finished college. I talked him into opening the construction company, scouting out some good used equipment—that sort of thing. When I got there, we were ready to go to work. At first the jobs were little ones, but pretty quickly I started to develop a reputation for renovating old places.

"After a year or so Tina showed up in Greensboro. Seems she still wanted Dolph—she'd had a breakdown after he sent her away, and she'd gotten into the drug scene. For a while I thought they were going to get together, but he started shoving her at me." Kyle stared at the flames as if they might help him go on.

"So you married her?"

"Eventually."

"What about the drugs?"

Kyle ran his fingers through his hair. "She was off them when she came back to Dolph. As far as I know, she was clean when we got married. But I was away a lot, working. She took a job at a dance joint while I was gone, one time. Told me she wanted to buy some things for our apartment." He hesitated, as if it hurt to go on.

"I was furious, ready to give her her walking papers. But Dolph begged me not to leave her. I owed him so much, I couldn't say no. So I went back home, apologized to Tina for what I'd said, and took her to bed.

"She wound up pregnant. Later I found out she'd been doing coke and heroin again, and she couldn't stop." Kyle choked back a sob. "She doomed my daughter to a living death before she was ever born."

"Kyle, I'm so sorry."

He stared at the fire, tears running down his cheeks. "I tried to get her to have an abortion. I tried to keep her away from the drugs. But she wouldn't listen. She had no idea what she'd done to her baby until she saw Alyssa in that incubator. When she realized, she checked out—just went home and shot up all the dope she could get her hands on. Her dealer came to collect from me right after her funeral."

Jill tried to imagine how he must have felt. She couldn't. "Is there anything I can do?" she asked, memories of her own suffering paling in comparison with Kyle's. "You must have loved her so much."

"I never loved her at all." Kyle sounded as if he were choking on words that conveyed sorrow—and shame. "What Alyssa is is more my fault than Tina's."

How he must have suffered! How he must suffer still! At that moment, as she watched Kyle relive the horror that he bore silently each day, Jill loved him more than she had ever dreamed possible. This man had lived for the past twelve years, trying to make amends for twists of fate—tragedies he blamed himself for, but that he could not have prevented.

"You can't blame yourself, Kyle," she murmured, but she knew he could and did—just as she held on to remorse over her own past blunders.

Silently Jill stood and held out her hand. When they lay together in the sleigh bed she had found for the remodeled master bedroom, she offered him the meager comfort of her battered soul.

Chapter
Thirty-One

THE GHOSTS

"They have shared their secrets, and still he shares her bed."

Laura snuggled next to Cyrus in the drafty attic, hearing rather than feeling the cold wind that rustled through air vents at either end of the long, narrow room. *"Yes. Cyrus, we will soon be free! Free to touch and love, and . . ."*

"Wed at last? That is my fondest wish. Yet I am not so certain. Young Randall appears reluctant—and Miss Carey has made no move to nudge him toward the altar."

Laura had to acknowledge the truth of Cyrus's words. Still, when she watched Kyle with Jill, she sensed the depth of their feelings for one another. *"Kyle is an honorable man. He will do what's right by Miss Carey."*

"They both carry guilt in their hearts."

"Cyrus, they are in love."

Cyrus shrugged, as though dismissing the value of that emotion. *"I fear we shall be doomed to an eternity alone, my love. That this love our young friends feel for one another will not be strong enough to overcome the obstacles from their pasts."*

"They will not be able to resist each other."

"No. They have made very little effort to resist the pull of lust. But neither have they resolved the issues that keep them apart." Cyrus floated over by the window and looked out at gently falling snowflakes.

Laura knew Cyrus was trying hard to hold on to the hope that had kept them going for a hundred years—but that he found it hard to believe they finally would be free. *"Kyle is not like Harry,"* she said softly.

"No. If he were, guilt could not control him. I doubt your murderous husband knew the meaning of the word."

Laura wished Cyrus could set aside the bitterness that had tarnished their relationship for so long. *"Please, Cyrus. Harry can't hurt us now. He has been dead and gone for years."*

"Dead but not forgotten." Cyrus hesitated. *"Forgive me, my love. I rarely think of old Harry. It is just that we have come so close to freedom, yet are still so far away. The thought of an eternity away from you makes me waspish."*

"It breaks my heart." Yet an eternity apart would be their fate unless they could bring Kyle and Jill together. Laura tried to sort out the couple's problems in her mind. *"Dolph."*

"What about him?"

"Dolph is the key. The key to bringing Kyle and Miss Carey together."

Chapter Thirty-Two

Dolph tried for the fourth time to concentrate on his reading for the following day's test. All he could see was his brother, uptight and defensive about Alyssa, and just plain uptight about Tina. And Jill Carey.

He sensed that Jill was more to Kyle than a convenient bed partner, no matter what his brother might say. As Dolph had reminded his brother more times than he could remember, he was crippled, not blind. He could see the love in Kyle's eyes when he looked at Jill—love he himself once felt for Tina.

"Shit!" He slammed the book shut, then slumped in the chair, exhausted.

What the hell was the point of trying to study? Dolph stared at the four walls of the living room for a few minutes until his gaze settled on the photo of Tina that Jill had held this morning.

He pushed his chair backward and rolled away from the desk. When he stared out the window at softly falling snowflakes, he saw instead a brilliant spring day.

Well and whole, he lay beside Tina on a plaid blanket under a stand of tall pine trees. He watched the sunlight play on facets of the tiny diamond in her ring, drank in its warmth and promise. When she begged him not to work on that logging crew anymore, he laughed. He, Dolph Randall, was going to bring his lady so much more than the old man had ever given his mother!

A house in Greensboro, pretty dresses. Maybe even one of those new minivans so she could haul the kids to school and Little League. Yeah. Dolph was going to be somebody, and it wasn't going to take him the years of studying little brother Kyle was suffering through in Chapel Hill!

Dolph closed his eyes. When he opened them again the light had dimmed.

He lay deathly still, half of himself in agonizing pain while the other half felt nothing. Nothing at all. Tina stood beside the bed, her dark eyes full of tears as he said the words that would send her away.

He couldn't take looking at her anymore, knowing he would never again hear her moan with pleasure when they made love—constantly being reminded that that part of his life was over. Having set the woman he loved free so she wouldn't have to face seeing his muscular legs wither away, watch the man he had been become a cripple bound to a wheelchair, he felt smug.

Darkness had set in outside, as black as the hole in Dolph's heart. How he hated becoming more helpless every day!

When he thought of Alyssa, doomed to so much worse, guilt washed over him. Had he been using her as an excuse for putting off the surgery that would restore him some mobility—if it didn't kill him?

Kyle might not love Alyssa the way he did, but Dolph knew his brother would never shirk his responsibility to

Tina's little girl. He had a feeling, if Kyle would take that step and dare to commit himself to Jill, she would come to care for the child as well.

No, he had used Tina's daughter as an excuse to refuse this surgery for far too long. He would take this test, get his degree, and make arrangements to check into the hospital just as soon as Kyle finished the work on Bliss House.

Prying a sleepy eye open, Kyle looked outside and saw it was still snowing. For the second time, he had spent the night in the master bedroom at Bliss House, this time without being locked in by his ghostly ancestor and her resourceful lover. He wondered how he would ever sleep again when this job was done and he no longer could look forward to waking up to feel Jill's warm body snuggled against him.

Reflexively he hugged her. Last night she had held him, almost made him forget the grim reality of his obligations to his daughter—and Dolph. They hadn't made love, but she had loved him.

Really loved him. And he had loved her, too. He did love her, in a way that went beyond the fantastic sex they had discovered and explored in depth. Suddenly he had to tell her how he felt, as much as he needed to hear her say the words he sensed she had been holding back.

"I love you," he murmured, his voice little more than a whisper against her cheek.

She turned her head and greeted him with a sleepy smile. "Say that again," she said softly.

"I love you, Jill."

He felt her arms curl around his neck. "I love *you*. So much."

He stroked her cheek. "I'm glad." All he wanted to do was stay in her arms in this room—the room where he had first made love to her in a dream that became clearer each day.

Kyle held her gently in his arms, afraid that if he let her go, his fantasy would turn to dust. There was so much he wanted to tell her, so much more than just the simple declaration of love he had just made and she had returned.

He had gone to college, but he was still a simple guy, not much for fancy words and sloppy sentiment—or for ghosts and magic, and destiny.

Destiny. Kyle tested the word in his mind and found it fit. What else could he call Jill, when he had made love to her in a dream before they had ever met? When the ghosts—or destiny—had created a warm, inviting haven and locked them in it to explore that hot chemistry that gripped them both from the first?

She was his destiny . . . his love. He leaned over to nuzzle her earlobe, pushing all the reasons he couldn't reach out and claim her for a lifetime to the farthest corner of his mind.

He had never experienced anything so mind-boggling as loving her, and making love slowly—so slowly and so beautifully—under the covers on that antique sleigh bed he had first seen in that dream.

In the hour after dawn, as snow fell silently outside Bliss House, Kyle felt more at home with himself than he had ever been before. He lay back, tightening his arm possessively around Jill's shoulder.

Her warm, damp breath played in the hair on his chest. He felt her words before he heard.

"Will you marry me?"

"Marry?" he croaked.

The sudden acceleration of Kyle's heartbeat and the way the muscles in his arms contracted warned Jill he wasn't taking her proposal all that well. "We could save Cyrus and Laura from whatever fate they're facing," she said lightly, deciding to keep this conversation light.

She felt him shake his head and waited for him to say something—anything—but it was as if he had suddenly turned mute. "Kyle? You okay?"

"No."

"No, you're not okay, or no, you won't marry me?"

He turned to meet her gaze. Suddenly Jill felt shy, lying there stark naked in bed with this man she had just boldly asked to marry her—the man she had made love with in every way she could imagine since shortly after he had come into her life. She pulled the covers the rest of the way up to her chin.

"Both. I'm not okay. And I can't marry you."

Jill couldn't help the tears welling up in her eyes and spilling down her cheeks. And she found she had no words to respond to his flat refusal. Still, she couldn't give up yet. She wanted Kyle more than she wanted her next breath.

"I—I don't understand. You said you love me."

He pulled one arm out from under the covers and brushed a tear off her cheek. "I do, honey. So much I can hardly believe it."

"Then, why?" She hesitated. "Is it about me and . . . Rob?"

"No!" The single-word reply practically exploded from deep in his chest. Then his expression gentled. "Never think that. I'd like nothing better than to tie you to me for the rest of our lives—but I have more responsibilities than I can handle already. I told you about them, remember—that night up at my cabin."

Jill shook her head. All Kyle had said was that the cost of taking care of Alyssa—and Dolph—left him with very little money for himself. Suddenly she realized *that* was what he meant—that he couldn't afford a wife. She couldn't help smiling.

"Kyle, money is not a problem. My grandmother left me a small fortune."

Suddenly Kyle sat up in bed and glared down at her. "It may not be a problem to you, honey, but it damn sure is to me. I may be a lot of things, but I take care of my own obligations. It would be a cold day in hell when I'd live off my woman. I'd better get up and get to work," he told her as he let go of her shoulders.

Jill watched him get up and jerk on his clothes. She

blinked away tears that she couldn't seem to control. When he came over to the bed and caressed her cheek, she reached up and clutched his hand.

"Let's just forget this whole conversation, honey," he muttered. "Let's not let it spoil the time we've got left."

When he pulled his hand away and strode out of the bedroom, the tears came again, this time with painful, heartbroken wails.

"Now, now, my dear, calm yourself," Laura murmured, more distraught because this dear young woman was hurting than losing her own hope of sharing an eternity with Cyrus.

"I—I can't. For the first time in my life, somebody loves me, but he won't let go of his silly pride so we can be together. I hate him!" Jill pulled the quilt tighter around her shoulders, as if the chill of the room had invaded her heart.

"Men are prideful creatures. I know my Cyrus chafed at the thought that much of his wealth had come from his late wife's dowry. How much more vulnerable Kyle must feel knowing that without your contribution, he could not provide you with even the basic necessities of life."

"But he could. He must know that I would go with him anywhere. That I need him, not luxuries he can't afford."

How could Miss Carey, obviously well taught in the carnal ways of loving a man, be so lacking in knowledge of the forces that shape a man's mind and heart? *Her family should be ashamed! How can I teach her in the piteously short time I have with her, what they neglected to impart by word and example over a period of years?*

Laura left a rocking chair that reminded her of the one she had bought to rock the baby who had died with her, and floated closer to Jill. *"My grandson needs to feel like a man. A good man. Good men do not accept the charity of the women they love."*

"Charity? I didn't offer charity."

"Obviously, my dear, my grandson views taking from you as accepting charity."

"What's money for, if not to make life comfortable for yourself and those you love?"

Laura paused. From all she had read and observed, the roles of men and women had changed much over the years. Married women often worked outside their homes, apparently with their husbands' approval. How was sharing wealth a woman brought with her to her marriage so different?

"Perhaps Kyle is being a bit irrational, my dear," she murmured sympathetically.

"Yes, he is." Jill paused, as if she was trying to figure out something of great consequence. "I don't think it's so much the money thing—although he certainly has an old-fashioned attitude about that—as it is that Kyle insists on punishing himself forever for his little girl. And Dolph."

Yes, Laura thought, *Dolph is the key to the tangle of regret and remorse that is keeping you and my grandson apart.* Yet she had no answer, no solution that would break through very real obstacles to these young people's happiness—and the freedom that now appeared improbable for her and Cyrus.

"Do not despair, dear. Circumstances can change." Laura started to float away. Yes, she thought, circumstances *could* change, but for the first time she began to doubt that the two young lovers would resolve their differences in time to save her and Cyrus from spending eternity apart.

"You know, young man, I felt much the way you feel today, some one hundred and twenty-five years ago. I had little choice but to swallow my pride and stand at the altar with Patience Delavan."

Kyle looked up from the piece of heart pine he was cutting to replace a rotted floorboard in a bedroom Jill planned to use for her mail-order decorating business. The ghost of Cyrus Bliss had appeared as if by magic, right there next to French doors that still needed a final coat of varnish.

"What do you and this Patience Delavan have to do with

me? If you've got eyes, you can see I'm busy." Kyle was still smarting from having rejected Jill's tempting offer of marriage.

"Patience was the reason Bliss House still stands—the reason my children could flee and live in comfort far away from the place they associated with shame for what I did. To save my home, to make my mother's last years bearable, I wed her for her dowry."

"Then you deserved to be miserable."

"But I was not. Patience brought me much besides wealth. Together we found joy in each other and in our children. When she passed away, I grieved deeply. It took ten years, and my beautiful Laura, to bring joy back into my life."

Kyle stared at Cyrus's shadowy figure, considering what he had said. "What does this have to do with me?" he finally asked.

"Merely that your misplaced pride may cost you the joy you could have with this woman you have come to care for."

Joy? Kyle laughed, a hollow and false sound even to his own ears. "The last thing I deserve is joy. You've seen my brother. You forced me to tell you my only child will live out her existence without ever seeing, hearing, or feeling anything except—just maybe—some pain she will never be able to tell anyone about. Damnit, old man, I have what I deserve—a life devoted to paying for my mistakes, without room for anything or anyone else."

"You caused your brother's paralysis? Your daughter's affliction?"

"Of course I didn't. Not intentionally. But they're the way they are because of me—of my selfishly putting my own needs above theirs. I owe it to them to give them the best care I can. That costs a ton of money. Just about all I can manage to make."

"Too much for you to support a family of your own?"

"Dolph—and my daughter—are my family," Kyle snapped, suddenly annoyed with Cyrus not just for interrupting his work, but also for his interference. "Look, what gives you the right to stick your nose into my personal life, ghost?"

"The desire to see your grandmother happy again." Cyrus floated over to lurk just inches from Kyle's face, and that made Kyle even angrier.

"Well, I'm afraid that if you're pinning your hopes on me, you two will just have to rot in hell, or whatever your fate is supposed to be, if you don't find some other relative to manipulate into a hasty marriage. I can't afford any wife, especially not one whose bank balance would have made you look like a pauper when you were alive. And there's no way in hell I'm going to live off someone I love. I'm not you."

"Shed that hair shirt, Randall. You don't fit the image of a penitent." Cyrus began to back away, shaking a ghostly fist as if in frustration.

"I wish you had the amoral nature of old Harry and some of your other Randall forebears from generations past," he muttered as he floated out of Kyle's line of vision.

Chapter
Thirty-Three

THE GHOSTS

"Cyrus, calm yourself. If you do not, I fear you will suffer apoplexy." Laura hurried over to her lover and tried to still his jerky, pacing motions.

"So near and yet so far . . . "

The attic where they had spent most of their time since their deaths suddenly made Laura feel uncomfortably closed in. She feared for Cyrus's well-being when he got anxious like this! *"That's better, my love,"* she murmured when he finally ceased his erratic motions and settled on top of a dusty trunk.

"He is as cussedly stubborn as any of your murderous husband's worthless kin. Unfortunately for us, this Randall lacks the usual family traits of greed, laziness, and lack of

conscience. He has too much of you in him. Laura, dearest, we must prepare to say good-bye."

The look in Cyrus's eyes made Laura want to cry. Poor dear, he had been so brave and strong for her over the years. Now was her turn to comfort him. *"We still have nearly three weeks. I want to talk to Dolph."*

"No!" Cyrus's reaction was as Laura expected. He had always told her he feared that one day she would slip into that ghostly trance that allowed her to see and communicate with others outside Bliss House—and not come back. She feared that, too, for the mind journeys left her drained.

Time was running out, though. And Laura sensed strongly that she had to talk with Dolph.

"Yes. Cyrus, you will always be my love. I'm leaving now," she murmured as she sat by the window and concentrated on visualizing her other great-great-grandson.

Chapter
Thirty-Four

As he lay strapped snugly to Dr. Granger's examining table, feeling naked and vulnerable under the flimsy white sheet, Dolph wished he had given himself a couple of weeks to think this over. He shivered, as much from apprehension as from the chill of the room.

"Doctor will be in right away. Will we be all right by ourselves?"

The young nurse who had gotten Dolph undressed and helped a coworker lay him out on the table in the hospital's outpatient clinic sounded nervous. She irritated the hell out of him, treating him as if he'd lost his mind as well as the use of his body.

"I'll manage." *Where in hell do you think I'd be going and how do you think I'd get there?* he thought nastily, his anger fueled by the memory of her reaction when she'd pulled off his pants and taken a good look at the parts of him that might as well not be there.

"You be good now." With that, the nurse flounced out. He heard the door open, then close, and he figured she was finally gone.

He didn't feel alone, though. It was as if there were a silent presence in the examining room, looking down on him. Dolph didn't have time to think much about that, though, because Dr. Granger appeared almost immediately.

"Feel that?" Granger asked in greeting as he ran a cold, blunt probe down the inside of Dolph's left arm.

"Yes." The damn thing nearly froze his skin.

The neurosurgeon took the probe away and looked Dolph in the eye. "You won't six months from now if you don't have this operation. I assume that since you're here, you're ready to get on with the program?" Not wasting any motion, he stripped back the sheet and quickly examined Dolph's lower trunk and legs.

Dolph hesitated. For a second he thought he heard a disembodied female voice say softly, *"Do it, Dolph."* Shrugging, he told himself his mind was playing tricks, reacting to the fear he had of leaving Alyssa alone, with Kyle to pay her bills—but no one to love her.

"Randall?" Granger rumbled when he finished dictating some incomprehensible data into the handheld recorder he never seemed to be without.

"Yeah. I thought I'd check in to the hospital in a couple of weeks—as soon as my brother finishes a project he's working on up near Gray Hollow."

"You're checking in today. Now. Your admission is arranged, and I've scheduled your surgery day after tomorrow—not a moment too soon. The MRI shows a lot of new damage, and I want to have a shot at making you better than you were, not just keeping your stubborn body alive."

"You could be better. Do more. For your sake, let this doctor work his magic on you."

There it was again, that gentle, high-pitched voice that

sounded as if it were coming from far, far away. While the unseen presence scared Dolph shitless, he couldn't help but listen.

"Okay. But I've got to let Kyle know."

"You can call him from your room. Meanwhile I'll send someone in to get you into a hospital gown and take you up to radiology for more tests." With that, Granger left as abruptly as he had arrived.

While he waited Dolph heard that voice again, murmuring encouraging platitudes he wanted yet feared to believe. Then the voice stilled. Soon he no longer felt that eerie presence that had been with him since they had left him here, alone.

Resigned to follow through with the decision he had made, Dolph imagined how he would live his life if Granger was right and the operation succeeded.

Lying on the metal table, Dolph shivered from the cold. Winter had never been his favorite season, but since his injury, he had come to hate it.

Florida. He would go to Florida, find a job helping troubled kids. He pictured himself playing wheelchair basketball—maybe even giving marathon racing a shot.

He'd laze on sandy beaches, let warm waves soothe his body. He imagined himself strong, self-sufficient, as he hadn't been for so long he'd nearly forgotten the feeling. For a brief moment Dolph even saw himself responding to the come-hither smile of a beautiful woman.

"Time for us to go to X ray."

Oh, God, he thought. That little nurse was back, with her penchant for plural pronouns. Dolph tried not to show his annoyance, but when the woman left him in his room two hours later, he lay back and said a prayer of thanks that he was rid of her. After a few minutes' respite he picked up the phone and placed a call to Kyle.

It had been a hell of a day, between taking a tongue-lashing from the ghost of Cyrus Bliss and feeling even more guilty than usual every time he looked and saw hurt and confusion stamped on Jill's face. It hadn't helped that he had been so distracted that he had smashed a hammer into two fingers, either. Morosely Kyle inspected the swollen thumb and middle finger on his left hand.

His cabin had never felt lonelier, but he had needed to get away from Bliss House to think things out. Damn it, it wasn't as if he didn't want to spend a lifetime with Jill. But she had known as well as he that he would never be in a position to offer her marriage. Why had she gone and proposed and put him in the position of hurting her by saying no?

And why, for God's sake, hadn't she dropped the subject when he had first refused? Kyle couldn't believe she actually thought he would allow her to support them!

Cyrus's lecture had bugged him, too. That ghost had no compunction about sticking his two cents' worth in whenever he felt like it—never mind that what he was butting into usually wasn't his concern at all. Kyle had wanted to throttle old Cyrus, and it frustrated the hell out of him that he couldn't grab hold of something that didn't exist—much less pound it to a pulp.

After the ghost had left, his words had remained, ringing in Kyle's ears and distracting him from his work. His thumb and finger throbbed, reminding him that he had stupidly whacked them with a hammer—something he hadn't done since he was a kid.

The cell phone's shrill beep caught Kyle's attention, and he fumbled to get it out of the pocket of his jacket. Hearing Dolph on the other end surprised him, since they had talked yesterday morning. The news that his brother was going to have surgery in just two days amazed Kyle.

After telling Dolph he would be at the hospital the next morning, Kyle set the phone on the table and tried to relax. He had been practically begging his brother to have this operation for months—but Dolph's sudden decision to go through with it shocked him. Kyle couldn't help wondering if Dolph's worsening condition had made the operation critical.

Since yesterday, dizzyingly rapid changes had overtaken Kyle's usually stagnant life. He thought again of Jill—and the proposal he would have loved more than anything to accept. Snatches of what Cyrus had said this morning rang in his head.

"... little choice but to swallow my pride and stand at the altar ... I wed her for her dowry ... she brought me much beside the wealth I needed ... we found joy in each other and in our children."

"Your misplaced pride may cost you joy. Shed that hair shirt, Randall."

Kyle recalled Cyrus wishing he was an ass like so many of his Randall ancestors. Ironic, he thought, since he had always held on to his stiff-necked pride largely so people wouldn't look at him and see another Randall good-for-nothing!

He had to admit, though, that by saving his pride and giving Jill up, he would make both of them miserable. And while he had been used to preserving his pride at the cost of his own pleasure, Kyle decided it was wrong to soothe his ego at the expense of the woman he loved.

She wanted him. He sure as hell wanted her. Kyle figured that since old Cyrus had made a success out of marrying for money, he should be able to succeed at marrying *in spite of* it.

His decision made, he picked up the phone. Just as abruptly, he set it down. What he wanted to say to Jill he needed to say face-to-face, at the haunted house where their relationship had begun. Grabbing his parka, he headed out into the snowy night and carefully wove his way down Hunter's Mountain.

A night without Kyle was hell. What would the rest of her life be like? Jill paced through the nearly finished rooms of Bliss House, seeing his touch in every hand-carved baseboard, each gleaming inch of the pine floors he had meticulously buffed and refinished.

Part of Kyle will stay here in this house. Jill wondered how she could live here, alone with the memories of a love that blossomed like the haunted house under Kyle's skilled hands.

What will become of Laura and Cyrus?

The ghostly couple weren't going to get their wish—at least not with Kyle and her. They hadn't told her, though, what would happen with them if the spell they were under wasn't broken soon . . .

"December tenth. Eighteen days now. If we cannot bring you and my great-great-grandson together by then, Cyrus and I will be doomed to spend eternity apart."

Laura had materialized just outside the parlor door. She sounded tired—and a bit hopeless, Jill thought sadly. "I'm sorry," she murmured to the ghost's wavering image.

"I haven't given up yet. You must not, either." With that Laura began to fade away.

Feeling sad for the ghostly lovers as much as for herself, Jill stared in the direction Laura had gone. Then she shook her head. She would go to the kitchen and try out the new microwave on one of those prepackaged dinners she had put into the freezer earlier. She doubted she would ever be hungry again, but going through the motions of living would fill a few lonely moments.

The wind played its mournful tune in bare limbs of the trees outside. The microwave's monotonous hum blended into the silence, too. Jill sat at the table, staring out into the darkness, not able to erase the memory of Kyle's gorgeous face—or the stubborn way his jaw set when he was determined not to listen to reason.

Before she saw him, she felt his presence. His big hands warmed her shoulders that had, just seconds earlier, been trembling from the cold. "Jill?" he said softly, as if he doubted his welcome.

"Kyle?" Why had he come back? To share her bed, as he had said this morning, until he had to leave?

"I've been thinking."

Jill turned to meet his gaze. Her breath caught in her throat at the sight of him, looking somber and more than a little bit afraid. "Well?" she prompted.

"I love you. You say you love me, too. I guess if you can take my living off you, I can live with having you help pay the bills. If you still want to marry me . . ."

"Oh, yes!" Then Jill saw the worry lines at the corners of Kyle's deep green eyes. She didn't want this, not unless he really wanted it, too. "Kyle, what's wrong?" she murmured, pulling him toward the table and motioning him to sit down.

He held her hand, gently massaging the finger he had just offered to adorn with his wedding ring. She felt rather than saw him shrug. "Too much going on. It's not every day that a guy gets proposed to, chewed out by a ghost, and smashed up with a hammer—or that he learns his brother will be going under a surgeon's knife in less than forty-eight hours."

Poor baby! Eyeing the swollen, discolored thumb and fingers now stroking her left hand, Jill figured Cyrus must have been at his ghostly, acid-tongued best to have made Kyle become so uncharacteristically clumsy. Since he had certainly appeared calm enough when he'd turned down her impulsive proposal, she doubted that *she* had contributed much to his little accident.

Suddenly Kyle's last comment registered. Dolph was going to have his operation—the one Kyle had said he thought his brother would keep postponing. "Dolph. Is he worse? Did something happen?" she asked, concerned.

"Not unless my brother's keeping secrets. I'm going to have to stop working here for a few days, though. Go back to Greensboro. I want to be there when he has the operation."

"Of course." Jill started to ask Kyle if he wanted her to go with him—then hesitated. She knew it would take her a while to believe he had changed his mind—that he wanted to spend his life loving her, in spite of it all.

"You're sure? About us getting married?" she asked, not able to shut her mouth before the impulsive question popped out.

"Yeah. I've thought things through. I won't lie, honey. It's going to bug the hell out of me, having to let you help support us. I didn't think I could do it. Bottom line, though, is that I really love you, more than I ever thought I'd love a woman." He paused, reaching over to tilt her chin up so she would have to look him in the eye.

"Other than loving you, living with you, there's nothing else that matters. You are going to marry me, aren't you?"

"Yes, I'm going to marry you."

How could she refuse, when a lifetime with Kyle was what she wanted most? Jill hesitated. She wouldn't be certain her dream was really going to come true until they said the words that would bind them together for the rest of their lives. "When?" she finally asked.

"When?"

"When do you want to get married?"

Kyle ran his fingers through the thick, dark blond hair Jill loved to touch. "We might as well do it soon—maybe if we do, our ghosts will vacate this place and leave us here in peace."

Laura had just mentioned a date. What was it? Jill strained her memory. "December tenth," she murmured. "That must be the hundredth anniversary of Laura and Cyrus's deaths."

Kyle shook his head. "That's less than three weeks away, honey. I don't know, with Dolph . . ."

"I thought just a small ceremony right here, in the parlor where I first saw you in that dream I told you about. You don't want a big wedding, do you?" She hadn't figured Kyle for a guy who would go for a splashy, three-ring circus, but then there were so many things they hadn't discovered about each other yet.

"No. I'd be kind of partial to doing it in the master bedroom," he said with a grin. "I just don't like the idea of getting married while my brother's lying helpless in a hospital."

"Neither do I. How long will his recovery take?" Needing to touch Kyle, persuade herself this conversation was for real, Jill stood up and moved behind his chair, rubbing her hands over the tightly knotted muscles of his broad shoulders.

She felt him shrug. "I'll know more after I get to Greensboro tomorrow and talk with Dolph's doctor. But I like the idea of making Cyrus sweat it out until the very last minute. How about planning for—the tenth of December, didn't you say? Then Dolph may be able to come here. But if he can't, we can be married in his hospital room."

Cyrus must have really let Kyle have it, Jill thought, stifling an evil grin. "All right. Do you have to go to Greensboro right away?"

"In the morning. I'd like to spend tonight with the woman I'm going to marry." Kyle got up and wrapped his arms around Jill, nearly taking her breath away.

"I'd like that, too," she replied softly, letting the feel of his big, hard body against hers lull her into a dreamy kind of anticipation.

"Have you had dinner yet?" The insistent beeps from the microwave oven reminded her why she had been standing here in the kitchen when Kyle arrived.

"No." A rumble from Kyle's stomach accompanied that single-word reply, so Jill pulled away from him and retrieved her dinner from the oven. Now, since he was here, her appetite had returned.

"I hope there's enough here for both of us." She set the plastic tray in the center of the table and carefully pulled the shrink-wrap cover off the prepackaged lasagna. She imagined it would be quite enough. It didn't look or smell a whole lot like the savory stuff she had eaten in Italian restaurants.

Kyle sat back down, and she went to find some eating utensils. "Don't go to any trouble, honey," he told her when she scooped out more than half of the lasagna onto a plate and set it down in front of him.

After shoveling the rest of the food onto her own plate, Jill sat down and watched Kyle take a bite. She followed suit. God, but the stuff was awful! "I don't know how to cook," she confessed.

He laughed. "That's okay. We can learn together. My stomach's gotten used to this stuff, but I think I'd like a real meal, cooked at home instead of some place like Maida's."

Jill pictured them here in the kitchen, having fun together while fixing dinner on a winter evening. That made her wonder. Would they live here, in this house she had come to love? "Kyle, where are we going to live?"

He looked up from his nearly empty plate. "I thought you'd want to live here, after you've spent so much money restoring this place."

"I do—but you've got your home and business in Greensboro. And Dolph."

Kyle ran a hand through his hair and stared out at the woods behind the house. Jill imagined this was the first he had thought about the mechanics of merging their lives. Finally he spoke. "I can store equipment anywhere. And I do very little in the way of actual construction work in Greensboro. Dolph could come here, stay at the cabin. . . ."

"He could even stay here. There's plenty of room," Jill interjected.

Kyle shook his head. "I don't think so. He wouldn't stay in the house with me when I was married to Tina. I love you for suggesting it, though." He took her hand. "Look, honey, we can sort this through later. Right now I'd like to take you to bed and show you how much I love you."

Jill had no problem with that! Kyle was right. They could work through the details later. Now she wanted to hold him, love him, persuade herself this all was real.

Chapter
Thirty-Five

THE GHOSTS

"Cyrus, they're going to set us free!"

Laura sounded so weak, so frail, Cyrus feared she would simply fade away. And for nothing! His Laura had risked her future, but it now appeared that it was his own stern talk with young Kyle Randall that had done the job!

"Do not excite yourself, my dear," he murmured, hovering as close as he could to his lover, his friend . . . his very life.

Laura lifted her hand, as though she could touch and hold him. *"December tenth. I must rest, regain my strength so I may help dear Miss Carey plan her wedding."*

"Harrumph!" He, too, had heard the young lovers set their wedding date—and he had seen the evil grin on Randall's face when he had mentioned waiting until the last pos-

sible moment, just to torture Cyrus. *"Randall should have thought of you, his great-great-grandmother, and insisted upon marrying her today!"*

"Cyrus. He set the date to give Dolph as much time as possible to heal, yet still marry Miss Carey in time to break this curse on us. It pains me to see you so bitter toward my children, my love."

"They are of old Harry's seed as well, Laura. Still, I make myself remember that Kyle and Dolph Randall carry something of you, too."

Deep in his heart, Cyrus knew that his rancor toward all Randall men dishonored the woman he loved. Still, old memories haunted him, just as he and Laura had haunted Bliss House for all these years.

He watched as Laura drifted off to sleep, praying that rest would make her strong again. Then, in the darkness of the late-November night, Cyrus relived the horror of those last moments of his—and Laura's—life.

The bedroom window shattered. A gust of frigid air made the dim light of the coal-oil lamp flicker out, and made the flames in the fireplace leap. A huge monster with a shaven head burst into the room, clad in grimy black-and-white prison stripes. No, not a monster, but a drunken parody of his lover's evil husband, Harry Randall. Cyrus gathered Laura's ripening body in his arms.

Harry cackled, an eerie, terrifying sound that froze Cyrus to the bone. Cyrus hesitated. Dare he get up to try to over-power this madman? Or would Harry go after Laura the moment he let her go? Frozen by indecision, Cyrus cradled Laura in his arms as her husband stared down at them with murder in his beady eyes.

Then in the space of a single tortured breath, it was too late. The oil lamp shattered against the headboard, and the bed went up in flames.

"You're going to die, bitch. You and your high-toned lover who got me locked away in hell are going to die for what you did. I've spent three years in that rat hole of a prison—now you are going to spend a hundred here in this house you seem to like so well. . . ."

Cyrus had never forgotten the wild look in Harry's eyes when he had doused the bed with coal oil from the lamp and painstakingly lit a match. The sound of Harry Randall laughing as he tossed that match onto the bed would stay with him for all eternity.

The rest of Harry's curse, etched in Cyrus's memory by excruciating heat and agonizing pain, faded as the ghost recalled the moment of his death, when Harry's twisted face faded from his vision as his own arms slackened, letting the lifeless body of the woman he loved slide relentlessly onto the flaming mattress.

Chapter
Thirty-Six

"You send me up in flames," Jill murmured, her fingers tunneling gently through Kyle's tangled hair.

Kyle chuckled. "You're pretty hot yourself." There was something magical about this room—some quality that made the staid, Victorian bedroom as sensual as he imagined a sultan's bedchamber must be. "I'm going to miss you for the next few days," he murmured as he idly traced around her pert, pebbly nipple with the tip of his index finger.

"Want me to come with you?"

He did, and yet he didn't. Kyle didn't know what to expect, with Dolph suddenly having this surgery, and he didn't want Jill there if things turned out badly. "Let me go alone first. If I need you, I'll call."

"Okay." She snuggled closer, stoking his fires.

Kyle responded immediately. It would never stop amazing him that he could drain himself into her eager body one, two, even three times in a night, and still get it up for more. Being married to Jill, sleeping with her every night, was going to kill him! "What a way to go," he mumbled as he levered his body over hers.

"What?"

"You're going to send me to an early grave, but I don't think I'm going to mind," he told her as he fit their bodies together and filled her in one hard thrust.

The next morning he woke her with a kiss. "I'll have to owe you an engagement ring," he said when he caressed her naked left hand. "Okay?"

"Okay. But if you're feeling sentimental, you can give me this. I think it must have been Laura's." Jill stretched out, then padded over to the Victorian oak dresser they had found at an antique store outside Greensboro. Curious, he watched as she rummaged through a drawer. "Here," she said as she slid the drawer shut, "this is a locket I found in this room, that first night we made love."

Kyle looked at the piece of jewelry Jill had dropped into his hand. The locket was small and delicate, like Jill, and the chain was thin and finely wrought. "Come over here," he said, and he fit it around her slender neck. "This looks as though it was made for you. You can consider it your engagement present from our ghosts."

"That's sweet, Kyle."

He didn't feel sweet, he felt horny. Kyle figured he had best get out of this magical room—out of Bliss House—if he intended to drive to Greensboro. "I've got to go, honey," he told her as he started pulling on his clothes.

"I'm going to marry her, Dolph."

"I'm glad. I think Jill is just what you need. I'm just surprised you gave in so fast, considering how you feel about not being able to support her." Dolph sounded drowsy, which shouldn't have surprised Kyle since he had watched a nurse add some kind of sedative to the IV that was dripping into his brother's left arm.

"She wants you to live with us at Bliss House," Kyle said, wondering how Dolph would feel about the idea of going back to Gray Hollow, and all the lousy Randall history they'd both sworn they wanted to escape.

"I'm not going back there." The words came out surprisingly strong, before Dolph's eyelids drooped and the muscles of his cheeks slackened. "Florida . . . warm sun . . . salt water . . ." Kyle caught just a few of his brother's slurred words before Dolph dropped off to sleep.

Picking up one of the magazines from the table by the bed, Kyle glanced at pictures of sunny beaches and towering palm trees. He'd never figured Dolph was serious those times he'd griped about how the cold winters made him ache in places he'd practically forgotten he ever had. But maybe he had been.

Kyle thought of Jill and the way she loved that old haunted house in Gray Hollow. He couldn't imagine asking her to pull up newly planted roots and move—not even for his brother.

"Kyle."

"Doc." Kyle stood up and extended his right hand. He'd known Bill Granger for five years, since he had remodeled the mausoleum of a house his wife had inherited from her parents. When Dolph's condition worsened, Kyle had been the one to insist he see the prominent neurosurgeon.

"What's going on with Dolph?" he asked when Granger pulled up another chair and motioned for him to sit back down.

"More of the same—but the deterioration is happening faster than it was when I examined him three months ago. I'd wanted to operate then, but he wouldn't hear of it. It's going to be touch-and-go tomorrow."

Glancing at the bed to be sure Dolph was still asleep, Kyle met Granger's solemn gaze. "He was finishing up his last semester at college. I didn't even know until a couple of weeks ago."

The surgeon shook his head. "I'm glad he got in when he did. He has just about lost the use of his left arm, you know."

"Yeah." Kyle had watched Dolph struggle to get himself out of bed the other day. He knew his brother's strength was damn near nil. "So what all are you going to do tomorrow?"

Granger flipped through the metal chart he had been holding and fished out a piece of paper. "This." He handed the paper to Kyle.

Dolph had already signed the consent for surgery, Kyle noted as he glanced at the list of scribbled-in words he assumed must refer to the operation Granger intended to perform. "Care to translate this into something I can understand?" he asked as he gave the paper back.

"I'm going to go in and release the pressure on his spine, fuse it in three places, and do whatever repair I can to the major nerves that branch off the central nervous system. The urologist who hooked him up to that bladder catheter a couple of months ago is going to undo that while Dolph's asleep and put in a standard one."

Kyle winced. He had watched a nurse work a tube up his brother's penis not long after Dolph's accident, and the procedure had made him cringe. "Why do that?" he asked, his own plumbing aching at the very idea.

"If I'm right, Dolph will regain bladder control. We'll never know, as long as he has that tube draining directly from his bladder. I don't like the idea of having a Foley put in me, either—but it really isn't painful. I hope in your brother's case it won't be for very long."

"I hope so, too. What about the surgery?"

"I won't kid you. I've booked the room for eight hours, and it might take even longer. That means Dolph will be under anesthesia a long, long time—and that's not good, especially for someone as badly debilitated as he is now." Granger paused. "We've taken every possible precaution, but Dolph understands the risks."

Dolph could die.

Kyle had known that for years. Still he felt as if he'd been hit. "Other than hopefully letting him pee like you and me again, what is this operation going to do to make Dolph's life better?" he asked, surprised at the catch he heard in his own voice.

Granger cleared his throat. "It should help him regain upper-body strength. Stop the shooting pains that he has been having more often in his middle and upper back, neck, arms, and head. Restore his ability to control his bladder and bowels. Possibly bring back some degree of sexual function."

"All that?"

"Yes. Dolph could even get some feeling back in his upper thighs, although that might be more a curse than a blessing since he will still be paralyzed. He will get painful cramping in those muscles every now and then, if he recovers to that extent."

"Then why in hell would you want to fix whatever you're going to fix that will make him hurt more, especially if it's not going to let him walk?"

The surgeon gestured toward Dolph. "Dolph wants me to do all I can. After twelve years of feeling nothing, he said he's ready to put up with a few aches and pains."

Kyle shrugged doubtfully. "Muscle cramps aren't my idea of minor aches and pains." He'd had them more than once, after especially rough football games and workouts, and they had hurt like hell.

"Let me put it this way, my friend. The more cramps your brother gets in his thighs, the more likely it will be that he can control his bladder fully. Have sex."

"Oh." That did make a difference, Kyle thought wryly.

"You understand now?" Granger stood up and set the chart down at the foot of Dolph's bed. "We'll be taking him to surgery first thing in the morning. I'm going to keep him pretty well sedated between now and then."

"Yeah. I'll be here." Getting up, Kyle walked with Granger to the end of the corridor before going back to Dolph's room.

Dolph slept through being poked, prodded, and stuck with needles by nurses Kyle hoped were more well-meaning than they looked. He woke up briefly when the anesthesiologist came in to explain what her role would be in the surgery, then drifted off into a narcotic-induced stupor. While Kyle ate the rubbery sandwich someone had brought him for lunch, he wondered how Jill was spending her day.

"You must have fresh flowers, my dear." Laura shook her head when she looked at the photos of silk bouquets Jill had set out on the kitchen table.

The ghost was much more herself today, Jill decided, recalling how wan and exhausted Laura had appeared to be last night. If she had her way, though, this tiny wedding was going to turn into a major event. "Not too many flowers bloom this time of year," she pointed out reasonably.

Laura's shoulders sagged. *"Of course you're right."*

"But I suppose I could order some from the florist in Greensboro," Jill offered as she realized she really didn't want to make this dear, sweet lady sad. "Roses, maybe." She fingered the locket Kyle had fastened around her neck this morning.

"White roses and forget-me-nots. Like the ones that used to grow out by the carriage house."

Laura had a dreamy look that made Jill wonder what memories those flowers evoked. She pictured Cyrus in his stiff-collared shirt, picking the posies and handing them to Laura, just to show her that he cared. Picking up her pen, she noted the ghost's choices to pass on to a florist.

"What will you wear?"

For a moment Jill pictured white satin, creamy embroidered lace studded with seed pearls and sequins—every woman's dream gown for the most wonderful moment of her life. Then she remembered. This wasn't going to be that kind of wedding.

She had done this before. Everything. More than any woman should do in a lifetime. And she had done it wearing puff-sleeved pink organdy Rob had picked out—a dress that should have warned her of the dark and shameful side of him.

"I—I don't know," Jill finally replied, choking on the words. Doubts had suddenly invaded her mind, making her positive she didn't deserve the loving commitment Kyle had made to her last night.

She was afraid to trust her heart, but even more frightened of denying her feelings for Kyle. She didn't doubt her feelings as much as she feared being unable to fulfill his needs the way she trusted that he would satisfy hers. "I'm so afraid," she whispered so softly she doubted if Laura could hear.

"Now, now, my dear. Do not fear. My great-great-grandson loves you. All will be as it should."

Haltingly Jill spilled out her fears to the gentle ghost. When she was done she unhooked the locket from around her neck and held it out to Laura. "This is yours, I think."

Laura looked at the locket in Jill's trembling hand, but she made no move to take it. *"You have told him everything, all the secrets that haunt you as surely as Cyrus and I haunt Bliss House. Kyle has bared his soul to you as well. All will be well if you but believe—in him and in yourself. Now put that locket back on. It was once mine, and I loved it, but ghosts have no use for baubles. Let it be my gift to Kyle, and his to you. I believe it will bring you joy."*

For what she thought must be the thousandth time since she had come to Bliss House, Jill felt tears stream from her eyes. These tears, though, washed away the past—fears, doubts, and most of all the guilt. Finally she could look to the future with Kyle with hope as well as love.

As she fastened the locket back around her neck, she heard Laura say, *"And now about that wedding gown . . ."*

Laura described while Jill sketched. At first Jill felt she was designing the dress of Laura's dreams, but soon she realized this would be her fantasy as well. *"We have the perfect material, my dear. Come with me, and we will find it."*

By noon they had found the fabric Laura had remembered, in one of the humpback trunks in a corner of the attic. And by one o'clock Jill had dressed and driven to Maida's in Gray Hollow, eager to find the dressmaker Laura had assured her could make her very special gown.

"It's to be very simple. Old-fashioned. Ivory watered silk, with a forest-green sash." Laura had wanted the sash to be blue, but Jill had finally insisted it be dark, wintery green because the color reminded her of Kyle's eyes. "Laura told me I'd find a dressmaker named Mary McGraw here in Gray Hollow."

She watched Maida's face get pale. *Oh, God,* Jill thought. *I've as much as gone and admitted I saw the ghosts.* "Are you all right?"

"Lord in heaven, girl! You've actually been talking with a lady who's been dead a hundred years." Maida sounded as if she had been the one to encounter some disembodied spirit. "You must have been. Mary McGraw's been dead fifty years or more, but her granddaughter Grace takes in a bit of sewing now and then. Her cabin's up on Hunter's Mountain, not too far from Kyle's place."

"Could I use your phone and call her?"

Maida chuckled. "She's got no phone. Lots of folks around here don't. Got no need for 'em. Couldn't afford them if they did."

The woman's eyes still practically bugged out of her head, and Jill sensed that Maida wanted to know all about her encounter with the ghosts at Bliss House. "Do you want to know what Laura looks like?" she asked, taking pity on the store owner for her uncharacteristic reticence.

"Have you seen Cyrus, too?"

Jill's offer had apparently restored Maida's natural curiosity. "Yes. They're both there."

"Then the legend must be true. Tell me, do they look like they're more'n a hundred years old?"

"No. They must have stopped aging when they died." Jill went on to describe soft, pretty Laura and her stern, unbending lover, right down to the quaint Victorian garments they had worn each time they had appeared.

"So are you and that big gorgeous man of yours going to get married in time to save them from Harry Randall's curse?" Maida asked.

Jill nodded. "I'd better head up Hunter's Mountain and see if I can find this lady who sews."

"Better not mention your ghosts, honey. Grace is a timid little thing—she's likely to run screamin' and hollerin', and jumpin' right off the edge of Hunter's Mountain. Probably it wouldn't be a good idea to mention Bliss House at all," Maida advised as Jill hurried out the door.

By the time she got home late that afternoon, Jill had arranged for Grace to make her dress. Now, after a call to a Greensboro florist to arrange for the fresh flowers Laura had described, she paced around the house, missing Kyle while she figured out what additional furniture she would need to buy right away. The parlors and dining room at Bliss House must look perfect for her wedding.

By nine o'clock Kyle couldn't wait any longer. Quietly he left his sleeping brother and went out to his truck. Hunkering down to fight off the cold, he picked up the phone he had left on the seat and dialed Jill's number.

"Hello?" Even from seventy miles away, the sexy sound of her voice turned him on.

"Hi. I miss you."

"I miss you, too. How is Dolph?"

Kyle gave Jill a brief summary of his conversation with Granger, then explained that Dolph had spent most of the day too drugged up to talk. "They're doing the surgery tomorrow morning," he concluded, wishing he'd had the guts to ask her to come be with him to hold his hand.

He smiled when she related her day. Talk of wedding dresses and bouquets would have scared him stiff a mere two days earlier, but now he was genuinely anticipating the day less than three weeks away when he would marry the woman he loved.

Remembering that roaming calls on his cell phone were anything but cheap, Kyle told Jill he had to go. "If you need me, call me here," he concluded, giving her the hospital phone number and the extension for Dolph's room.

As he hurried back into the hospital, out of the biting winter wind, he briefly considered what he would wear to his wedding. Then, while he sat in the snack bar and ate two greasy hamburgers, he pictured the ring he wanted to buy for Jill.

He had seen it somewhere, not long ago. Kyle searched his memory. Angie's Antique Boutique. That was where it had been. When he had been there a few weeks ago, looking for a handmade brass door knocker to replace the one that had practically rusted off Bliss House's old front door, the ring had caught his eye.

Hell. He'd imagined it on Jill's dainty finger the minute he'd seen it. Sensual curves of antique gold filigree blended into a cluster of red-hot rubies and diamonds not so big they would overwhelm his petite lady—or his depleted wallet. That was her ring!

Trudging over to a bank of pay phones and fishing out a quarter, Kyle called Angie and asked her to set aside the ring and a band she had assured him was a perfect match. He laughed when Angie asked if he might be in the market for a book of hundred-year-old erotica—then told the lady to keep it with the rings, and he'd be glad to look it over.

When he got back to Dolph's room, though, Kyle had a sudden sense of foreboding—that some unforeseen event was going to tear his life apart. As he watched his sleeping brother he prayed that his premonition was simply the result of nerves.

Chapter
Thirty-Seven

Jill couldn't sleep. She had never wanted to do anything more than she wanted to go to Kyle tonight. Even though he had tried hard to sound casual and upbeat when he'd called her earlier, she sensed his anxiety.

Lying there alone in the room she associated with him, she tried to calm her own fears about Dolph's surgery. He was Kyle's brother, and Kyle loved him——but even though they had met just three times, Jill felt Dolph already was a friend.

She went so far as to get up and start packing an overnight bag, but just as quickly she dumped her clothes back into the drawer. Kyle had told her to stay here——that he would call her if he wanted her at the hospital. She imagined he needed this time alone with his brother, and that her presence would just add an unnecessary complication.

It was snowing again, harder than the previous night. Jill

fretted over that as she stared through the panes in the French doors, knowing that if the snow didn't stop falling and the temperature stayed below freezing, getting down the mountain from Bliss House might prove difficult. At that thought, she laughed.

Make that impossible.

She had never driven on ice or snow. Until six months ago she had never driven at all. Driving hadn't fit Rob's picture of her as a perpetual little girl, she thought with a fleeting sense of disgust. If the weather worsened, Jill would be stranded here at Bliss House. The prospect of being alone, except for her resident ghosts, unnerved her.

"I'm going to have to get Kyle to give me some lessons about driving in this kind of weather," she muttered to those pesky snowflakes. "He'd better not want me to drive out with all of you tonight!"

Wrapping herself in the quilt she had pulled from the sleigh bed that felt too big, too lonely when Kyle wasn't sharing it, Jill curled up in the padded rocking chair and stared out into the night.

Kyle didn't know how many times he had lifted the phone to call Jill, then set it down again. There hadn't been much point in staying at the hospital, watching Dolph sleep—so he had come back here to get some rest.

His house wasn't a whole lot warmer than the outside, Kyle decided as he heaped some logs on the hearth and started a fire. The pine starter crackled as it burned hot and fast, igniting the logs.

Kyle shrugged out of his damp parka and tossed it on a chair. Then he sat on the edge of the sofa and tugged off his boots before leaning back and stretching his legs out along the sofa's length.

Damn! He might as well have kept working up at Bliss House for all the conversation he'd had with Dolph. Whatever medication Granger was feeding his brother through that IV had zonked him out but good.

Kyle mulled over what little he'd understood of Dolph's mutterings. He was glad that before the drugs had taken effect, he'd told his brother he was marrying Jill—and that Dolph had enthusiastically approved. But the other?

Dolph had been adamant about not living with them at Bliss House—but after saying so, all he had done was mutter about warm winters in Florida. Did he want them all to move there? Or did he have some demented notion of taking off on his own, leaving Kyle and all they had worked for together?

No. Dolph couldn't seriously be thinking of trying to live alone. He knew damn well, even if this operation did all Granger hoped it would, that he would still be tied to a wheelchair. How would he get along without Kyle close by to ease his way?

Kyle decided the drugs must have caused Dolph to have weird fantasies—ones he wouldn't even remember when his mind cleared after his surgery.

That puzzle solved to his satisfaction, Kyle lay back and tortured himself by thinking of Jill. He didn't want her driving here tonight, not in the snow—but sleeping without her in his arms was going to be hell!

Pulling a crocheted afghan off the back of the sofa, he wrapped up in it. Wide-awake, he stared at the crackling flames in the fireplace until it was time to go back to the hospital.

Dolph should be going into surgery about now, Jill thought as she glanced at the clock on her dresser. Getting up, she stared out the window, mouthing a silent prayer that the operation would be successful.

It had stopped snowing, and the sun shone bright. But all Jill could see was a bright, white panorama broken by the deep blue green of native spruce limbs peeking through a light dusting of the snow. Figuring that all Kyle needed today was to hear that she'd crashed into a snowbank, she gave up the idea of driving to Greensboro to keep him company while he waited for word about Dolph.

I can't drive through a little snow. I can't cook. I haven't the vaguest idea of how to sew, not even to fix a hem or put on a button. Kyle certainly isn't getting much of a bargain in me.

Determined to stop feeling sorry for herself—and Kyle, she added with a shrug—Jill slipped into warm sweats and wandered out into the kitchen. Since she couldn't go to him, and she couldn't shop for the furniture pieces she had decided she must have before the wedding, she decided she might as well do something productive.

As she sipped her instant coffee she thumbed through some magazines. Surely anyone can learn to cook, she told herself as she skimmed through some recipes. One for mocha brownies caught her eye.

Flour. Sugar. Coffee. Butter, eggs, and chocolate. Jill was certain she had bought all those items when she had stocked her pantry and refrigerator last week. She looked at the list of ingredients more carefully. The only thing she didn't think she had was vanilla. She was pretty sure *that* was just for flavoring, since the recipe only called for two teaspoonsful of it.

She figured she'd just use a bit of Kahlúa instead. Surely it wouldn't matter—no more than it would make a difference that her chocolate was Hershey bars instead of the bitter chocolate the recipe called for! "Who would want to eat chocolate that's bitter anyhow?" she asked aloud as she dug through a cabinet in search of a bowl and some kind of pan.

For the next half hour she measured and mixed, then poured the batter into a roasting pan she had found. She popped it into the oven and turned it on. Even though the kitchen now looked like a war zone, Jill felt smug. Kyle would be so proud of her when he sampled these brownies she was making with her own hands!

She set the timer for fifteen minutes, just as the recipe said. But when she pulled the pan out, she stared disbelievingly at the brownies that bore absolutely no resemblance to that mouthwatering photo in the magazine. Jill didn't know whether she wanted to laugh or cry!

"Something smells . . . interesting." Cyrus floated into the kitchen, shooting the smoking pan of brownies a hasty glance.

"They're scorched. And they're too skinny. But I'm sure they will taste just fine." Better to defend one's cooking to a ghost than to one's real, live fiancé, Jill thought as she watched one of Cyrus's elegant eyebrows lift doubtfully in the direction of her masterpiece.

"Perhaps, my dear, it would be wise for you to procure a cook before you marry young Randall."

Jill grinned in spite of herself. She had been thinking the same thing before Cyrus had appeared to witness the debacle she had made of one pan of brownies. "It would be. But Kyle is having enough problems with us using some of my money to live without my wasting it on frivolous things like cooks."

Cyrus eyed the brownies again before glancing pointedly at the disaster area Jill had created from a perfectly good kitchen. *"I would think the prospect of going hungry or contracting some dread disease would cause him more serious problems than accepting that his wife's talents lie elsewhere than in the kitchen. If he has a grain of sense, he will realize he is fortunate that his wife can afford to hire someone to prevent such misfortune,"* he replied, his tone deadly serious.

"Mr. Bliss. I resent that! Look, I'll show you. These brownies may not look perfect, but they taste just fine." She used a knife to scrape out a hunk and shoved it into her mouth.

"Ugh," she sputtered, sprinting to the sink to spit out the scorched, bitter morsel before rinsing her mouth with water straight from the tap.

Cyrus chuckled, and Jill silently seconded Kyle's suggestion to keep *this* ghost on edge until the last hour of the last day before doing the deed that would set him and Laura free.

"Cyrus Bliss!" Laura appeared beside Jill and encouraged her to drink more water, this time from a glass. *"Leave this poor young lady alone! If she feels she needs to learn to cook, I will teach her. Make yourself useful now. Take that pan outside and bury it. My grandson does not need to see it, or this."*

Jill watched Laura float around the kitchen, gathering up the ingredients she had strewn all around and putting them away. "Don't," she protested. "At least I'm able to do that."

"Describe how you made those brownies," Laura suggested while Jill scrubbed damp flour off the floor.

When Jill obliged her, the ghost shook her head and chuckled. *"I believe they meant you to use brewed coffee, not coffee grounds, my dear,"* she commented.

Jill recalled having carefully measured half a cup of instant coffee from the jar to dump into the batter. "I suppose you're right. Do you think that was what made the brownies so bitter tasting?"

"That, and the fact that they were burned. When baking, you should let the oven get hot before putting in the batter." Laura floated over by the windows and peered outside. *"Have you heard from my grandson this morning?"*

Shaking her head, Jill glanced down at her watch. "I don't expect Kyle to call until Dolph is out of surgery—and from what Kyle told me last night, I don't imagine that will be until late this afternoon." Disastrous as it had been, her cooking experiment had helped her pass the lonely morning, at least. It had surprised her to learn it was nearly one o'clock.

"I cannot imagine doctors daring such long, complicated operations. In my day, if the operation lasted longer than an hour, the person was well assured of dying." Laura shook her head, as if she seriously doubted Dolph's wisdom in consenting to this operation.

Jill had her doubts, too—not about the wisdom of Dolph's

decision but about Kyle's grief if his brother didn't survive. "Dolph will be all right, Miss Laura," she murmured to the ghost, but it was Kyle who filled her thoughts.

Kyle crumpled what he thought must be the tenth paper cup that had held foul-tasting coffee from the machine in the surgery waiting room. For the third time in the past ten minutes he looked up at the big round clock on the wall.

One o'clock. Dolph has been in there six hours, and I haven't heard a word.

Getting more anxious by the minute, he got up from the worn vinyl-covered lounge chair where he had been sitting for the last hour and strode to the information desk.

"No word?" he asked the sweet-faced volunteer. Since he had asked several times before, he didn't figure he needed to give his or his brother's name.

"Not yet. Be patient, son. I'm sure Dr. Granger will come out and talk to you as soon as the operation is finished. He's real good with families. Not like some of the doctors who work in the OR." The lady's soft drawl should have soothed Kyle, but it didn't.

"I know." What Kyle didn't know was what the hell Granger was doing to Dolph for six damn hours in that operating room! Not knowing was playing havoc on his exhausted mind. "You'll call me as soon as you hear something?" he asked for the fourth time. And for the fourth time the volunteer nodded patiently before she turned her attention to a stack of papers on her desk.

I should have brought my laptop computer, used this time to work up some estimates for that job Dolph lined up to keep the crew busy for the rest of the winter.

Fat chance! Kyle's mind was in no condition to calculate how much material it would take to remodel an outhouse, let alone a four-thousand-square-foot antebellum home!

For ten minutes, or so that ticking clock said, Kyle paced the floor of the waiting room, pausing occasionally to stare out at the snow-covered park across the road. Then he reclaimed his chair, closed his eyes, and tried hard to catch a few minutes' sleep.

Sleep wouldn't come. Kyle guessed he had drunk too much of that thick black mud the vending machine dispensed as coffee. He was wired—running on nervous energy and pure, unadulterated fear.

God, but he wished Jill were here! When he concentrated on her, he found himself relaxing and letting go of enough apprehension about Dolph to fall asleep.

"Mr. Randall?"

Kyle came awake instantly when he heard his name. Blinking his eyes until they focused on the volunteer's cherry-pink uniform, he cleared his throat. "Dolph. Is he all right?" he asked as he met the woman's steady gaze.

"The OR nurse just called. The surgery is over, and Dr. Granger will be out to see you soon."

"Thanks." Glancing out the window, he noted it was getting dark outside, so he looked down at his watch. Five-thirty. He could hardly believe he had slept almost four hours—or that Dolph had spent more than ten hours under the surgeon's knife.

How was Dolph? Had the operation been a success? Kyle paced the waiting room, wishing to hell Granger would hurry out here and end his apprehension. When he saw the doctor, still wearing surgical scrubs with a wrinkled white lab coat slung over his shoulder, Kyle strode quickly to meet him.

"Dolph is doing well, considering the time he was under anesthesia," Granger assured him quickly.

"And the operation. How did it go?"

The doctor shrugged. "I did all I set out to do. Now we just have to wait until your brother wakes up and starts to recover before we'll know just how much his condition will improve."

"Certainly you've got some idea. . . ."

"Yes. I believe Dolph will ultimately be better than he

was before. How much better, as I said before, we'll just have to wait and see."

Granger looked tired—more exhausted than Kyle felt. "Thanks, Doc," he said sincerely, knowing the man had done his best for Dolph. "When can I see him?"

"Tomorrow. I've left orders for them to keep him in ICU overnight—just a precaution. If he's come out of the anesthesia completely by morning, and if everything looks good with the surgical sites, I'll send him back up to the surgical floor."

"All right." Kyle decided there was no reason for him to stay here when Dolph would be out cold as well as inaccessible. He figured he would stop by Angie's and pick up that ring for Jill.

"I'll run some errands, then go home and get some sleep," he told Granger. "The number to my cellular phone is on Dolph's chart, in case anyone needs me." He checked his jacket pocket to be sure the phone was there.

Granger smiled. "Good idea. I'll see you in the morning." They took the elevator downstairs together, then Kyle headed toward the visitors' parking lot.

Thoroughly chilled by the time he had scraped frost off the windows of his truck, Kyle shivered as he drove along Greensboro's snow-slick streets, bringing Jill up to date on Dolph as he talked to her on the cell phone. The heater didn't kick in until just before he pulled up in front of Angie's.

The sign said CLOSED, but Kyle saw a light inside, so he rattled the door until Angie opened it up. "Didn't expect to see you today. How's Dolph doing?" she asked.

"Doc Granger says he's getting along okay—but he kept him in ICU tonight. I'd had about as much as I could take of the hospital, so I thought I'd stop by and take a look at those rings we talked about."

The soft-spoken antique dealer stepped back, inviting him in. "I put them in my office," she said, leading the way through a jumble of furniture and glassware toward the little cubicle where she did her bookkeeping. "Come on, now, tell me all about the lucky girl you're marrying."

Making his way through the maze of stuff Angie had piled in every spare spot in her office, Kyle sat down. In spite of his exhaustion, he found himself getting hard as he talked to Angie about the woman he loved. "You have the rings?" he asked, trying to keep his mind off the empty bed he'd be sleeping in tonight.

"Here. If this is the one you want, the band I told you about is its mate. They're a set." Angie handed over the pair, and Kyle examined them closely.

Up close, the ring appeared more perfect for Jill than he had thought when he first noticed it in Angie's locked display case. And he loved the narrow matching wedding band with its tiny diamonds and rubies.

"How much?" he asked, meeting Angie's gaze as he handed her the rings.

"For you, since you bring me so much business, I'll sell them at cost." The dealer named a figure that made Kyle grin.

He could handle that! "Then consider them sold. What was this book you were talking about?" he asked as he watched Angie dump the rings into a bottle of jewelry cleaner.

Reaching into a drawer inside her desk, she fished out a slim volume bound in dark green leather. "Here. Books aren't my specialty, but this one came along with a mixed box lot I bought at an estate auction a couple of months ago. According to the copyright, it dates back to 1897. Has some interesting illustrations in it, if you're into that sort of stuff. If you want it, I'll throw it in with the rings."

Handling the fragile old paper carefully, Kyle thumbed through the pages. "I'd always heard the Victorians were a bunch of prudes," he commented as he looked at beautiful illustrations of men and women making love. Some of the illustrations piqued his curiosity as well as his libido. "Looks like I was wrong."

Angie laughed. "I'd say so. Well, maybe they wrote this for the soiled doves. You think your lady will like it?"

"Yeah." He'd never met a woman as unabashedly sexy as Jill. Making love with her was like a guy's wildest dream come true. "I'd like for you to meet Jill," he added, thinking Angie might have some of the antique pieces his lady was searching for to furnish Bliss House. "You going to open up on Saturday?"

"For you, sure. What time do you want to come by?"

Kyle gave Angie's question a moment's thought. "Would around one o'clock be all right?" he asked, figuring they could go see Dolph in the morning then stop by here on the way back to Gray Hollow.

"I'll be here, doing paperwork. Just knock on the door if I've got it locked." Angie fished the rings out of the cleaning solution and dried them with a small, soft cloth. "Hold them for a minute. I think I have a box that will be perfect for them."

Kyle watched the light play off facets of the stones, glancing occasionally at Angie, who was rummaging through a box full of stuff he guessed she hadn't had time to put on shelves.

"Found it!" she exclaimed, turning back to Kyle with a big smile on her face. "If your Jill is fond of pretty things, she should love this."

A tiny box just the size to fit a ring! Kyle opened it and set the matched bands inside. Fitting the lid back on, he picked up the box and looked more closely. Angie was right. Jill *would* go nuts over this gracefully carved old mahogany box someone had buffed to a satiny sheen. "Whoever made this was a master," he commented.

"*I* thought so."

Pulling out his checkbook, Kyle paid Angie. Then he zipped the rings into a pocket of his parka and picked up the book. "Angie, thanks. You're a lifesaver," he told her as they made their way to the front door. "Jill and I will see you Saturday."

When he arrived at the house, Kyle called Jill again just to hear her voice, then called to check on Dolph and crawled into bed. The next morning, after stopping by the hospital and sharing a few words with his still-groggy brother, he headed back to Gray Hollow.

Jill's heart beat faster when she heard the crunching sound of heavy tires against the blanket of snow on the driveway. Dropping the cloth she had been using to clean an ornate humpback trunk she had brought down from the attic, she ran to the front door. Kyle was back!

Heedless of the cold in her slipper-clad feet, she met him halfway between his truck and the house. His strong arms felt so good, his mouth tasted heavenly as they came together, surrounded by the landscape of a winter wonderland.

"You're going to freeze," he said when he came up for air. Before she could protest, he lifted her in his arms and headed for the house. She wished she could stay this way forever, safe and loved.

When he set her down inside the master bedroom, Jill noticed deep circles under Kyle's eyes. He must not have had a moment's rest while he was in Greensboro with Dolph. "You need to rest," she told him softly.

"Yeah. But first I've got something for you."

She watched him shrug out of his parka and unzip one of the small side pockets. When he handed her the tiniest, most beautifully carved wooden box she had ever seen, she couldn't have been more surprised.

"Open it up," he said as he sat down and worked off his boots.

"How?" The gleaming box felt solid, the way she prayed their marriage would be. Then she felt a tiny groove that went all the way around the sides and gently pulled the two sections apart.

"Look inside." Kyle met her gaze, and she thought he looked as if he weren't quite sure how—

It was a ring, gleaming gold, with a round-cut, glittering

diamond surrounded by perfect tiny rubies and diamonds. "Kyle, I love it. Thank you!" That he had taken time to buy this while he was worried to death about Dolph meant more to Jill than she could put into words.

Tears streaming down her face, she picked up the ring and handed it to Kyle. Sitting beside him on the bed where they had first made love, she held out her hand and silently invited him to slip the ring on her finger.

"It's like you, honey," he told her as he complied with her request. "Fire and ice. Want to lie down with me for a while?" he asked, pulling her into his arms and holding her.

"Anytime at all." Even as she voiced the teasing reply she sensed that Kyle needed rest more than passion—loving companionship more than sex. "Let me hold you while you sleep," she murmured against his cheek.

As he slept Jill dreamed about their life together—and what life would be at Bliss House after the spirits of Laura and Cyrus were set free.

"Randall's back."

Laura hated the tone that came to Cyrus's voice when he spoke about her kin. While she could understand and accept his hating Harry, it wounded her for him to forget that Kyle and Dolph Randall were as much her descendants as they were her murderous husband's.

She resolved to hold her tongue. *"Yes, he is,"* she murmured politely. *"Now perhaps our two young lovers can get this wedding planned."*

Cyrus cleared his throat. *"Young Randall had best not play her false,"* he muttered, clearly in no mood to set aside old prejudices.

That made Laura furious! For a hundred years—no, longer than that, she amended—she had let Cyrus demean her. Yes, he might not realize it, but when he scoffed about her Randall kin, he scoffed at her. *"Cyrus, I am quite aware of your feelings about my family—however, I do not care to hear them just now."*

*"My apologies, my love. Much of the time I can keep
memories of our deaths at bay. Of late, however, they have
returned with a vengeance."* He crossed the parlor and settled close enough to make Laura feel vaguely uncomfortable.

Still, she understood Cyrus's feelings. The prospect of
freedom after all these years of imprisonment in Bliss House
had unsettled her as well. Always scrupulously honest, she
reminded herself that she, too, had recently relived her and
Cyrus's horrifying last moments.

"We must look to the future, Cyrus," she murmured, picking up a sketch Jill had made and handing it to him. *"Look.
Miss Carey is going to have the parlors looking even more
lovely than they were when we were alive."*

She watched his expression soften as he looked at the
drawing that depicted both rooms, opened into a single area
the way they were the first time she had entered Bliss
House. The first time she had ever seen Cyrus Bliss up
close.

*"You must have described the furnishings to her, my
love,"* he said as he took one last look, then handed the
drawing back to Laura. *"Except for the colors, she has re-
created almost exactly the look of these rooms. . . ."*

His words trailed off, and Laura imagined Cyrus was
thinking about the glittering parties—parties he had held
here with his wife, and with his children after her death. Parties she had never attended—except for that first one, the
one where she had helped to serve his guests.

Harry had been her husband then, in truth. Cyrus had
merely been her employer. It had only been later, after Harry
had turned more and more to his homemade liquor—after he
had beaten her children and threatened her—that she had
seen Cyrus as her salvation.

Remembering all that made Laura sad. *"There were never
parties here after you took me to your bed,"* she murmured
as she recalled all Cyrus had sacrificed to make her his.

Cyrus reached over as if to take her hand. *"There would*

have been, had Harry had the decency to divorce you in-stead of breaking out of prison and murdering us in our bed," he ground out, his tone and expression fierce. Then he lowered his voice. *"I am sorry, sweetheart. I'd not hurt you for the world. Soon we shall be together for eternity, and for that we have your great-great-grandson to thank."*

Laura nodded. As darkness gave way to dawn she sat next to her long-ago lover and let herself remember all that had brought them to this state of life-in-death. Her heart ached when she thought back on those first good years with Harry . . . their two strong sons, who had grown up to curse her in the streets of Gray Hollow . . . her little boy, who had died before he had truly had the chance to live . . . and the unborn child of the man she loved, whose life Harry had brutally ended before it had begun.

Perhaps, if the fates willed it, Kyle and Jill would lift the curse Harry had placed on her and Cyrus, and open the way for them to spend eternity together in a peace they had never had in this fickle, often cruel world. Perhaps this freedom would rid Cyrus of the hatred that ate at his soul. Laura could only hope.

Chapter Thirty-Eight

"I hope you got a good rest," Jill murmured when Kyle nuzzled hungrily at her neck.

He'd slept like a baby, curled up tight against her back. It felt good, waking up hard and ready, with the woman he loved warm and willing in his arms. "Uh-huh," he said, nudging her legs farther apart and burrowing his way inside that wet, welcoming heat.

This morning he wanted her slow and easy, in this cozy bed where he'd first dreamed of making love to her. It appeared she wanted it that way, too, from her languid motion, the soft sweet way she milked him . . . the gentle sigh of contentment when she convulsed inside and came, sweeping him along with her like a gently running mountain stream.

"Want to go shopping today?" he asked when he'd come down from the most profound climax of his life. A voice inside Kyle's head told him sex would keep getting better with Jill as their love grew stronger and more committed.

"Sure. But shouldn't we call and check on Dolph?" Jill rolled over to face him, her left hand reaching out to caress his stubbled cheek.

Kyle nodded, then captured her hand. He liked seeing her wear his ring—knowing he was soon going to claim her as his wife. "We'll call in a little while," he told her as he rolled over and crawled out of bed. "Want to go to Maida's for breakfast?"

"Sure."

He thought Jill had started to say more before she got up and began to dress, then shrugged off the nagging concern that something might be bothering her. It wasn't until they sat down at a booth in Maida's that he read uncertainty in her expressive eyes.

She toyed with her engagement ring. That bothered Kyle. "What's wrong, honey?" he asked, and laughed out loud with relief when she confessed her disastrous attempt to make brownies the day before. "I told you, we'll learn to cook together. Besides, with Maida's just five minutes away from home, I don't think we're going to starve." He picked up a fluffy biscuit and spread butter and jelly onto it.

"Kyle, why do you want to marry me?" Jill asked quietly.

He grinned. "So I can make love with you every night." Watching her features tighten, he decided he'd said the wrong thing. "Honey, I love you," he told her, trying to get her out of her funny mood.

She gave him a tiny smile. "Kyle, I can't cook or sew or even iron your shirts. I've never been around children, so I will probably be a terrible mother. You're not getting any bargain in me."

Children? Mother? Kyle hadn't given the first thought to having more kids. He wasn't planning to, either. Not after watching Alyssa lie there year after year, living proof that he didn't deserve the family he had once dreamed of. "I'm getting what I want," he said, forcing a bright smile as he curled his fingers around Jill's hand.

For the rest of the day they made the rounds of every antique and used-furniture store in the area. By the time they finished shopping, they had loaded the pickup truck with everything they needed—except for an elusive dining-room set.

That night he suggested they go to Greensboro on Saturday to look for the buffet and dining-room table as well as visit with Dolph. Her good mood apparently restored, Jill agreed before teasing Kyle into bed.

Feeling happier than she could ever recall, Jill rested a hand on Kyle's muscular thigh as they drove into the parking lot at the hospital. When she saw him tense at the sight of the stark, brick building, she wondered if the place held painful memories—of Tina's death . . . Alyssa's birth.

"Ready?"

Kyle sounded okay about the place. Jill guessed her mind had been playing tricks on her when he opened the door and helped her out of the truck cab, giving her a brief hug before half dragging her to the hospital entrance. Then, when he first saw Dolph, she felt him tense up again.

"Welcome to the family," Dolph said, his voice hoarse and indistinct—a contrast with the pleased expression on his face.

"Thanks." Following Kyle to the bedside, she watched him settle onto a chair before sitting down beside him. "How are you feeling?" she asked Dolph when she met his gaze.

"Like somebody ran me over with a truck."

Jill thought Kyle's chuckle sounded forced, but he came back with a light reply. "That bad, big brother?"

Dolph's face suddenly contorted with pain. "Yeah," he ground out between clenched teeth, but just as suddenly his smile returned. "That bad. That good, too. I hurt in places I haven't felt for years."

"You need some medicine?"

"It's right here if I need it, Jill." He gestured toward a pump hooked to the IV tubing that led to a vein in his left hand. "I can push that button, and feel less than nothing in just a few minutes. Being able to feel gives me such a high, I almost enjoy the pain, though."

Briefly Kyle told Dolph about their wedding plans, and Dolph related the doctor's optimism about his recovery. Because they didn't want to tire Dolph out, Kyle and Jill left after less than an hour, promising to return in a couple of days when he was stronger.

"I want to go by Angie's first. She might have the dining-room set we want," Kyle told Jill as he turned out onto a still-unplowed street.

The truck fishtailed on a patch of ice, then dug in. "How'd you do that? Did you use the brakes?" she asked, motioning toward the steering wheel as she murmured a prayer of thanks that it was Kyle, not she, who was driving.

"I let up on the gas and let it slide. If I'd hit the brakes, we'd have probably slid into one of those parked cars—or maybe a building." Pulling to a stop in front of a dingy-looking shop, he looked at her. "Didn't you drive on snow or ice in Atlanta?" he asked, a puzzled look on his face.

"No. I just learned to drive last summer. Winter weather makes me a prisoner just as surely as iron bars would."

"Well, I'll have to give you some lessons," Kyle said lightly as they waited for someone to answer his knock at the shop door. "If old Harry could break out of his prison all those years ago, you should be able to as well."

"Kyle. And this must be the lady you're going to marry!"

"Hi, Angie. This is Jill."

Jill smiled at the spare, tall woman as she and Kyle stepped inside the store. Then she spied the buffet—a rich-looking, ornately carved walnut piece that reminded her of the one she had seen in that first, prophetic dream at Bliss House. "Oh!" she cried, her hand reaching out without her conscious direction to touch the satiny wood.

Chuckling, Kyle turned to Angie. "I have a feeling you've made a sale."

About to concur, Jill turned and watched the dealer shake her head almost imperceptibly. "That sideboard is—"

"Not for sale?" Jill's spirits sank as she noted Angie's guarded expression, then saw Kyle shrug his broad shoulders.

"Oh, it's for sale all right. It and a matching dining-room table. And eight chairs."

Kyle turned to Jill. "I think Angie assumes quite correctly that I can't afford them," he said, his expression closed.

"How much are they?" The question came out before Jill could choke it back.

She watched as the antique dealer disappeared into a back room and returned with a tattered ledger. "I can't break up the set. It's on consignment from a family here in Greensboro. The least they'll take is eight thousand. I'd let you have it for that," she said, giving Kyle a shamefaced look.

"Jill?" He obviously was going to leave this decision up to her, but from the look on his face, she could tell he was not enjoying this conversation.

Her gaze shifted from him to the beautiful sideboard, and she pictured how it would look in their newly renovated home. Then she turned to Angie. "It's too much," she said regretfully. "Do you have anything similar—but less expensive?"

"If you want it, get it," Kyle said, his voice tight.

Jill shook her head. Buying some old hunks of wood, no matter how much she wanted them, wasn't worth wounding Kyle's pride.

Angie finally spoke. "If you're willing to do some major refinishing, there's a dining-room set out in the warehouse I could give you a pretty good price on."

"Could we see it?" Refinishing was one job Jill knew she could do—after all, she had rescued an old rocker from the attic, the one that now occupied a cozy corner of the master bedroom.

The oak sideboard Angie showed them bore evidence of hard use, but Jill liked imagining it had been part of some family's history over many generations. She pictured its surface satin-smooth again, its luster restored by the efforts of her own hands.

The matching table and chairs, though, appeared to be beyond repair. "Kyle, what do you think?" she asked, frowning as she traced a warped board in the tabletop with a finger.

"Do you like the style?"

Less ornate than the heirloom set she had first picked out, the oak set had a solidity Jill loved. "Yes," she told him, "do you?"

He walked around the rickety table, then knelt to check out one of the matching chairs. "Yeah. It will take a lot of work, but most of the wood can be restored. What can't, I can replace. But, honey, if we get this, there's no way we can fix it up before the wedding," he noted, echoing her thoughts.

"I know." Mentally Jill pictured the empty dining room at Bliss House before glancing at the antique sideboard again. There was something about the piece that called out to her. "We could clean that up and wait to refinish it later," she said tentatively.

She watched the conflicting emotions play across his face. "If you want the other set, honey, go ahead and buy it," he said after a long pause.

"No. This one will be perfect." There was no way Jill was going to sacrifice Kyle's ego to have that priceless mahogany dining set.

She studied the damaged table before turning to Kyle. "If you can make that table sturdy enough so it won't collapse, we'll put a piece of plywood on top and cover the whole thing with a tablecloth for the wedding. We aren't going to be using the chairs anyhow, so we can put them in the attic and repair them as we find the time."

The tension appeared to drain from Kyle's body, and he

met her gaze with that lazy, sexy smile that never failed to turn her on. Then he turned to Angie. "How much?" he asked, and they quickly settled on a price Jill thought was more than fair.

"You could have gotten the other dining room set," Kyle told her after they loaded up the furniture and settled in the cab of his truck.

Jill smiled. "I've got what I want," she replied softly as she stroked his cheek.

I should stop by and see Alyssa, Kyle thought as they began the trip back to Gray Hollow. But he wouldn't say the words out loud. These past few days, planning a future with Jill, had been so good. He wanted to savor the good times a little longer, without letting realities intrude.

The light, sexy scent of Jill and her cologne filled the truck cab, making Kyle need nothing more than to touch her, reassure himself she was real and not a dream. Taking a hand off the wheel, he covered the small hand that rested on his thigh.

As he approached the turnoff to Angels' Paradise, Kyle wrestled with his conscience. *No one will visit her today,* a voice inside him whispered. He beat that voice down. *Alyssa will never know if anybody's there or not.*

Without thinking, he squeezed Jill's hand hard as he passed that turn. "We're not stopping by to see Alyssa?" she asked, apparently surprised.

Kyle patted her hand. "Not today. We need to get that beat-up furniture out of the weather before it warps any more. Besides, I want to get you home and love you." He could see his daughter any day. Today he'd pretend it was only him and Jill—and the ghosts he hoped would make themselves scarce so he could have her to himself.

Chapter Thirty-Nine

THE GHOSTS

"Cyrus, we must leave them alone. Can you not see the way they look at each other? We may glimpse whatever it is they have brought with them much later, when we will not be intruding."

Laura settled beside Cyrus at the foot of the attic stairs. She knew he yearned to see how Jill and Kyle were refurnishing the dining room where he had insisted they eat each meal in formal splendor.

"The wanton Miss Carey and your randy descendant always look as though they can hardly wait to devour each other, my love," he pointed out, his tone resigned. *"I only wish we could gaze that way at each other again—and that you would let me glimpse the new furnishings the young lovers have brought."*

Reaching out to grasp his hand and succeeding only in stirring the air about them, Laura yearned for form and substance, too.

"I believe, Cyrus, that existing without the ability to touch and feel has been the most hurtful result of Harry's curse. Being here in your home with you for a century has otherwise been most pleasant. Please, wait here with me, at least until the children go to bed."

"Children. Those two are hardly children." Cyrus paused. *"I shall do as you say, my dear, and leave them to their mortal pleasures, for they will soon free us from this curse you say you have found somewhat pleasant. For me, the past hundred years have tried my soul."*

Laura gasped at the vehemence of Cyrus's words. *"Has this time alone with me been so vexing to you as that?"* Sometimes she thought that if Cyrus could have reached out, struck something or someone—even her—he could have worked off the bitterness he stung her with even now, when they were about to be set free.

Sighing, Cyrus leaned back against the stairs above them. *"To see you yet not touch you, hear your lovely voice as pure as it was the night we died . . . to want and yearn and have not the power to act on those wishes and needs—my love, Harry could not have devised a form of hell more devastating. Can you truly blame me for despising him and his for all eternity?"*

He sat up straight and looked deeply into Laura's eyes. *"You are all too kind. The sins of the father shall—"*

"What of the mother's sins?" Laura granted that her own transgressions had placed her beyond her children's love. Cyrus, though, had sinned as much as she, by taking another man's wife to his heart and his bed.

"And yours?" Those last words came out so softly she could barely hear them. For a moment she hoped they had not reached Cyrus's ears.

"You committed no sin. As for myself, my sin is that I failed to protect you from that brute you married."

Laura gave up. When they had been alive, she had found ways to bend Cyrus's rigid opinions toward reason—but those methods had involved the abilities to touch and soothe that their deaths had taken away. As they floated, formless now, around their attic prison, Laura tried to picture spending eternity with a man whose hatred for her family she sometimes thought nearly overwhelmed his love for her.

Chapter
Forty

Jill's heart nearly burst with love for Kyle. As she worked linseed oil into the long-neglected sideboard, she watched him set up the dining-room table he'd spent the day repairing. If she lived to be a hundred, she didn't think she'd ever tire of looking at him, even disheveled and wet with sweat.

"This thing should be safe now," he muttered, lifting the oval piece of plywood Jill had watched him cut and positioning it gently over the warped oak tabletop. "The top will have to wait. Need some help over there?"

She grinned. "Another pair of hands would make this go much faster," she said, pausing to stand on tiptoe and brush a quick kiss across his smiling lips. "I like this better than the other sideboard," she said later while they put away the cleaning supplies.

His fingers moved over the clean but still-scarred wood. "Me, too. Because we're going to make it good as new together. How about us taking a quick shower and going down to Maida's for supper? I'm starving."

"Sure." Jill's stomach growled at the thought of food, which she figured was just about normal since they had hardly eaten a bite all day after staying in bed long after they should have been up and getting ready for the wedding.

At the memory of them lying together, leafing through that book of Victorian erotica Kyle had pulled out of his parka last night and told her was Angie's engagement gift for her, Jill felt heat rush to her cheeks. Those pictures—demure, she supposed, by the standards of today's adult bookstores—had given Kyle—and her—so many delightful new games to try, to enhance the pleasure they shared.

While she dressed she looked at the little book on the bedside table. "Want to read some more when we get home?" she asked Kyle in a teasing tone.

"Yeah."

"Okay." Jill couldn't resist a longing perusal of Kyle's big, muscular body and the way it rippled when he pulled on clean jeans.

"Look at me that way, honey, and we're going to be skipping another meal," he grumbled, but she could tell he wasn't too upset.

"We could live on love." The cliché seemed appropriate as a teasing reply, until her stomach growled again to let her know it wasn't kidding.

"Come on, woman. I don't want you to starve before the wedding." With that Kyle shrugged into his parka, grabbing Jill's jacket and tossing it playfully in her direction.

Chapter Forty-One

THE GHOSTS

"They're gone now."

"All right, Cyrus, we can go downstairs. I know how anxious you are to see how they've furnished your dining room."

Side by side, they floated from the attic to the room Laura knew would be the last one Jill would furnish before the wedding. When she reached the opened double doors, she heard Cyrus gasp.

"By God, that's my mother's sideboard!" Cyrus kept going until he could have reached out and touched the scarred top of the huge oak piece if he had been a mortal. Laura watched his stern expression soften with what had to be nostalgia as he visually traced each curve, every flaw in the satiny, polished wood.

"Look, Laura. Mother's silver punch bowl made this dent," he told her, indicating a spot on the broad tabletop.

For a moment Laura thought her memory had failed. This simple, sturdy piece was certainly not the one she recalled polishing every day so long ago. There hadn't been a punch bowl on top of it, either. That heavy, ornate bowl with its twenty-four matched cups had rested on its own mahogany table in the other corner of the dining room—when it was not in the kitchen being polished, she remembered with the tiniest bit of rancor.

"Cyrus, are you certain?" she asked as her own memories of the room became more vivid.

He had turned to inspect a heavy table topped with a flimsy oval piece of some man-made substitute for wood. Laura couldn't hold back a cry of distress. *"Certainly they are not going to serve their wedding breakfast on that— that—"*

"Table. The very table I pulled chairs like those to at dinnertime when I was young. Apparently young Randall has chosen to cover the top with this unfinished wood rather than making proper repairs."

Of late, Laura thought, Cyrus hadn't missed an opportunity, however small, to speak of her descendant with disdain. Since she had started this, however, she felt it prudent to hold her tongue. *"I cannot recall this furniture,"* she murmured neutrally.

"Of course you cannot, my love," Cyrus replied in a softer and kinder tone of voice. *"My late wife replaced this with a set more to her taste soon after we were wed. But certainly you do recall the punch bowl?"*

"Yes. I never envied Prudence or her descendants the chore of polishing it—or the cups. I was a simple woman, my dear. One who would have much preferred a simpler set of milk glass—or even that machine-made cloudy pressed glass that had come into vogue before we died."

Cyrus chuckled. *"If you had voiced your preferences*

then, I would have gladly complied with them. I would have done nearly anything for you, sweetheart."

"I had no right to ask. I was your mistress, never your wife."

"In my heart you were mine. You will be mine forever." As Cyrus voiced the words that reassured Laura of his love, he floated around a rickety chair, as if trying to decide if it were strong enough to support a mortal's weight. *"Randall is going to have to work on these chairs,"* he commented casually, as if uncomfortable with the tender words he had just said.

Not wanting to hear more of Cyrus's criticism of the young man she was proud to claim as her great-great-grandson, Laura encouraged him to share his childhood memories of Bliss House—memories of events and possessions they had not shared in life.

Chapter
Forty-Two

"I wonder where our ghosts have been hiding," Jill commented sleepily the next night as she lay in Kyle's arms. The scent of rose potpourri sweetened the pleasantly musky smell of man and woman and sex that filled her nostrils.

"I'd be just as happy if old Cyrus would stay out of my sight. You miss my ghostly grandma, though, don't you?"

Jill snuggled as close as she could and nodded. "He's a character, but I miss him, too."

She felt as well as heard Kyle chuckle. "Not me. The old guy damn near cut me to ribbons the last time he got me cornered. Figuratively speaking, of course."

"He teased me about my brownies."

"Poor baby. He wasn't teasing me." Kyle shifted positions, nudging her thigh with his renewed arousal. "Roll over, honey. Let's see if the guy who wrote that book knew what he was talking about."

They had read that chapter together earlier, the one that advised lovers on how to stay linked in sleep. The stilted roundabout language had made them laugh, but Jill had found the delicate illustration incredibly erotic. Tingling with anticipation, she rolled to her other side and fit her backside in the cradle of Kyle's muscular thighs.

His hands caressed her tummy as he found and filled her. "Be still, honey, if you want this to work," he cautioned when she began to move gently to take more of him inside. "Think of something calm and peaceful."

He felt so good, so warm and firm as they lay there in the dark as one. Soon Jill drifted off to sleep.

When she woke up, Kyle pulsed hard and hot inside her. Nothing had ever turned her on so fast, she knew as she began the motion that would bring him with her to sweet oblivion. Afterward she lay her head against his hard-muscled chest, lazily listening to his heart beating strong and slowly beneath her ear.

She could stay like this forever, she thought as she relished the mind-boggling joy of loving and being loved. Then Kyle's cell phone rang, its strident tone intruding on the precious interlude.

She got up and looked for the source of the noise. "On the dresser, honey," he directed her sleepily. "Go ahead and answer it."

Having located the phone, she pressed a button and put it to her ear. Then she handed it to Kyle. "It's a nurse at the hospital," she told him.

"What the hell? Why didn't someone call me yesterday?" he yelled, apparently wide-awake now.

Concerned, Jill sat down on the edge of the bed and watched Kyle's expression change from relaxed to irate to scared out of his wits. She didn't say anything until he tossed the phone into the covers and practically leaped from the bed.

"What's wrong?"

"Dolph's critical. Pulmonary embolism, whatever the hell

that is. He wouldn't let them call me when it started last night. Now they're getting ready to take him back to surgery. I've got to go."

Jill had never seen Kyle pull on clothes so fast. "Can I help?" she asked, feeling helpless.

"No. I've got to go. Stay here. I'll call you from the hospital as soon as I know anything." With that he shoved his feet into his boots, grabbed his parka, and headed out.

Spying the cell phone on the bed, Jill picked it up, wrapped herself in the quilt, and ran as fast as she could to catch him. "Kyle, wait!" she yelled from the porch, but his truck was already halfway down the drive.

She stared at the truck until it rounded the downhill curve into Gray Hollow, then looked at the phone. Nearly sick with worry over Dolph—and Kyle, driving hard on the icy roads to get to him—she returned to the house.

No use trying to get more sleep, she told herself as she tossed the quilt onto the bed. Staring at the phone, Jill just stood there naked, shivering against the early morning chill.

"What is wrong, child?"

Her great-great-grandson had just run out of Bliss House as though the hounds of hell had been chasing him. Now dear Miss Carey was standing in a chilly room, naked as a babe as she clutched some mysterious machine between her trembling palms. Laura hovered in the bedroom doorway, concern—and curiosity—overwhelming her natural sense of embarrassment over having invaded the privacy of Jill's boudoir.

Her motions jerky, Jill picked up a robe and slipped it on before meeting Laura's gaze. "Kyle's brother is having another operation. Oh, Miss Laura, Dolph may die," she sobbed.

No! Hadn't this elder of her two living descendants suffered enough? Laura could not have hurt more if she had still been alive. Just yesterday she had overheard Kyle say

Dolph was recovering nicely. Now he was back under a surgeon's knife? *"Surely you are mistaken, my dear,"* she murmured.

Jill shook her head as she used one of those fancy boxed hankies to dry her tears. "Someone from the hospital called Kyle. He said he would call as soon as he knows anything."

No one knew better than Laura how fragile life was. Still, the ghost's kind heart went out to this young lady who had done nothing to deserve such pain. *"We must be brave, then,"* she murmured, *"and try to go on with what must be done. Dress. I will await you in the kitchen."* With that, she floated away.

In the cozy kitchen with all its miraculous modern inventions, Laura wished she had a mortal's powers. That young woman certainly appeared in need of some strong, hot coffee and a nutritious breakfast. Wishing, however, would not change the fact that Laura was a ghost, able to see and talk and move about Bliss House—but not to do the household tasks that had been so simple when she had been alive.

As if she could will the fancy faucet to turn on, the shiny pot that made whistling noises to fill and set itself on the stove to boil, Laura stared fiercely at them until she heard the sound of human feet treading across newly polished floors. She looked up and saw Jill, attired now in what those fashion magazines had called a sweatsuit.

"What will we do today?" she asked Jill before floating over to the table and perching on one of the straight-backed chairs.

Jill shrugged. "First I'm going to have some coffee." Filling the silvery pot with water, she set it on a glowing coil and sat down across from Laura. "Maybe you'd like to tell me how to cook something?"

As Jill drank her coffee along with bread she had toasted in a machine that popped it out as if by magic, they decided on a menu. For the rest of the day Laura tried to distract her young friend—and herself—from fretting over Dolph's condition by helping her prepare a home-cooked dinner.

"What is that noise?" Laura asked when a shrill, repetitive beep kept interrupting her explanation of how to roast the chicken now thawing in the sink.

"The phone." Jill reached over and picked it up, then set it back in its cradle. "Excuse me. It must be Kyle's cellular phone." With that, she hurried into the bedroom. When she came back with the phone clutched against her chest, she was trembling uncontrollably.

"Calm down, honey." Kyle could barely understand Jill, the way she was sobbing between every word. "I was just about to call you. Dolph's out of surgery. Doc thinks he's going to be okay."

"Alyssa. It's Alyssa."

"What about her?"

"Y-you left your phone here. A lady—I think she said her name was Ellen Draper—called from her school. She's got a fever."

Alyssa had had fevers before. That tended to happen once in a while, since all she did was lie in that bed. "Calm down, love. I'm sure it's not serious. Did you catch what I said—about Dolph?"

"Y-yes. That's good. But Kyle, the person who called talked like Alyssa was pretty sick."

"Alyssa will be fine. But I'll call to check on her just as soon as they bring Dolph up to his room."

Kyle was itching to get back downstairs to the recovery room, where he hoped he'd be allowed to see his brother. After Doc Granger had told him that he had gotten rid of the blood clot, he came here to Dolph's room to call Jill—after realizing he had left his cell phone back at Bliss House. When he walked in, picked up the ringing phone, and heard her voice, he had taken it as a sign of their perfect attunement to each other.

He heard her sigh. "Don't worry, honey. I'm sure Alyssa will be all right." Then he told her how much he loved her, said good-bye, and hurried back to the surgical suite.

"Kyle, I've had the volunteers looking all over for you," Dr. Granger told him when he stepped off the elevator. "They've taken Dolph back to the OR."

"What? And why in hell are you out here?"

"He threw another embolism—a massive one. Glenn James, a thoracic surgeon, is going to try to place a vena cava umbrella."

Kyle clasped Granger's shoulders. "Speak English, damn it!"

"Embolisms are blood clots. They form in veins and travel toward the lungs and heart. A vena cava umbrella is a device sort of like a porous filter. Hopefully it will trap the clot before it can enter a lung."

What the hell has Granger been doing to Dolph for the past two hours? Kyle wondered nastily. Out loud, he simply murmured what he supposed was a polite response. "What happens if a clot does get in the lungs?" he asked.

"The person can die."

"So Dolph's life is on the line again?"

Granger nodded. "These things happen sometimes, especially when a patient has to be immobile for a while after long, extensive surgery. Glenn's the best, though. I've seen patients of his pull through when no one thought they had a snowball's chance in hell."

That endorsement gave Kyle small comfort. It was *his* brother, not Granger's, going through the third trip to surgery in less than a week! God, did he feel helpless! And did he hate that feeling!

Forcing everything except Dolph out of his mind, Kyle collapsed into the waiting-room chair he had seen more of in the past few days than he had his own bed. Drained, he propped his elbows on his thighs and used his hands to support his throbbing head.

And he prayed. Prayed as he hadn't prayed for more than twenty years, since he and Dolph had stood together at their mother's deathbed.

*   *   *

"Perhaps if we pray . . ."

"Yes. Cyrus, take my hand."

Jill didn't know the words to the vaguely familiar prayer Cyrus intoned in a hushed, reverent baritone. Somehow, though, the sound of his voice invoking God's help for Kyle's daughter and brother soothed her troubled soul. "Thank you," she murmured when he raised his ghostly head and met her gaze, then Laura's.

"Could we pray for Kyle, too? My heart goes out to him, having to cope with all this," Laura said, her voice strained.

Cyrus bowed his head again as the cell phone beeped its strident message. *Kyle! Let it be Kyle, telling us Dolph and Alyssa are both going to be all right!* Jill thought as she brought the phone shakily to her ear.

"Hello . . . I'm sorry, Ms. Draper. Kyle is in Greensboro, as I told you earlier." Jill felt her skin grow cold as the woman recounted the efforts she had made to reach Kyle. "I'm Kyle's fiancée," she said, desperate now to know if Alyssa's condition had worsened.

In clipped tones, the nursing supervisor from Angels' Paradise informed her that Alyssa's flu had progressed into pneumonia. She told Jill that Kyle's little girl was dying— that if he wanted to see the child again, he should hurry.

"Can't you do something? Take her to the hospital? I didn't know people still died of pneumonia!" Jill knew she sounded like a ninny, but she didn't care. Ms. Draper's matter-of-fact declaration seemed so cold.

She's a DNR. Most of the children here are. The woman's words reverberated through Jill's brain as she tried desperately to reach Kyle. *DO NOT RESUSCITATE. Let her go in peace.*

No answer. Dialing the hospital's main number, Jill asked for the nurse on Dolph's floor and learned he was in surgery—again. Kyle was nowhere to be found. Defeated, Jill left a message for him and turned to the ghosts of Bliss House.

"What is it, child?" Cyrus's voice was uncharacteristically hushed.

Jill quickly repeated the nurse's words. "I have to go to Alyssa. Apparently Dolph has had some kind of relapse. I can't reach Kyle. If the phone should ring, answer it—I'll have Kyle's cell phone with me."

She felt rather than saw the ghosts follow her as she hurried to the bedroom for her boots and parka. *"We can't answer the phone,"* Laura told her plaintively.

Damn it! "Why not?"

"Because we can touch and feel only those things that have remained here from the days when we were mortal," Cyrus said gently. *"Take care, my dear. I am certain your newfangled automobile is even more hazardous on icy mountains than a horse and buggy."*

Jill figured Cyrus was right as she tried to control the Bronco around hairpin curves to the main road that snaked through Gray Hollow. The trip to Angels' Paradise, which had taken only forty minutes before, stretched to three terror-punctuated hours as she negotiated roads now scraped free of snow but still dotted with treacherous patches of ice.

"She couldn't! My God, Jill will kill herself driving down those icy mountain roads." Kyle stood up, not wanting to believe the terse message Jill had left with the unit clerk at the nursing station.

Then the rest of her message registered. Alyssa might be dying. Surely Jill was wrong, he told himself as he strode to the bank of pay phones by the elevators and punched in a number. He couldn't recall the exact number of times he'd been called to his daughter's bedside, only to find her recovering from whatever ailment the attendants had been certain would be the last.

He started to punch in the number to his cell phone, then paused. Jill would need to have all her attention focused on the slippery road—he didn't dare distract her with a phone call! From memory, he dialed Angels' Paradise.

"I'm Kyle Randall," he said when someone answered the phone. "Let me speak to the nurse on my daughter's ward."

Pneumonia. Labored breathing. Rising fever. And Jill risking her neck, trying to get to Alyssa's bedside because some hysterical nurse thought his little girl was dying. Hell, Alyssa had had pneumonia half a dozen times before and recovered from it, Kyle thought dismally as he hung up the phone.

His brother might be dying on an operating table somewhere beyond those swinging doors marked STAFF ONLY. There was no way Kyle could walk out now. Scowling, he turned to the volunteer he figured had to be tired of seeing his face by now.

"No word yet, Mr. Randall," she told him before he could ask.

"Thanks."

Kyle walked over and stared out a window. The day was as gloomy as he felt. Briefly he thought about leaving, hurrying to his daughter's side where he hoped to hell he would find Jill.

No, Kyle couldn't leave. If—no, when—he woke up, Dolph would need him. And, in spite of Jill's insistence that his daughter recognized his presence on some level despite her handicaps, Kyle couldn't believe that being with Alyssa would make the slightest difference in her recovery.

Leaving wouldn't affect whether the woman he loved made it safely down those treacherous mountain roads, either, Kyle reminded himself. He tried hard to squelch a picture of that red Bronco of Jill's smashed into a snowcapped evergreen tree—and Jill slumped unconscious against the wheel.

He glanced at his watch. Three hours had passed since they had taken Dolph back to surgery; two and a half hours since he'd called Angels' Paradise. If none of the horrible accidents he'd been imagining happened, Jill would surely be there by now. Rubbing his gritty eyes, he stood and headed back to the pay phone.

The quarter Kyle had fished out of his pocket hadn't even dropped all the way into the phone when the soft-spoken volunteer called out his name. Setting the receiver into its cradle, he whirled around and strode quickly to her desk.

"You can see your brother in recovery now, Mr. Randall," she told him.

Totally focused on Dolph, Kyle bolted through the forbidding doors, his quarter and his concerns for Alyssa and Jill temporarily forgotten.

Jill's arms and shoulders still tingled, and it felt as if a dozen hammers were pounding away at her head. "Is Kyle here yet?" she breathlessly asked the receptionist.

"No. Would you like to go on upstairs?"

As she rode the old-fashioned cage elevator to the second floor, Jill silently said a quick prayer for Dolph. Kyle would have come here right away, she knew, unless something had gone terribly wrong with his brother.

At the entrance to Alyssa's ward, a stern-faced attendant stopped her. "You are . . . ?"

"Jill Carey—Kyle Randall's fiancée. How is Alyssa?"

"Not good. The nurse is with her now." The attendant looked concerned. "We moved her to a private room across the hall. You can sit with her if you like." She motioned toward the only closed door along the hallway.

Jill's throat tightened with apprehension as she opened the door. A nurse glanced up and met her gaze. "Miss Carey?"

This must be the woman who had spoken with her on the phone. Jill forced a nervous smile as she tried to remember the woman's name. "Yes. And you must be . . . Ellen Draper," she said. "How is Alyssa?" Coming closer to the bed, she observed the child's pale, clammy skin and the sound of her labored breathing.

"Critical. Have you reached her father?"

Her throat too tight to speak, Jill shook her head. "I gave a message to the unit clerk at the hospital. She told me she would see that he got it right away." She glanced down at her watch. "That was over three hours ago. I'll try again now."

"Sit down before you collapse." Ellen indicated a chair beside Alyssa's bed. Pulling the phone from her pocket, Jill hung her parka on the back of the chair before perching on its edge, phone in hand.

Before she could dial the hospital's number, the phone on the bedside table rang. Jill listened as Ellen spoke. "She's here. Mr. Randall, I believe you should come now. Your daughter . . . yes. I'll tell her."

Kyle. Jill reached out and cradled Alyssa's limp, hot hand between her palms. *Please God, don't let him lose her and Dolph, too.*

After making a few comments that barely registered in Jill's mind, Ellen set the receiver back in its cradle. "That was Alyssa's father. He said to tell you his brother is out of surgery, and that he will be here soon. He asked that you wait for him."

Where else would I go? Jill wondered, squeezing Alyssa's hand, as if she could will the child to live. "What are you doing for her?" she asked, watching Alyssa's frail chest heave with every gasping breath she took.

Ellen's expression sobered. "Trying to make her comfortable."

"It must be difficult for you. . . ."

"You mean, taking care of children like Alyssa?" Jill nodded. "It can be."

"Do you think they know you care about them?"

Ellen nodded as she placed a stethoscope against Alyssa's back. When she straightened up she frowned. "Yes, I do. If I didn't, I couldn't work here."

"Kyle doesn't talk much about Alyssa," Jill said quietly as she smoothed a damp, dark strand of the little girl's hair. "He doesn't believe she has ever responded to him at all."

"He's wrong. After his visits—or his brother's—Alyssa's vital signs always perk up. Even now, as sick as she is, I see tiny changes in her breathing that make me think she knows someone who cares for her is here."

Jill shifted her gaze from Ellen to Alyssa. "Is—is she going to die?"

"I think so."

"Has a doctor seen her?"

Ellen nodded. "Just before you came. Miss Carey, sometimes the kindest act is to let a loved one go. Your fiancé made that decision when he brought Alyssa here from the hospital nearly seven years ago. He put his baby in my arms when she was six months old, telling me Alyssa had suffered enough high-tech medicine and that he wouldn't let them hurt her more."

Jill shuddered. *What hell Kyle must have gone through!* He'd told her Alyssa had spent six months in the hospital, that Tina had been so sure the doctors could fix what she and her drugs had broken. He must have brought Alyssa here almost immediately after burying her mother.

"May I hold her?" she asked, choking back tears as she looked up at the nurse.

Nodding, Ellen lifted Alyssa off the bed, carrying her as easily as she would that tiny, flawed infant Kyle brought here seven years ago. She settled her into Jill's arms, then positioned Jill's hands to support Alyssa's limp body. Jill welcomed the feel of the little girl, so tiny for her age, yet ageless in her delicate, otherworldly beauty. Rocking gently back and forth, she hummed a lullaby she remembered from long ago.

It could have been five minutes—or it could have been an hour later—when Jill heard silence where there had been heartrending rales and rasping sounds of labored breathing. Numb, she barely felt it when Ellen lifted Alyssa's body from her arms.

Shrugging out of his parka as he sprinted up the stairs, Kyle tried to fight off a sense of foreboding. He wasn't successful. Somehow he knew, before he opened that door to the room where they isolated sick kids, that this time his child was going to die.

Jill's dark head was bowed, her body rigid against the back of the old straight chair. Kyle forced himself to meet Ellen Draper's sympathetic gaze.

"She's gone, Mr. Randall. About ten minutes ago."

"No." The denial came out as an anguished cry, and as it did so Jill sprang out of the chair and wrapped him in her arms. "I should have been here," he said between guilty sobs before breaking free of Jill's embrace and moving to the bed.

Ellen touched his shoulder. "She died peacefully in your fiancée's arms. Do you want to see her?"

Zombielike, he reached up and pulled back the stark white sheet. His little girl was dead. Gone. Yet she looked the same—beautiful and innocent, unmoving in death as she had been in life.

"Kyle?"

He turned at the sound of Jill's voice, and felt Ellen gently pull the sheet back over Alyssa's face. "Thank you for staying with her," he said woodenly. "Holding her."

"I wish I could have done more."

"I've got to go tell Dolph," he muttered, dreading the task of informing his ailing brother of his niece's death.

Ellen cleared her throat. "Have you made any arrangements?"

"No." How could he have, when he'd just now learned the news himself? "Do you . . . ?"

"I can, if you want me to. But you'll need to talk to the funeral home sometime soon."

"Do it," he snapped. The last thing Kyle felt like dealing with now was a funeral director. He had to come to terms with the fact of Alyssa's death first, and he had no idea how long that would take. He had had over seven years to come to terms with the facts of her life—and he hadn't managed that, either, he reflected guiltily.

Jill put her hand on his arm. "You can call Kyle on his cellular phone," she told Ellen quietly as she picked up her purse and jacket.

He was glad Jill had her Bronco, because he needed time alone. In just two days life had come crashing down around him, damn near crushing the breath out of him. First Dolph—although Doc Granger had assured him his brother should come through this last crisis just fine—and now Alyssa!

She hadn't been the child he'd imagined cuddling and teasing, taking camping . . . worrying about when she started school. Kyle had never reconciled himself to Alyssa's fate, never stopped regretting or feeling guilty that his daughter would never *really* live. He had hurt for Alyssa since the day Tina had delivered her two months early, her future destroyed by her mother's coke and heroin.

Yes, Kyle thought, he had hurt for his baby. He had spent damn nearly every cent he could make seeing that Alyssa had the best of care. But he had never given her a father's unconditional love—and for that he raked himself emotionally over white-hot coals.

"I don't deserve a kid," he muttered as he pulled into the driveway at his house in Greensboro and slumped wearily over the steering wheel. He couldn't make himself move to open the door. All he could think of were the times, as recently as last weekend, when he'd avoided visiting Alyssa for no better reason than that he didn't want to be reminded of her flawed existence.

His tears felt icy against his cheeks in the rapidly cooling cab. "Damn it, I should have been there," he choked out when he thought of his daughter dying. "For Jill, if not for my baby."

"Kyle?" Jill's voice—and a cold blast of air through the opened driver's door—halted Kyle's recriminations. "Are you okay?"

"Yeah." He'd burdened her enough, having her be the one there, alone, when his daughter died. "We'd better go inside."

For the next hour Jill stayed at Kyle's side as he talked to the funeral director Ellen had called and decided how and when they would finally tell Alyssa good-bye. For a long time afterward he let her cradle his head in her lap, giving him love and comfort he knew he didn't deserve. Finally he let her drive them to the hospital so he could break the news to Dolph.

"Alyssa's dead."

Dolph seemed poleaxed by Kyle's stark announcement. Jill shifted her gaze to Kyle and saw a portrait of grief colored with emotions she knew very well—remorse . . . guilt . . . shame.

She had felt that way when she'd stood beside a pauper's grave, watching them bury the runaway girl who might still be alive if not for her own inability to keep Rob satisfied. Jill felt herself tremble.

Kyle had no reason to feel such guilt. He had given poor Alyssa the best care money could buy. Moving to his side, Jill took his hand to try to give him comfort.

"How?" Dolph spoke with what appeared to be almost superhuman effort as he met Jill's gaze.

"I don't know. I wasn't with her." Kyle sounded as if he were about to cry.

Jill squeezed his hand. "Alyssa contracted pneumonia, Dolph. When she stopped breathing, she was in my arms." Small comfort that might be, but at least she could assure both Dolph and Kyle that she had given the child love and comfort as she passed from this world to whatever might follow.

"I—I'm glad you were there for her." Dolph's eyes closed, and Jill hoped this sad visit wouldn't cause him to have another relapse.

Kyle straightened his shoulders and cleared his throat. "I've arranged to bury her next to Tina. Friday."

"I want—I want to be there."

Friday was just four days away. Dolph's voice appeared

strong enough, but when Jill observed the tubes that snaked from various parts of his body, she doubted he could make that wish a reality. "Kyle has arranged for a priest to say a few words at the grave, Dolph. There won't be a regular service."

"Priest?" Dolph sounded surprised.

Rubbing a hand across eyes swollen and ravaged by tears, Kyle hesitated. "Tina had Alyssa baptized Catholic. Remember? I think she would want her baby laid to rest that way, too."

Dolph nodded and slowly opened his eyes. Jill's heart went out to him as she sensed his pain . . . regret . . . and that sense of helplessness she herself had felt when Kyle's daughter had died in her arms. "I wish I could have seen her again," he murmured after a long while. Jill wondered whether Dolph was referring to Alyssa or her mother.

"Yeah." Kyle's single-syllable response left no doubt in Jill's mind that his regrets were for not having reached his daughter in time to say good-bye. "I should have been there."

"You were here for me, instead. Kyle, you couldn't have known that this time Alyssa wouldn't snap back the way she did so many times before." Dolph let out a sigh as his head sank back against the pillow.

Jill could feel the tension in Kyle from the death grip he had on her fingers. "Look, Dolph. I'm not fit company for anybody right now," he said gruffly. "You going to be all right if we go?"

"Sure."

Reaching out to squeeze Dolph's hand, Jill said, "Are you sure?" After all, from what little she had observed, Kyle's brother had felt closer than Kyle himself to Alyssa.

The corners of Dolph's mouth drew up in a weak imitation of a smile. "I'll be all right. Alyssa will be whole and strong in heaven, the way she never would have been on earth. You concentrate on taking care of Kyle."

"Damn it, I'm not a snot-nosed kid who needs a keeper!" Kyle spat out as he snatched his hand from Jill's.

"No. You're a guy who thinks you can engineer a good life for everybody you care about. One who blames yourself when something happens that isn't in your plan. I know you—I know damn near everything you're thinking about now, and I know you need all the comfort your lady can give. Now you two get the hell out so I can rest. I've got to persuade Doc Granger to let me out of this place long enough to say good-bye to my niece."

"Let's go, Jill," Kyle growled as he grabbed her hand and practically dragged her from Dolph's room. By the time they reached the car, she could hardly breathe.

Chapter
Forty-Three

THE GHOSTS

"Calm yourself, my dear."

"I cannot. Cyrus, can you not sense some tragedy?"
Laura felt as though the walls of Bliss House were closing in on her. Something terrible had happened, some event so catastrophic she dared not try to envision it. Cyrus's deep, gentle voice belied the strained expression on his distinguished face.

She watched him float to the glass-paned windows of the front door. *"I feel pain, a pain that is not my own but that of the young people chosen to end our imprisonment. In due course I feel certain Miss Carey or your great-great-grandson will return to enlighten us."* Cyrus whirled around to meet Laura's gaze. *"I forbid you to destroy yourself, Laura,"* he said.

Cyrus knew. Over the century they had haunted his fine old home, he had somehow learned to read her mind. Her feelings mixed, Laura forced her mind back from the journey it had painfully begun and focused on the tragedy that weighed so heavily on both hers and Cyrus's minds.

"Cyrus, I must know."

"I came close to losing you, when your soul left this house before, to learn Kyle Randall's shameful secrets. I will not allow you to go again. Come, my love. Let us rest in the parlor."

"All right."

Laura knew Cyrus would never countenance her risking herself for any of Harry's kin. She would make her journey, but she would do it in secret. With any luck, Cyrus would drift off to sleep, and she could journey into Kyle's mind and heart to learn of this tragedy that had cast a pall over Bliss House.

Chapter
Forty-Four

Gloom lay heavily on Kyle's broad shoulders, Jill thought as she walked beside him to a canopied spot in an ancient Greensboro cemetery. These past days she had seen a different man than the one she had fallen in love with—a solemn, guilt-ridden shell of the vital, sensual Kyle she knew.

Barren white, muted browns, bleak grays of winter—and crumbling markers barely visible against the newly fallen snow—brought Jill vivid memories of other places, other graveside funeral services. Her heart went out to Kyle as he strode to the small casket suspended above frozen ground and stared into the hole beneath it.

Had he reacted this way when Tina had died? she wondered, staring at a simple marble slab next to the spot where Alyssa would be laid to rest. Only Tina's name and the years of her birth and death marred the smooth surface of the marker.

A strong, icy wind whirled around the grave site, piercing the thin wool of Jill's coat and dress and seeping right through her sheer stockings. At that other funeral she had been too numb to feel the cold—now, through her concern for Kyle, her senses were heightened.

She hadn't wanted to leave him long enough to return to Bliss House for proper clothes, so she had made a quick trip to a Greensboro mall late yesterday afternoon. Kyle's uncharacteristic depression had unnerved her so much that she prayed he would snap—curse and rail at the fates that had taken his child and threatened his brother's life.

Instead, he had barely spoken two words since they had left Dolph's hospital room on Tuesday. Now, as they waited for the priest—and the ambulance that would bring Dolph to see his niece put to rest—Jill watched Kyle's gaze shift from the hearse to the gaping hole just inches from where he had planted his feet.

His eyes were dry, his expression stoic. When the cleric arrived, muttering platitudes about the unfulfilled promise of a child he obviously had never met, Jill heard Kyle make wooden, correct responses. Then an ambulance pulled up, and an attendant opened the rear door so that Dolph could see and hear from the shelter of the vehicle.

Through chattering teeth, the priest murmured a prayer Jill barely heard. Then the casket was lowered. A few more prayers were said. It was as though they all had suspended their emotions, she thought after she and Kyle walked to the ambulance and said a few words to Dolph before going back to her Bronco and heading to Bliss House.

As they sat silently in the front seat Jill realized she had shrunk into a shell of regret and recrimination when she likened Alyssa's death to the child's Rob had killed. Thinking that her own depression might have fueled Kyle's, she forcibly shoved those old guilts and hurts to the back of her mind and vowed to bring back the Kyle she loved—the Kyle who loved her in return.

As Kyle reached to open the door, a gust of wind wrenched it from his hands and flung it open to reveal the scowling face of Cyrus Bliss. *Cyrus! The last person—or thing—I need to see today,* Kyle thought nastily as he met the ghost's censuring gaze.

"Laura has been frantic for damn nearly a week. What can you mean, leaving her here without a word of your whereabouts, you—you inconsiderate Randall reprobate?"

Before Kyle could take a futile swing at the ghost, Jill grabbed his hand and spoke in the soothing voice that had kept him halfway sane since this nightmare had begun.

"Mr. Bliss, Kyle's daughter died on Tuesday, not long after his brother had to be operated on for the third time. We've just come from Alyssa's funeral," she explained to the formless creature Kyle believed had stayed here for the sole purpose of making his life miserable.

The stern set of Cyrus's features softened. *"My sympathies, young man. From what you have told your grandmother and me, the child's passing has to have been a blessing. I trust your brother is faring better now?"*

Kyle nodded. "I can't handle talking now," he said shortly, heading toward the bedroom where he hoped the ghosts of Bliss House wouldn't dare intrude. As he went he half listened to Jill's soft-voiced account of all the sad events since they had laughed and loved together here.

Pausing only to take off his shoes, topcoat, and suit jacket, Kyle sprawled across the bed. Riddled with remorse he couldn't shake, he lay there in the late-afternoon shadows and tried to clear his head. The last conscious thought he had was of Jill, standing by him even when she had firsthand proof of what a selfish bastard he really was.

He felt her hands on him, gently loosening the burgundy-striped tie he had put on this morning—unbuttoning his light blue dress shirt and slipping it off his shoulders—loosening his belt and unzipping his slacks. The scratchy wool material tugged at the hair on his legs as she pulled the slacks off, and her fingers tickled his feet when she rolled down his dress socks. The soft quilt she spread across his naked body soothed and warmed skin that had prickled from the chilly air in the room.

Kyle figured he had to be dreaming. Before the funeral, Jill had lain at his side at night, stood by him all day while he went through the motions of putting Alyssa to rest—yet he had felt a distance between them, one he figured he had earned by his callous refusal to go to Angels' Paradise the moment he knew his daughter had become sick again. Hell, why should he expect Jill to understand and forgive when he couldn't begin to forgive himself?

"Jill?" He sounded scared, even to his own ears. Opening his eyes, he watched her step out of the somber dress she'd bought for Alyssa's funeral and peel off sheer, dark panty hose.

"Just relax, darling. Let me love away the hurt," she murmured as she let her slip slide down to the floor, leaving her wearing only scraps of black lace that passed for bra and panties.

He felt rather than saw her settle on the bed beside him, but he realized she was real—and here. Kyle wanted nothing more than for her to love him the way she had before he had proven himself unworthy of anybody's affection. "You don't have to do this," he murmured just in case she was caring for him out of some misplaced kind of pity.

"I want to." Lifting his head onto her lap, Jill used her fingers to soothe the tense flesh of his neck and shoulders.

Her touch felt cool and tender, sort of like what he imagined heaven would be—and Kyle knew he deserved to be someplace much hotter than that. He felt more tension ease as her fingers pressed harder into the knotted muscles of his upper arms.

As he relaxed he found himself talking . . . about Dolph's

accident, his travesty of a marriage to Tina . . . Alyssa's birth and Tina's death.

"The doctors begged us to let Alyssa go, but Tina insisted they use all they had to keep her alive. The morning she took that last shot of heroin, we sat in one of those little rooms outside the intensive-care nursery and listened while one of those guys said our baby would never see, hear, or think— much less do all the other things we sort of take for granted.

"After Tina ran out screaming, I sat there like a zombie, wishing I had the balls to tell that doctor to forget what Tina wanted and let Alyssa die—when I should have followed my wife and kept her out of trouble. I didn't. And Tina died instead."

Jill kept stroking gently down his chest, in spite of what she must think about all he had done. "Kyle, it wasn't your fault. It wasn't," she murmured as if she knew his thoughts before he voiced them.

Jill moved her hands up to cup his face. He had to set her straight. "I could have stopped it, but I was too goddamn tied up inside, feeling sorry for myself." Her hands stilled against his cheeks, then slid back to his shoulders as if his words had finally struck a chord in her mind.

"Don't you mean you were hurting for your baby?"

He could lie. Hell, he'd lied to himself for years. If anyone deserved the truth from him, though, it would have to be the woman who had promised to marry him.

"No. I was hurting for me—for the times I'd miss because my kid would never be right, for what I would never see her accomplish. If you want the whole unvarnished truth, honey, I was hurting for what I knew it would cost me to take care of this baby I'd made."

She cradled his upper body in her slim arms. "I don't think any of those feelings you say you had make you a monster, Kyle. I can't say I wouldn't feel that way myself, if I were faced with the same situation."

"It took Dolph years to get over Tina dying the way she did."

Jill prodded him to sit up, then tilted his chin down until he had to meet her gaze. "Kyle, even if you'd kept your wife from killing herself the day it happened, you couldn't have prevented her doing the same thing later. Why are you so hell-bent on taking responsibility for events you couldn't possibly control?"

Sitting there on the bed in Bliss House, Kyle thought about Jill's fairly simple question. The answer he came up with made him sound like the selfish bastard he was.

He drew in a deep breath before he spoke. "Because everything I've done for years I've tried to make people think I did because I cared for Dolph—or Alyssa. Hell, I've almost made myself believe it.

"Truth is, marrying Tina made me feel a little less guilty over Dolph's getting hurt. And making the doctors honor Tina's wish to keep her baby alive after she killed herself— that made up in a twisted way for my not having been enough of a husband to make Tina want to stay around.

"I let them condemn Alyssa to seven years of hell, so I could tell myself how goddamn noble I was, shelling out for her care and coming once a week to see her—when I couldn't think up a good enough excuse not to go. I even put off see-ing my own flesh and blood the day she died." Kyle sat up and buried his face in his hands, not wanting to see the ex-pression of disgust he was sure he would see on Jill's face.

"Kyle. Stop it! You couldn't have been in two places at the same time. Don't do this to yourself. Don't do it to us!"

He felt Jill's hands on his shoulders, pushing him down against the pile of pillows at the head of the bed. "Shut up. Don't say another word," she warned as she lay down beside him and clasped his hand.

"You're the man I love. A good man. No, you're not per-fect. Neither am I. But you're not the selfish monster you've been telling me about, either. Close your eyes. Don't let the past destroy you. Don't think, just feel."

He wanted to. God, but he wished he could forget, even for a little while, how he had disappointed everybody who had ever trusted him. He couldn't, though. Wide-eyed, Kyle stared up at the cream-colored ceiling . . . the ceiling the color of his daughter's small wooden casket.

"Close your eyes."

Kyle felt Jill's gentle fingers cover his eyelids and force them to close. Too drained to fight her, he lay there in the dark while she massaged his throbbing temples.

"Relax, Kyle."

Gentle, soothing—he had never thought of Jill that way before. He had fallen under her spell of tantalizing, uninhibited sexuality . . . a spell so strong, it must have masked this gentle feminine side of her.

"I never thanked you for being there for Alyssa," he said as he imagined his little girl dying peacefully in Jill's tender, loving embrace.

She slid her hands into his hair, soothing his scalp with her nimble touch. "I was glad I could be there," she murmured. "Hush now. Don't think about anything."

By the time Jill had rubbed down every aching muscle in his body, Kyle felt as though he had turned to a quivering mass of jelly. Where her hands had soothed, now her lips and tongue were working their magic, creating a tension of a different kind than what she had so sweetly eased.

His nipples puckered and hardened at the touch of her nimble tongue. The feel of her breath tightened the muscles of his belly and made him want her to keep delving into his navel at the same time as he yearned for her to move lower. When she shifted to the foot of the bed and began to suck his toes, his sex started to twitch with need.

Kyle couldn't move. He couldn't think. All he could do was feel Jill's warm, wet breath as she made her way up the inside of his calves, loving him with her mouth . . . nipping carefully . . . moving slowly, so slowly, toward the parts of him that she was so lovingly bringing back to life.

When she finally took his aching cock into her mouth and suckled it, he thought he'd come right then and there. But she lifted her head and lapped up the beads of moisture from its throbbing tip, and he managed to hold on.

He wanted to come inside her, to feel the slick heat and friction. He wanted the gut-wrenching pleasure. More than that, though, Kyle needed to be part of her, to take the comfort and courage she so sweetly offered.

Forcing his arms to move, he clasped her waist and dragged her up his body until his aching sex felt her welcoming heat through the skimpy veil of black lace and silk.

"Rip them," she said, the words coming between quick, raspy breaths that told him she wanted this as much as he did. The sound of fabric tearing preceded his own moan of pleasure as she took him into her body and began the slow, sensual motion of mating . . . of love.

If he opened his eyes, he knew he would explode. He'd had sex with Jill before—mind-boggling sex—but until now Kyle had never felt so loved.

"Cherished," he murmured as he shifted his hips and sank deeper into her body.

"Hmmm?"

"Nothing." His hands tightened around her waist to slow her movement. He was close, too close. And he wanted this to last.

Warmth spread through his body with each loving stroke of her hands on his chest and belly. As her tight internal muscles gripped and released him with every languid rise and fall of her hips, Kyle's guilt fell away, leaving only the sensation of loving and being loved by Jill.

The tension built. He had to see as well as feel her. Opening his eyes, he glanced down their bodies to the spot where they were joined.

His control shattered, and he poured himself into her, barely registering her own gentle climax as he gathered her into his arms and savored the closeness he figured it would damn near kill him to lose.

Lying there as darkness settled over Bliss House, Kyle tried to figure how the hell he was going to protect Jill from the pain he knew he would somehow inflict on her—just as he had done to everybody who had ever gotten close to him.

He relived Dolph's injury, his loveless marriage to Tina, the tragedy that was his daughter's existence for seven years—and the events of the past few days. No matter how Jill might try to gloss over his actions, Kyle knew he had proven again that he was a selfish bastard who deserved nothing more than fate had handed him.

He couldn't give Jill up. Yet he had to, because she had already been through hell and she certainly didn't deserve to go through more for him. Holding her as if he'd never let her go, Kyle made up his mind to do just that. Loving her, he could do no less.

Chapter
Forty-Five

THE GHOSTS

"He is going to leave her, Laura. We are to be doomed to an eternity apart, all because your precious great-great-grandson is such a lily-livered coward, he will not follow through with his promises. He plans to leave Miss Carey dishonored, ruined, after having taken what she should have saved for marriage."

Laura moved a bit away from the master bedroom door. How like Cyrus, she thought sourly, to condemn her kinsman for having done what they—he as well as she—had done a hundred years before!

"Leave them alone, Cyrus. Surely Kyle has reason for being distraught! Can you show no pity? You yourself told me that he buried his daughter today."

"And after you nearly destroyed yourself to learn what

disturbed Randall so, you told me the child was so afflicted that death would be a blessed release. I would say her dying would remove rather than create obstacles to Randall's marriage."

Cyrus scowled, but Laura refused to cower in the face of his anger. *"Cyrus, get away from that door. You have intruded on Kyle's mind for far too long as it is."* She floated into the dining room, where she hoped the newly returned furniture he remembered from his childhood might distract him from his tirade.

"I can read his mind from here as well as from where we were," he said peevishly as he settled in the middle of the table. *"Because the blood of your precious grandson's scurrilous Randall ancestors has surfaced, we shall be condemned to eternity in hell—apart."*

"Being apart becomes more appealing, the more you vent your irrational hatred against my kin, Cyrus. Mine. Not just Harry's." For a century Laura had tolerated Cyrus's rantings against the man she had married, but now he had gone too far! *"I begin to doubt you are much better a man than Harry was,"* she said, perching on the sideboard and skewering him with a disdainful gaze.

"Now, now, my dear. You were ever too good for that family of vermin that polluted Hunter's Mountain." Cyrus's silky voice belied the venomous feeling in his words.

"And you were ever too wicked to head the fine Bliss family, especially after you took another man's wife to your bed," Laura retorted. *"Do you not recall how the townspeople—even your own son—reviled you?"*

She watched his expression change to sadness and, she thought, regret. *"They were wrong."*

"Yes, they were. Just as you are wrong to base your judgment of Kyle on hatred you rightly felt for Harry. Cyrus, I have loved you for a hundred years, but I cannot keep loving you unless you can let go of this hatred."

"You cannot?"

Laura willed herself to be strong. She had lied to Cyrus

for the first time, because she would love him for all eternity no matter how angry he might make her. If they were to help Kyle and Jill, and set themselves free, they had to face the young couple without the animosity she sensed Kyle had read in Cyrus's words and actions since he had come to Bliss House.

She gathered her courage. *"No, Cyrus. If you wish to have my love, you must rid yourself of hate."*

Watching him as he appeared to consider her ultimatum, Laura hoped his love for her was as strong as it had been when they were alive. Then he had defied convention and given up his place as a pillar of the community of Gray Hollow to embrace her publicly as his lover. She held her breath when he cleared his throat to speak.

"Hate is a hard thing to relinquish, but I believe that letting go of my love for you would be even more difficult. I cannot willingly lose you, so I shall endeavor to keep my opinions of your kin to myself."

Laura shook her head. *"That will not suffice. You have promised that before, only to renege each time something Kyle does angers you."*

Tilting his head to the side as though he were considering what she had said, Cyrus made another offer. *"I could never feel anything but hate toward Harry, as much because he hurt you as because he burned us alive and condemned us to haunt Bliss House. I will, however, strive to keep your young descendant's strong points at the forefront of my mind."*

"I will accept that, my love. I cannot think charitably of Harry myself, so it would be wrong for me to expect you to do so after all he has put us through." She paused, smiling at Cyrus. *"Now, what can we do to help Kyle transcend the turmoil that is tearing him apart?"*

Cyrus grinned. *"Come closer, my dear, and we shall discuss our options."*

Chapter
Forty-Six

You need six months' worth of intense outpatient therapy, but I can safely tell you now that your surgery was a complete success.

Exhausted from the routine his physical therapist had just put him through, Dolph lay back in his hospital bed, considering options he hadn't dared dream would be his until Dr. Granger had spoken those words this morning. Unhampered now by tubes and drains, he rolled onto his side and looked at the small framed photo of Alyssa that he had brought from home.

Convinced that Tina's daughter was now well and whole in heaven, Dolph couldn't bring himself to mourn her death. He worried, though, about whether Kyle was torturing himself with guilt.

Dolph was looking forward to seeing Kyle and Jill this afternoon. He grinned when he imagined his brother's reaction to the news that he would be taking a job in Florida as soon as he completed his therapy. Alyssa had held him here, but now she was gone—and Kyle had Jill to help him put his tangled memories to rest. It was time—time for Dolph to get on with his own life.

Still staring at Alyssa's picture, he fell asleep, only to wake up two hours later when the door to his room opened and his brother stood there—alone.

"Where's Jill?" Dolph asked, half-awake by the time Kyle got to the side of his bed and sat down.

Kyle shrugged. "I left her at the house. I'll follow her back to Gray Hollow later. Don't want her driving those icy roads alone."

Dolph watched his brother pick up Alyssa's photo and stare at it. Kyle was guilt-tripping again, he guessed. "She's whole and happy now, little brother," he said as he reached out and took the picture, setting it back on the bedside table. "Don't grieve. You've been doing that since the day she was born. Let go."

"I can't. Maybe if I'd been there for her . . ."

"Bull. She wasn't alone. You've said a hundred—hell, probably more like a thousand—times, Alyssa couldn't have known whether it was Jill, or a nurse, or you, or me there with her when she died."

Dolph noted Kyle's shocked expression. "That's right, Kyle. I always argued that she knew us. You handled your guilt your way. I handled mine the way that made it hurt me less."

"You, guilty? Of what?"

"Of many things. Life's too short to let past mistakes destroy the future, though. Granger gave me a clean bill of health this morning," Dolph added, changing the subject.

"Great! No more problems with blood clots?"

"Not since the blood thinner started working. Doc said there shouldn't be any need for the medicine after I get to moving around more. He took out all the plumbing and sent me down to therapy this morning."

For the first time in too long Kyle's smile reached his eyes. "You sore?"

"Hurting like hell. It feels good." He grimaced with pain. "Even the goddamn cramping in my legs."

"Can I do anything?"

"For the cramps? You could grab that hot pad over there and shove it between my legs. Heat helps."

Kyle picked up the pad, settled it against Dolph's thighs, and replaced the covers. "No catheter?" he asked as he stepped back from the bed.

"So far, so good. It came out yesterday, and everything seems to be working fine down there. Granger apparently knows his stuff."

"Everything?"

Dolph laughed. "The plumbing, anyhow. Haven't had the chance to check out *the other.*"

"I'm glad." Kyle settled back onto the chair.

"Me, too. Looks like I'll be getting out of here in time to be your best man."

Kyle suddenly appeared to be examining his boots in minute detail. "There's not going to be a wedding," he mumbled so softly Dolph barely made out the words.

"What the hell do you mean? Jill's perfect for you!"

"I mean I'm not about to take the chance of fucking up the life of somebody I love as much as I love Jill."

Grunting with discomfort as he raised the head of the bed so he could face Kyle eye to eye, Dolph sounded strained even to himself when he spoke. "And what does Jill think about this sudden attack of conscience?"

"I haven't told her yet." The tortured look on Kyle's face said more than words.

Dolph wished briefly for the strength to shake some sense into his brother's stubborn carcass. "You're a goddamn idiot," he observed.

"How do you figure?"

"You're going to ditch a lady you love—and who loves you—just because you've got some insane notion that you have some supernatural kind of power to mess up lives of people you get close to." Dolph shifted in the bed to ease another cramp that popped up in his right hip.

"Look, you're hurting," Kyle said, getting up and reaching for the button to call for a nurse.

Not about to let this conversation go unfinished, Dolph reached down and stayed his brother's hand. "Not yet," he said. "I'm not done with you."

"Yes, you are."

"Sit down." When Kyle just stood there glowering at him, Dolph decided to use Kyle's guilt to his own advantage. "By your own reckoning, you owe it to me," he added silkily.

Kyle sat down, but he appeared none too happy about it as he muttered, "Have at it. But you're not going to change my mind."

"I'm not wasting my breath, rehashing arguments I've made a hundred times. Here it is, straight out. You didn't cause my accident, or Tina's death, or Alyssa's handicaps. You never had the power to cause them even if, for some dumb reason, you had wanted to. You didn't owe it to Alyssa to be there with her on the off chance that she was going to die."

"Stop, damn you!" Kyle choked out the words through tightly drawn lips.

"You stop playing God. Get it through your thick, football-battered skull that bad things happened because they happened, not because of something you did or failed to do. Grab Jill and make yourselves a life together—be happy."

"For how long? How long before I screw up and have to watch helplessly while something awful happens to her?"

Dolph paused for a minute. "No one knows how long. But wouldn't whatever time you have be better if you weren't looking over your shoulder for some dark tragedy that exists only in your mind?"

Lifting his head from his hands, Kyle looked at Dolph. "I can't take the chance," he said, his tone one of sad resignation.

"Well, I can. As soon as I finish therapy I'm heading for someplace warmer. Florida. Like I told you, I'm tired of living off your generosity—I'm going to make it on my own."

"You can't . . . I mean, what the hell are you going to do without someone to look out for you?" Kyle's gaze settled on Dolph's useless legs.

"Plenty of paraplegics manage just fine on their own. Damn you, who do you think has taken care of me while you've been out of town on jobs? Me. That's who!"

"Sorry. I just don't like the idea of you going so far away, where you couldn't pick up the phone and call if you needed anything." Kyle stood up and paced across the room, stopping to stare out the window.

"It's time. Both of us need to get a life. Forget about what's past and go for now and the future. Kyle, do you have any idea how much you'll hurt Jill if you walk away from her?"

Kyle knew. That was why he hadn't been able to tell her, not before Alyssa's funeral or in the three days since. "I'm afraid I'll hurt her more later," he ground out, looking toward the park where he had spent countless miserable hours more than seven years ago, trying to dredge up the courage to let his infant daughter go in peace.

"You can't be sure of that. Damn it, Kyle, you know you would never hurt Jill if you could help it. With Alyssa gone and me finally living on my own, you two will have every chance in the world to have a good life together."

Kyle mulled over Dolph's words. Did he dare to believe them? The thought of living without the responsibilities he had embraced for so long frightened him yet filled him with hope.

"Love her. Marry her. Have a couple of kids."

Spinning around at those words, Kyle met Dolph's gaze. *"Kids?* No way. I wouldn't wish a father like me on any poor child. Look at the way I deserted Alyssa!"

"You gave her all you could, Kyle."

"And it wasn't enough."

Dolph spoke so softly, Kyle could barely hear him. "Then don't have children with Jill."

A load lifted off Kyle's chest. "I could get a vasectomy," he murmured, wondering how Jill would respond to the prospect of not having children.

"Or you could just be careful. You might change your mind someday."

"Yeah." Knowing how Dolph felt about kids, how much he regretted the fact that he could never father a child of his own, Kyle felt sheepish. He shouldn't have voiced his own desire not to create another new life—not to Dolph.

They talked for another half hour, until Kyle noticed Dolph's eyelids begin to droop. Leaving him to his rest, Kyle headed back to his house in Greensboro to get Jill and follow her back to Gray Hollow.

As he drove he replayed Dolph's arguments in his mind. Concluding as he had before that he couldn't bear to let Jill go, he resolved to bring up the subject of children, just as soon as they had a moment alone, away from his great-great-grandmother and the obnoxious former owner of Bliss House.

Jill had sensed a change in Kyle as they had loaded the contents of his closet into the back of her Bronco and lashed down two cane-back rockers to the bed of his pickup truck. Driving on a stretch of road that miraculously was free of snow and ice, she glanced at the rearview mirror to find him following closely behind her.

She wondered why Kyle had insisted on seeing Dolph alone, but she had used the free time to check that the flowers she had ordered would arrive at Bliss House early on the morning of their wedding. In any case, she figured the visit had to have been successful because Kyle had come back without most of the gloomy attitude he'd demonstrated these past few days.

It was nearly dark when they pulled into the driveway at Bliss House after stopping for a quick sandwich at Maida's.

Looking forward to a relaxing soak in the claw-foot tub, she hurried to help Kyle store his belongings in their bedroom.

Steam rose from the tub, filling the master bathroom. Her dusty clothing in a heap on the floor, she was stepping into the water when she noticed Kyle standing in the doorway— just beyond the warm, soothing fog.

"When you're done in here, we need to talk," she heard him say through the sound-muffling wall of steam.

"Okay. I'll be out in a little while."

"He's going to tell you he doesn't want children," Laura whispered after Kyle had closed the door. *"Of course, we both know his wishes will have little to do with whether God blesses you with little ones."*

Laura was so innocent! "That might have been true in your time, but it certainly isn't now." Straining her eyes to see the ghost, Jill shifted her gaze around the foggy room. "Where are you?" she asked.

"Here." Jill could barely make out Laura's shape against the dark wood of the bathroom door.

"How can you possibly know what Kyle is thinking?" Ghostly powers were strange, Jill thought as she compared the limited freedom of the ghostly prisoners of Bliss House with their ability to read minds.

The steam began to lift in time for Jill to catch Laura's enigmatic smile. *"We just can,"* she said calmly. *"Do not let Kyle frighten you out of marrying him."*

Jill shrugged. "Kyle is his own master. If he doesn't want to get married, nothing you or I or anyone else can do will change his mind."

"Cyrus is trying to make the boy see reason."

The last being, human or ghost, in the world who could successfully coerce Kyle into anything would be Cyrus, Jill thought even as she shot Miss Laura a pleasant grin. "I'd best hurry and get out there, then, before they come to blows," she quipped, and watched the ghost fade away.

*   *   *

Cyrus materialized between the parlor chair where Kyle was sitting and the cheery fire he had just started. It unnerved him to watch the flames through the ghost's translucent body. Hell, seeing that ghost unnerved him, period!

"You must not walk away from Miss Carey now. To leave her, despoiled and dishonored, would break your great-great-grandmother's heart."

What was Cyrus babbling about? How could he possibly know Kyle had been thinking about doing just that? "I've got no intention of walking away, old man. Not unless Jill tells me to go," he added sourly.

"Good. Your sense of honor is stronger than I had thought when I read your mind the other night."

The damn ghost read his mind? Kyle snorted. "Don't make me laugh. Nobody dead or alive can get inside someone else's head!"

Cyrus shot Kyle an evil grin. *"No? Shall I tell you what you have been thinking these last few moments?"*

"Take your best shot."

"You are terrified of fathering more children. At this moment you fantasize that you can tell Miss Carey there will be no babies for her to hold—and that somehow you can prevent nature from taking its course. You fear she will believe this fantasy of yours, and turn away from you in favor of some faceless man who will promise her a family."

Kyle shuddered. Either Cyrus had an uncanny knack for guessing—or he could actually read minds. "Okay. Part of what you say is true. I don't think I want to know how you did that, though."

"Part?"

"I do not want children—not now, not ever. That I can ensure not having them is hardly fantasy, though."

Shrugging his shoulders, Cyrus let out a fiendish sort of laugh. *"Somehow I can't see you staying out of your wife's bed. Unless of course you intend to follow some of your more illustrious Randall kinsmen and slake your lust on the soiled doves above the Old Mill Saloon outside Gray Hollow.*"

"I intend to honor my marriage vows."

"Then how can you be so sure—"

"Times have changed. There's an operation that will prevent conception, totally and permanently."

Cyrus's horrified expression made Kyle laugh. "Don't get your hopes up. Since you've been dead the doctors have found something less drastic than castration."

"I should hope so," Cyrus sputtered.

"Why, good evening, Mr. Bliss," Jill said politely as she sat down next to Kyle. "Were you and Kyle having a nice visit?"

"Harrumph."

Kyle shot a disgusted look at Cyrus, then turned to Jill. "We were just discussing birth control," he told her, hoping to hell the ghost would take a hint and disappear.

"I believe I will bid you young people good night," Cyrus said stiffly.

"Good night to you." Kyle took pleasure in noting the uncharacteristic color on the cheeks of the annoying spook as he floated slowly from the room.

Jill tucked her hand cozily between his thighs, making Kyle think of everything except the conversation he had planned to have with her.

Resolutely he removed her hand and met her questioning gaze. "I love you. More than I ever dreamed I could love. I want to marry you, live with you until we die. Before we marry, though, there's something we have to talk about."

"Children?"

Damn! Had Cyrus taught her to read minds, too? "Yeah. Jill, I don't want kids. Ever." Might as well spit it right out, Kyle thought as he observed Jill's dark eyes fill with tears.

"Because of Alyssa?"

He nodded, then shook his head. "Partly. Honey, I know you'd never destroy a baby the way Tina did Alyssa. I just can't . . . won't . . . be part of creating another life. I made a goddamn lousy father."

For a long time he watched her sit there, toying with the antique ring he had given her before all his mistakes came crashing around his head. "Might you change your mind?" she finally asked.

"No. I don't think so. Damn it, I don't know. Maybe after a few years, if—"

"Kyle, are you planning to have a vasectomy?" she asked flatly.

Fifteen minutes earlier he would have said yes without hesitating. Now he wasn't so sure. If Jill would wait . . . if everything went well with them, and Dolph . . . then maybe, just maybe in time he could bring himself to risk giving her a baby.

"No. I'll use condoms. And I'm hoping you'll stay on the Pill."

He loved the way her soft lips curved up in an accepting smile. "I will. For however long it takes. Have you got some of those condoms with you now?"

Big Al twitched, as though he sensed the pleasure Kyle was anticipating. "I sure do, honey," he said as he scooped her into his arms and headed for their bedroom.

Chapter
Forty-Seven

THE GHOSTS

"What a beautiful day for a wedding!" Laura exclaimed as she floated around the dining room. Cyrus could almost smell the sweet scent of pink-tinged ivory rosebuds that graced the table and sideboard.

He glanced through window glass Jill had polished to a crystal sheen, at the brilliant sunlight reflecting off a dusting of pure white snow. It *was* a gorgeous day—the kind of wedding day he had dreamed of. Turning and looking at Laura, it struck him that instead of fading, her beauty had remained as fresh and ethereal as it had been the day he had first discovered it.

"I would wed you today if I could, my love," he murmured, reaching out his hand to touch her only to feel the nothingness of air between his fingers.

She, too, reached out, as if to caress his cheek. *"Soon we will be free, Cyrus. Free to touch, to love . . . to escape this prison Harry—"*

"Do not defile this day with that man's name." As always, Cyrus burned with fury when he remembered Laura's brutal husband. *Her husband.* When he and Laura left this limbo, would she still be bound to Harry?

That prospect terrified Cyrus. He reflected on the weighty question silently. Old Harry must have been dead and buried for years—his rotten soul securely ensconced in hell. Surely the fact that Harry had murdered her broke all bonds between them.

Cyrus sighed. In life, he had never had reason to consider such twisted relationships. Death had ended his vows of fidelity to Patience—or had they?

"My dear?"

"My apologies. I was merely thinking. Laura, would you become my bride in truth today, as your great-great-grandson recites his vows with Miss Carey?"

He watched Laura's delicate features soften, her eyes grow bright with what looked suspiciously like tears. *"What a dear, dear thought!"* Then she frowned as she said, *"Cyrus, I am not certain ghosts can enter into vows meant for mortals."*

Not to be deterred from his purpose—to ensure that when they finally entered heaven, they would be viewed as man and wife—Cyrus floated to Laura's side and called on every power of persuasion he had ever possessed. Earnestly he related his fear that old Harry's spirit, or even the spirit of his long-dead wife, might yet conspire to tear them apart.

"Whether we can wed in the purest legal sense of man is immaterial, don't you see? I wish us to be one in the eyes of the angels we will soon be joining, to know we can pass through those gates together to eternity. There must be no question that you are mine, and I yours," he concluded forcefully.

Laura nodded. *"Then we will speak our vows with Kyle*

and Jill today, if doing so will ease your mind. In my heart you have been my husband forever."

"*And you my wife.*" His soul nearly bursting with the joy of loving and being loved, Cyrus leaned close to Laura and whispered in her ear. "*God willing, by the time the sun sets this day, we will be free to touch . . . to feel . . . to love.*"

Chapter
Forty-Eight

Creamy ivory roses and tiny forget-me-nots gave off a scent Kyle knew he would associate with weddings for the rest of his life. Arranged in crystal vases with leathery fern and velvety bows the deep green color of the parlor drapes, the flowers lent a festive air to the parlor and dining room he and Jill had worked together to restore.

He looked down at Dolph and grinned, then glanced around at George Wilson, Maida, and a handful of other Gray Hollow folks he recognized. It pleased him that Jill had asked these people he had known all his life to share their special day.

"Feels good to come back to Hunter's Mountain, knowing you've disproved what folks have always thought about us, doesn't it?" Dolph asked quietly.

"Yeah." Stopping his hand in mid-motion, Kyle restrained

himself from tugging at the tie that was constricting his neck.

Dolph grinned as he straightened his own hunter-green-and-gray-striped tie against the front of his white dress shirt. "First time I've had on a suit in years," he said.

Briefly Kyle recalled having put on the gray suit he was wearing for Alyssa's funeral, then shoved that memory to the back of his mind. This was his wedding day, a time for celebrating his love for Jill and making a commitment to their future.

His tension evaporated when he heard soft music fill the room and noticed that the justice of the peace had come to stand next to them by the antique table with its sweet bouquet and shimmering ivory candles.

When he turned to the parlor door, expecting to see his bride, Kyle had to hold back a startled gasp. Laura, in something white and soft looking . . . and Cyrus, wearing a stiff-looking shirt and shiny black suit, materialized before his eyes and floated down the aisle to stand at the other side of the justice of the peace.

"Do you see anything strange?" he whispered.

Dolph shook his head, giving Kyle a look that silently asked if he was losing his mind.

The volume of the music rose, and Kyle turned toward the doorway again, forgetting the ghosts as he got his first look at Jill in her wedding finery.

She looked like a fairy-tale princess, gliding toward him in a simple ivory dress with a dark green sash she must have had in mind when she'd bought his and Dolph's matching ties. When she reached his side, his nostrils flared at the heady smell of roses mingling with her own elusive scent.

She was Kyle's angel . . . his temptation . . . his friend and his lover . . . his every sexual fantasy come true. This woman was his love and his life, and she was about to become his bride. He took her hand and listened as the justice of the peace read the words of the ceremony.

"Do you take this woman . . ."

"I do."

"*I do.*" Kyle looked over to see the ghost of Cyrus Bliss repeat the vows as he made them to Jill.

Jill made her promises in the soft, husky tones that brought thoughts of naked skin, sweaty straining bodies, and mind-boggling sex. Then Laura repeated the words in that sweet, high voice Kyle knew he would never forget.

Dolph handed Kyle the antique ring he had chosen, and Kyle smiled as he placed it next to its mate. As he felt her ring slip over the knuckles of his finger, he knew he had finally come home.

"You may kiss your bride."

Kyle didn't have to be told *that* twice. Gathering Jill's slender body close to his heart, he joined their lips just as her eyelids fluttered and closed. Out of the corner of one eye, he watched the ghost of Cyrus Bliss enthusiastically embrace his great-great-grandmother.

When he came up for air, Kyle chuckled. When Jill shot him a questioning look, he bent over to whisper in her ear. "I bet we weren't the only couple to get married just now."

"What kind of mayhem are you two plotting?" Dolph asked as he released the brake on his wheelchair.

Jill smiled. "Kyle believes the ghosts of Bliss House joined us when we said our vows."

"They did!" Had Kyle been the only one to see Cyrus and Laura strolling into the parlor as though they'd been members of the wedding party?

Just then the ghosts appeared, blushing like newlyweds. Cyrus cleared his throat. "*Yes. We have finally wed. Now we must take our leave.*"

Looking around to determine whether the guests had seen the ghosts and run for their lives, Kyle saw they were all in their places, apparently oblivious to the proof that Bliss House had indeed been haunted for a hundred years. "Stay. Share our happiness," he told Cyrus, his usual annoyance at the sometimes surly ghost forgotten.

"Yes. Do stay. You two have become my family." Jill

curled her arm through Kyle's as they stood there beside the star-crossed lovers of long ago.

"My dear, we would love to stay. But we must go now, since you have broken the curse that bound us here. Be happy with my grandson and enjoy your life at Bliss House. Kyle, I am happy that I was able to come to know you and Dolph."

Cyrus boomed out his good-byes in that deep, solemn voice he had used with such success to cower Kyle. Then the ghosts of Bliss House locked their hands together and faded from view.

Kyle blinked, then met Jill's gaze. Her loving smile warmed him, and the good wishes of the people of Gray Hollow made him feel welcome here on the mountain where he had grown up under the shadows of scandal.

As he and Jill bid their guests good-bye Kyle finally found himself looking forward to a future with his lady in this old house, no longer haunted by specters but bewitched by love.

Epilogue

Swinging out of his sporty red convertible, Dolph wheeled himself along a newly shoveled walkway and up a steep ramp he supposed Kyle had put up in honor of his visit. No sooner had he twisted the antique doorbell at Bliss House than the door swung open and his brother greeted him.

"Kyle. Good to see you." Dolph grinned as he shed his jacket and warmed his hands before a cheery fire. "Snow makes it seem more like holiday time," he observed, recalling the eighty-degree weather he had left in Sarasota.

Kyle sat back and glanced toward the back of the house. "It's damn good to see you. Sunshine must agree with you—you're looking great!"

"I feel better than I have in years—hell, better than before I tried to wrestle the damn tree. How's business?"

"Good. Keeping the crews busy. I'm taking it easy this winter myself." The corner of Kyle's mouth turned up in that lopsided grin that usually meant he had some interesting news to impart. "How about you?"

"Hopping. You wouldn't believe the number of kids we get at the shelter—or what brings them there."

Kyle lifted an eyebrow. "I thought you said they were neglected or abused kids. You get others?"

"We get an occasional preteen who has gotten in trouble with the law. And we took in our first orphan last week. Prettiest little girl you ever saw. Parents were killed in an accident."

"No relatives to take her?" Kyle asked.

If only there was just one relative! "Too damn many of them. Grandparents. An uncle. An aunt from the other side of the family who is certain the others want the kid just to get their hands on the money she's going to inherit. We've got Katie until a judge decides which one gets to adopt her."

A choking sound coming from the hall bathroom interrupted him.

"Jill, honey, are you all right?" Kyle called out.

"I'm f-fine," a muffled voice responded.

"Don't you think you should check on her?" Dolph asked, wondering at his brother's seeming lack of concern for his wife.

Kyle smiled—that same lopsided grin he'd given Dolph just minutes ago. "She's okay. Just can't keep anything in her stomach. It makes her madder than hell when I chase around after her, holding her hand every time she throws up, so I try to give her space."

"Is she . . . ?"

"Yeah. You're going to be an uncle again, next August."

This pregnancy must have been an accident, considering how adamant Kyle had been about not wanting more children. "You okay with this, Kyle?" Dolph asked, concerned until he observed his brother's sappy smile.

"I'm fine. Thrilled. Ready to do it a few more times if Jill is, after getting sick all day and all night with this one."

Dolph laughed, then looked up as Jill entered the room,

looking sheepish when she bent to give him a hug. "Happy Thanksgiving," she said as she perched on the ottoman beside the fireplace.

"Congratulations."

"Thanks. I think. Look, guys, how would you feel about eating Thanksgiving dinner at Maida's?" When she met Kyle's gaze, Dolph envied the contentment he read on his brother's face.

"Fine with me," Kyle said, sliding his fingers through Jill's hair. Dolph had noticed right away that she'd let it grow out, and he liked the soft, feminine look of dark curls brushing gently against her shoulders. "Makes no difference whether we eat *at* or *from* Maida's, honey. You sure you feel like going out?"

"I'll live—I think. What about you, Dolph? Shall we start a tradition of eating Thanksgiving dinner out?"

A year ago he would have said no—the effort of getting in and out of the car and restaurant would have been too much. Now Dolph welcomed all kinds of challenges— marathon swims and wheelchair basketball. Joining Jill and Kyle for dinner out would no longer tax him at all. When he laughingly told them he'd pick up the tab, he felt good.

When he left Saturday morning, it struck Dolph how life had come around for Kyle—and he figured Jill for having made the difference. He took one last look at the welcoming home they had made from what had been a haunted house complete with resident ghosts, and shook his head, smiling.

And now for a preview of the next
Haunting Hearts romance

Shadows in the Flame

Coming in September 1997 from Jove

VIRGINIA CITY, NEVADA
JANUARY 1862

He arrived too late to shoot the groom.

Rose Gallagher fumed at such luck. No doubt the guests figured it a blessing for the newlyweds, but the gunman standing spraddle-legged in the saloon doors might have taken the bride for himself and given Rose the groom as her escort back to the hereafter.

Of course, it mightn't have worked that way.

Ghosthood was a wry riddle, indeed. For instance, Rose wondered why, after months of haunting her own cottage, she stood in the middle of the Black Dog saloon, barefoot and clad in a white nightgown, watching renegade Lightfoot O'Deigh break up her daughter's wedding party.

Lightfoot's smile might make her Molly's heart flip like a flapjack under her bridal gown, but he was proving himself to be as useless as a milk bucket under a bull.

325

Once, Rose might have fancied Lightfoot herself. With his Cornish blue eyes, black hair, leather chaps and hard rider's body, he made quite a picture. Murdering the groom might earn him what he deserved—a short drop, a stiff neck, and a honeymoon in Hell. With her.

But her darling Molly loved the rogue, even though he'd stolen her horse, heart and decency before spurring out of town. And Rose, brazen trollop in life, now shameless matchmaker in death, blamed herself for her daughter's downfall.

With only a wee bit of ghostly meddling, she'd taught uppity Moll, God love her, how hard it was to be good when a handsome lad took you in his arms.

Now, the barroom fiddle faded to a cat's yowl and the piano's clink-tink hung amid cards flicking down. One last glass slammed on the bar and Rose knew she'd barter her soul—what remained of it—for a sip of throat-stinging whiskey.

With every eye in the place following, Lightfoot crossed the saloon, spurs ringing, chaps slapping. Following just behind him, riding the breeze of his wake, Rose heard the whispers.

"Right down cocky—"

"—he'd fight a rattler and give him the first bite—"

Lightfoot heeded nothing but Molly.

"What are you doing here?" Molly, furious and trembling, stood firm beside her legally bound husband.

Lightfoot stopped. His arms rose past his holsters and lifted above his gun belt. His fists opened and closed. Would he fight Molly's husband? Or run his rope-rough hands over Moll's satin gown from her nape to her crinoline's flare?

Though she had eternity to fill, Rose felt even less patient in death than she had in life. If the men planned to sling fists, she wished they'd get after it.

Rose hovered behind the gunman, but only Molly, wide-eyed and exasperated, noticed her. Lightfoot took full advantage of Moll's distraction and squared off with Richard

Griffin. Candlelight glittered on Griffin's diamond shirt studs, marking him as more gambler than husband.

"Here now, Richard." Lightfoot flashed a joker's grin and reached for the gambler's beer, abandoned on the bar. "I only came to drink a wedding toast to my best girl."

Get on with it. Rose gave the gunman a thump between the shoulder blades. *Enough of your jawing.*

Lightfoot's arm stopped short of the glass.

Are you a jester or a man? Rose swatted his backside, enjoying the chore, though her fingers slipped right past him. *Take Molly back, or take to the hills, boyo.*

Suddenly Lightfoot caught the bride to him, bending her backward with a branding sort of kiss.

Fluttering commenced where Rose's own heart had been. Full of herself and the blessed whiskey fumes floating above the bar, Rose celebrated the passion she'd set in motion.

Her jubilation stopped short.

No! Rose wished for a voice to scream that Richard Griffin had dug a pearl-handled derringer out of his fancy gambler's vest. *No!* She wished for a fleshed finger to point at Griffin, coolly aiming at the couple lost in embrace.

Lord, no. Had they held off love so long to lose it now, in a belch of fire and lead?

Shadows swirled through the saloon, candles flared and flagged as Rose's silent howls bemoaned the cold autumn morn when Lightfoot O'Deigh first rode into town and saw green-eyed Molly Gallagher, the witch of Six Mile Canyon.

VIRGINIA CITY, NEVADA
SEPTEMBER 1861

Widow's weeds streamed behind her, riding the wind like a flag of warning. Beneath the signs of mourning, her hair burned bright as the autumn leaves skittering down the boardwalk. She stopped before a rough-looking freighter and pushed her shawl away from a cheek like an ivory Madonna's.

Certain she'd speak with the tongue of an angel, Lightfoot eavesdropped from behind Abner, his vicious mule.

"Your choice, Mr. McCabe," she said to the hulking driver. "Trade the milk cow or I'll offer no remedy for that gut pain. What did you say of it last time? It could split an iron bucket?"

The Madonna shrugged and the giant stood, dumbstruck. Ah, well. Mam had railed at his "poet's imagination," demanding to know how such fancies profited the son of Cornish fisherfolk and why he'd leave the sea and strike off for a land filled with heathen—red, white and yellow—who'd lead a poor boy astray.

Mam'd had *that* right enough.

But he'd wager she couldn't explain away this plainspoken Madonna with a voice sweet as midsummer pipes over meadows. The beauty was a flesh-and-blood omen, proof he'd chosen well in selecting these mountains to hide himself in.

Lightfoot cinched down Abner's tie rope on the steep-pitched rail behind the general store. He tugged the knot, testing, before sneaking another look. They'd passed beyond view, the freighter McCabe storming after the widow as shushing leaves parted for her slippers.

Alert for her voice, Lightfoot heard only the pounding stamp mill down the hill and the slam of hooves hauling loads of rock along the town's main street. Beneath both sounds, his caged cats mewed complaints.

"Well, hell, Molly—" The freighter's growl broke over the smack of the coiled bullwhip he slapped against his boot.

Molly. The villain addressed her rudely, but the widow let him talk as she smoothed wrinkles from the cloth covering the basket she carried.

"I'm not saying that I have a milk cow. But if I did, if I *did*—" The freighter bellowed as if increased volume would make her attentive. "I could lead a cow down to Persia's, stake it in trade and have myself a ha-reem—"

"And your belly would still hurt." The widow's veil fluttered with her nod. "Good day, Mr. McCabe."

Lightfoot slipped his index finger through the wire cage. He let the calico she-cat give it a bite and hoped the widow would toss a reprimand over her shoulder.

Wind gusted, bringing a whiff of fresh bread mingled with pine. Warm bread then, nestled in that basket over her arm. Retrieving his finger from the cat, Lightfoot leaned around the corner of the store for a last glimpse, and rammed heads with the freighter.

Big as a bull and almost as smart, judging by the matchstick space between his eyes, McCabe stood undazed.

"What in hell're you lookin' at?" McCabe spat. "Cussed witch and her potions." The behemoth's forearm guarded his stomach as he shoulder-butted past.

Before his left hand could drop, Lightfoot clenched it into a fist. *No gun on your hip and no call to use one. Settle, man.* He would not look after the blustering giant. He would not consider the nasty glob beside his boot. *Roarin' pride is a luxury just a bit out of pocket-range.* He breathed deliberately and rubbed his brow. *Settle.*

The aroma of bread and pine lingered on the high desert air.

No reason he couldn't look after her, though he'd gain nothing *settling.* Sweet Mother, no.

A widow's hips, swathed in layers of black, shouldn't sway like one of McCabe's imagined harem girls. Shouldn't, but there she went, proceeding down the boards like Cleopatra of the Nile.